Despite th

and the blanket

One side of the carriage house had become completely engulfed in flames and thick smoke.

Burning branches waved to me as they flew off into the black night sky. I waited for David to rush out, or perhaps be miraculously carried out over someone's shoulder like I'd seen on television. I regretted my earlier words were likely our last.

The fire chief stood close enough for me to hear the radio messages from the firefighters inside. "Command, from interior one."

"Go ahead, interior one," he responded.

"We have a body, Chief."

Ice cold shot through me. "Jake?"

My world went black.

****

Pulling at an oxygen mask, I came to in the back of the ambulance. Jake sat facing me, holding my arm, taking my pulse. I shook off his hand and sat up. "My heart is fine. Are you okay, Jake? Did you find David?"

His eyes answered me without words as he pulled me toward him. I stretched my arms around him, clutching his coat. His gear smelled like smoke. Everything smelled like smoke. The urge to throw up burned my throat. I spoke into his chest while he rocked me. "What have I done? If I had left things alone, none of this would have happened. David's dead. You could have been hurt."

Kudos for Sue Jaskula and *ALL FIRED UP*

Finalist in the New Jersey Romance Writers'
Put Your Heart in a Book contest 2019

~

Finalist in Romantic Suspense category
Indiana Golden Opportunity Contest 2019

~

"I loved it, it was a true page-turner…couldn't put it down."

~Teri Kielbowich

All Fired Up

by

Sue Jaskula

This is a work of fiction. Names, characters, places, and incidents are either the product of the author's imagination or are used fictitiously, and any resemblance to actual persons living or dead, business establishments, events, or locales, is entirely coincidental.

All Fired Up

Contact Information: info@thewildrosepress.com

Cover Art by *Diana Carlile*

The Wild Rose Press, Inc.
PO Box 708
Adams Basin, NY 14410-0708
Visit us at www.thewildrosepress.com

Publishing History
First Crimson Rose Edition, 2021
Trade Paperback ISBN 978-1-5092-3495-0
Digital ISBN 978-1-5092-3496-7

Published in the United States of America

Dedication

For my amazing, loving mom, who is an inspiration for the way we should all live our lives, with kindness and courage; and, for my amazing, loving dad, who graciously passed along his creative gift of storytelling.

Chapter 1

The walls were gray, the blinds contrasting bright white. His glass-topped desk screamed pretentious male, too dark, too big, and too modern. He had placed a pair of dark gray, soft leather chairs strategically in front so clientele could relax while he maneuvered their investments from behind the desk, in a chair made of the same luxurious leather but larger than any man needed, let alone his toned, six-foot frame. He assured me the layout and contemporary design exuded power and confidence. I argued that without color, a book or a picture in sight, the office felt cold and impersonal. Now, I realized, he was right, his space represented him perfectly, as much as it unsettled me.

My husband didn't like the dog in his office, but having my faithful golden retriever follow me in helped calm me and defying my husband gave me a small degree of satisfaction. I rubbed the top of Sunny's head with my trembling hands. "If David finds us in here, we're both in for it!"

While my conscience argued, respect his privacy, show him some trust, my instinct told me I had reason not to. Exhausted from too many sleepless nights running worst-case scenarios in my head, I sat behind his desk, shuffling through papers, and pulling at locked drawers, questioning my own insecurities.

The only unlocked drawer in the center of his desk

revealed nothing but a few strewn Post-it Notes, paper clips, a stapler, a gift-boxed pen set, and a tin of fruit candies. The pen box held the predictable matched silver set. With a sigh of resignation at another dead end, I reached for a candy from the colorful tin, gasping when I found tiny keys in place of the expected contents. "Really, you hide the keys in your candy tin, that's the best you can do?"

Sunny's head raised toward my voice.

"Talking to myself, girl."

She dropped her chin back on her extended front legs. I tried the keys in each of the side drawers. The top drawer held basic desk paraphernalia, a stack of unused folders, computer paper, and replacement ink for his laser printer. My suspicions mounted when the second drawer wouldn't budge after trying each key unsuccessfully. Moving on to the bottom drawer, I took two attempts before I found the correct key. Lifting out a large batch of clipped papers revealed nothing underneath that screamed evidence.

"Why does he need to lock the drawer on a bunch of old…what the heck? These are registered mortgages, stamped from the Registry Office and recently. Why would he have these locked up in his home office instead of in clients' files in the city or even scanned into his computer?" Again, I spoke to the empty room, gaining the dog's sideways glance.

Continuing to flip pages, my heart pounded as apprehension came over me. It made sense to have an electronic copy of a mortgage if he had investors putting money in, but these printed copies with original signatures didn't seem right.

I bolted upright when I noticed my name on a

mortgage against our house, a mortgage I had never seen, but which bore my signature. Scanning the papers more thoroughly, my gut knotted. I found the signatures of my father, our friend Jake, and a few others I didn't recognize, all presumably well-forged. The satisfaction of discovery mixed with dread.

Hearing his car on the gravel drive outside, I yanked the bottom drawer ready to toss the papers back inside, allowing me time to think before I reacted to what I had discovered. The force of my tug caused a framed photo to slide forward.

My sudden intake of breath was loud in the silent room. Rage boiled when I glanced down at an enlarged photograph of my husband on the beach, our beach, in front of our Lake Huron cottage, happily arm in arm with his business partner, Sharlene Hayward. She wore a billowy summer dress showing bare, slightly sunburned shoulders. Her dark hair was pulled up in a clip, small curls escaping, blowing into her happy sun-freckled face. David squeezed her close to his side, his half-unbuttoned palm tree shirt revealing evidence of too much sun on him too. He gazed lovingly at her with a relaxed, truly happy smile on his face, a smile I hadn't seen in years. Their expressions spoke volumes, and their colorful umbrella drinks told me they had spent a fun day soaking up the sun. That one glance confirmed my worst-case scenario.

The car door slammed. The front door opened and closed. I didn't have time to digest what I had found. Tossing the incriminating evidence back and closing the drawer quietly, I stifled a gasp when the office door opened and in walked the cause of my grief.

****

"Here you are. I've been calling from the front door. Didn't you hear me?" He carried a giant bunch of colorful flowers, smiled at me as he entered, then glared at the dog.

Sunny jumped to attention and cowered out of the room, her head low, tail between her legs.

When our eyes met, his expression turned dark. "You look like a deer in the headlights. What are you doing in here? And why is the damn dog with you? You know I hate dog hair on everything."

I wished I could retreat like Sunny, head down, without a word, giving myself time to recover my shock before facing him. Instead, I slipped the tiny keys into my pocket, clenched my shaking hands in my lap and met his eyes with a half-smile. "You're right and I'm sorry. I shouldn't be in here snooping around, but I'm at the end of my rope. I've asked you what's going on lately and you don't, that is, we haven't—"

"There's nothing going on, Christine. We've been through this. You have no right to be going through my desk. My clients' investments are confidential. I don't rummage through your cases. You need to stay the hell out of my office!" He came around his desk and yanked me out of his chair.

Snatching my arm back from his grasp, it took everything in me not to accuse him of the fraud and infidelity I had discovered. But I knew, if he destroyed the contents of his drawer, I'd have a hard time proving my accusations. "You're lying. Your anger tells me you're hiding something."

"I'm not one of your crooks to be cross examined on the stand," he said, his voice forceful. He stepped away, to stare out the window.

He had a way of taking over a room, holding himself straight, shoulders back, appearing taller, in charge, confident. That dark and handsome charm had won over many situations, including me initially. I knew him better now. I'd seen it before, his ability to change from anger to calm to avoid confrontation simply by walking away from the situation. The tapping together of his thumb and middle finger, the long stare at nothing, his deep inhale, letting it out slowly all told me, he was struggling to regain his composure.

"You may as well be counting to ten out loud. I get it, you're pissed off," I said.

Turning back with what looked like a forced smile, he stepped closer and put his arm around me. "I'm not pissed off, and I'm not a criminal. There's no need for this interrogation. We've loved each other for years. I'm your husband. You can trust me. You're searching for something that doesn't exist."

I held silent, unable to trust myself not to scream out accusations.

He picked up the bouquet as if to start over. "Here, I brought your favorite sweetheart roses. We've both been busy, and things have been difficult, but we can get back on track. Let's have some wine, plan a weekend getaway, just the two of us?"

Ignoring the flowers, I shrunk from his touch, pushing his arm off my shoulder. "Changing the subject also tells me you're hiding something. Our marriage has felt like one big lie for the last year, and I'm done with it. I'm not interrogating. We need to talk. I want some answers."

Dark eyes stared at me. David tossed the flowers onto the desk. He didn't back away, but I held my chin high, maintaining eye contact, challenging his intimidating stare.

His calm dissipated once again. "Jesus, you're impossible. You're the one who's never around, always working late on your damn cases. Things are falling apart, and you want to put all the blame on me."

"I'm never around? You've been away six weekends out of the last two months. I hardly saw you all summer. You said expenses were tight at the office. Where's the money coming from for all these business trips and where did you get that sporty new Rolex?" I demanded.

He ignored my prodding which I expected. A flash of the framed photo came to my mind. "Are you having an affair?" I glared, eyes wide, begging for some honesty.

"Holy shit, now you're really losing it. I try to bring you nice flowers and I'm thinking we'll have a cozy night together, maybe rekindle some romance and you throw all this crap in my face!" He closed his eyes and shook his head.

"Rekindle? Are you kidding? Wine and a couch make out session to fix our broken marriage? You never give me a straight answer, let alone time for a full conversation. The cozy couch nights are long gone, David. I don't know you anymore."

"You don't ask questions. You throw accusations like you're at work, prosecuting a criminal in front of a jury. I haven't done anything wrong, and I'm not sticking around to listen to your bullshit." He stormed out of the room, stomped down the hall, and slammed the front door behind him. Gravel flew as he sped out of the driveway.

"Once again, you avoided my questions by throwing blame back on me. You're good at that." I fell into his chair and reached for the flowers, knowing guilt drove him to the purchase.

Anger overtaking defeat, I threw the roses across the room. "Daisies damn it. My favorite flowers are daisies!" I yelled, swiping a tear that threatened to fall.

Chapter 2

I stared at the window then down to the damaged stems now scattered on the floor. *Now what do I do?* Turning back to the desk, I pulled the bottom drawer, retrieving the papers and the photo once again, needing to confirm my worst nightmare.

My phone rang in my pocket, startling me from the silence of the room. It wouldn't be David. Hell would freeze before he'd call to apologize. Lifting my cell, I wasn't surprised to see Jake's number on the screen. He had been my best friend since childhood, and my only confidante since I became suspicious of David. Jake and I had done some crazy things in our younger days, but always came out laughing. He almost always put me in a better mood when I felt down. Today, I wasn't so sure even he could cheer me up.

"Hey, Jake."

"You okay, hon?"

"I guess you saw David screech out of here again."

"Kind of hard not to notice when gravel flies and tires screech on the road. Again, is right; what's up with his temper these days?"

"I just can't…"

"Can't what?" he asked.

"We're done." A sob threatened my voice.

"I know you are. So, maybe that's all there is left to say." His voice was soft, understanding.

I cleared my throat. “That would make life really easy for him. David is up to no good. There’s money involved and there’s another woman.”

“You’re speculating. It comes from your crown attorney mind, always trying to find an angle for everything. You don’t need to prove anything; you just need to end it. Call it irreconcilable differences. Go get the divorce papers signed before he hangs himself in his own career, so you have no association with whatever he has going on.”

“You don’t understand, it’s not that easy anymore.” I choked, glancing at the lovers’ picture.

“What are you saying? Are you crying?”

“I found some things in his desk, incriminating things. I might need your help,” I said.

“I’m on my way.”

I stood at the window watching him walk the path between our properties. His dark brown Irish Wolfhound, Finnegan followed at a distance stopping occasionally to investigate random scents. Jake made me smile despite my anger. He stood over six feet tall, stocky, but not overweight. His dark blond hair fell over his brow today like it did most days. Wearing his standard off work uniform of jeans, a plaid shirt and a dark jean jacket, he walked purposefully but with a relaxed pace. He looked more like he should work as a ranch hand than a captain on the fire department in a busy city. He never seemed rushed or preoccupied and it touched my heart that Finnegan went everywhere with him.

He rounded the back of the house, and I returned to David’s desk, knowing Jake would let himself in, and leaving Sunny to greet them at the door. The dogs whimpered excitedly, their nails clicking on the kitchen floor as they circled each other in greeting.

"Back here," I called.

Watching Jake come into the office, it occurred to me how much his confident, relaxed appearance contrasted David's superior, tense image. It gave me courage to have Jake on my side and reassurance that he too knew something was terribly wrong. I stood to accept his hug when he walked toward me, arms outstretched.

"You okay?" he asked, rubbing his hand up and down my back.

Allowing myself a moment to indulge in the comfort of his support, it also struck me, the difference in my physical reaction to each man's entrance. Feeling tears brim again, I stepped away from his embrace, sitting back behind David's desk. I swallowed the lump in my throat and smiled at Jake.

Several seconds passed before I spoke. "Can I just say, my life is simply better when you're around. I don't know what I'd do without you."

"Okay, I love you too, now talk to me; what's going on?" he asked.

I handed the clipped stack of papers to him.

His brows knit. "What's this?"

"Mortgages, registered mortgages," I said.

"So? I don't get it." He lifted one hand and shook his head.

"These are originals, with supposedly original signatures."

"What difference does that make and what do you mean supposedly?" he cut in.

"Original mortgages get registered by lawyers'

clerks at the Land Titles Office. The lawyer keeps the original document and sends a copy to his client and one to the bank to get the money to close a purchase or make an investment. Maybe they would scan a copy to the investor or a broker like David, but he shouldn't have these originals locked up in his home office," I explained.

I stood, came around the desk, and leaned over his shoulder. "More importantly, they're our mortgages. See, it's your name on this document." I pointed. "Right here, Jacob Anderson on a loan for over two hundred thousand dollars, secured by your property, and registered three months ago. There's one on this property too with my name on it and my Dad's condo and a few others."

"What the hell? Give me that." Jake grabbed the paper with his name from the pile, his voice louder now that fury replaced his concern.

"This is it, Jake. This is the proof I've been looking for." My voice was calmer than my emotions.

I returned to David's chair. "He must have arranged money on the pretense he'd invest for a client and then drawn up these mortgages on houses he knew had no liens, keeping the amounts low enough not to cause suspicion. Then he could forge the signatures and have Sharlene register them.

"The lawyers wouldn't even have to be involved. In his position as an established investor, the bank would transfer him the money in exchange for a copy of a registered mortgage, no questions asked, allowing David access to hundreds of thousands, all without the knowledge of any of the homeowners. He could make minimal monthly payments, easy enough to do when you handle people's money and especially when you have a big chunk of change like that coming in once every few weeks."

"I can't believe it. How could he do this to his own family and friends?" Jake asked, still flipping pages.

I shrugged when he glanced up. "That is a question I cannot answer. He'll never be able to pay all this back, and he's definitely looking at jail time."

Jake stood and began to pace. "I'm going to kill him first."

"I'm so sorry," I said.

"You have nothing to apologize for. Let's get out of here and let the cops deal with this."

"I need to think." I held up my hand. "Just give me a minute," I said.

"I don't like either of us being here in his office. If he finds out you have these papers, I don't trust what he might do."

"I'm not afraid of him. He's all hot-headed talk, but he would never hurt me," I said.

"This is different than discussions about divorce. You've got hard evidence that will end his career, and ruin his life," Jake said.

"David won't come back. He doesn't know I have anything on him, and he always disappears for a couple of days when we have a blowout. I just want enough time to clear my head, figure out what to do next."

"And where's Annie?" Jake alternated pacing and stopping to check out the window.

"Annie was working in the back yard when I came home from work; I'm surprised you didn't pass her when you walked over. She hovers lately; like she thinks I still need a live-in nanny. I don't even need a housekeeper. We're never here to mess anything up."

"Maybe she thinks she's helping since David's never around. But, whatever, I don't want to run into either of them. Let's get out of here."

"There's more," I said, flipping the photo I had faced down on the desk.

He came to stand beside me. "Awe, maybe it's not what it seems." His tone softened. "Maybe it's a work thing and they just made the most of the day?"

"Yeah, okay. You don't believe that any more than I do. Neither of us ever brought work to the cottage. I assure you; she's never been to the lake when I've been there. But there have been a whole lot of business trips this summer when I should have asked a lot more questions. Why would he take her there of all places? People know us up there and who could have taken this picture and why would he have it printed out and enlarged?"

"Okay, look at me." Jake pulled my face away from the photo, forcing me to pay attention to his words. "You've found your proof. You've already told him your marriage is done. We need to go before he comes in and I strangle him myself."

I clutched the papers so tightly; the folds dug into my palms. My mind raced with dates, explanations, supposed business trips. All lies. Glancing at the picture again, my shock and sadness had been replaced with rage that clearly matched Jake's.

"Let's go." Jake tugged the papers from my clenched hands. "I know you're furious, and I'm ready to destroy him myself. But we need to calm down, take the information to the precinct and talk to your Dad. There's a lot going on here."

I stared, bewildered, at one of my best friends, David's friend too. "Our marriage has been over for a long time, and I guessed something shady was getting him extra money, but I didn't expect this double whammy. Did you have any idea it would be something like this?"

Before Jake could answer, Annie came through the office door, smiling, her hair windblown like she had been outside playing in the leaves instead of working in the yard. Now in her mid-fifties, she appeared much younger, with her shoulder-length layered cut, no gray hair in sight. She dressed like I did, casually in jeans and sweaters, but mostly her constant energetic attitude made her seem closer to my age than my dad's.

She looked first at my face and then at the papers in Jake's hands. Her smile disappeared. "What are you two doing in here?"

She stared at me, her brow drawn close, clearly irritated, which was a mood I rarely saw. "You shouldn't be poking through David's work, certainly not with him in here." Her tone and dismissive flip of her hand at Jake also took me by surprise.

I snatched the papers back from Jake and shook them in front of me. "David has been scamming people's money, and now I've got proof."

"That's impossible," she said with an angry shudder.

"Why would you jump to defend him? Is there something you know, Annie?" I asked.

Glancing back and forth from Jake to me, she didn't answer. I turned the picture of David and Sharlene toward her. "Do you know anything about this?"

Her eyes widened and her mouth dropped open. "Oh dear, no, I'm sure it's not what you think." She sounded more composed as she approached.

"Well, I'm sure it is. Can you leave us alone please? Actually, never mind. We were just leaving, and these papers are coming with me." My voice quivered. I pushed past her wanting to confront David while I was still angry, not have Annie around to tell me to work things out.

I reached for my coat at the back door, dogs skirting around Jake and me. "Can I call David from your place? I need some space to think." I tilted my head back to where Annie had been. "Away from her," I whispered.

"Of course, you can." He patted his leg, inviting the dogs to follow us out the back door.

****

After stashing the papers and the framed photo into a fireproof box Jake kept locked in his storage room, we returned to the kitchen. I took a deep steadying breath and called David on my cell.

He answered on the first ring. "I'm sorry for what I said earlier."

"Save it. I presume you didn't want me in your office so I wouldn't find your bogus mortgages and cozy lovers' picture? Well, they're not in your office anymore, so don't bother trying to find them."

My words hung in the air for several seconds, then finally, he offered the standard cliché. "Chris, let me explain—"

"How dare you use my family and our friends for your scam? And how dare you try to blame me for our sham of a marriage when you've been up at our cottage with that tramp? Did you make out right under the stars like we used to?"

I didn't expect a reply. Taking another steadying breath to keep my angry tears at bay, I continued. "I'll see you hang for this, you arrogant, manipulative cheat. And that home-wrecking bitch is going down with you."

Again, he offered no reply.

The standoff seemed like minutes but I'm sure only seconds passed before Jake took the phone and motioned me to sit on his back deck. He was silent at first, but then his voice rose to a threatening tone. "You better hope the cops take you in before I get my hands on you. And wait until the press gets a hold of this. They're going to have a heyday. You and Sharlene won't be handling anybody's money after today."

Jake paused briefly. "Don't buddy me. Stay away from me and from Christine if you know what's good for you."

He joined me on the deck, a glass of red wine in one hand and a bottle of water in the other. I stared off, lost in my thoughts. He put the wine and my phone on the table and sat down beside me.

I reached for the glass. "Water?"

"I'd love to join you in a glass of wine or better a shot of something stronger, but I'm going in on nights."

"Right." I took a sip and felt the warmth of the wine flow through me. A choked half laugh escaped my lips. "He used to be so charming. We had such a whirlwind romance back in university. Remember the wedding in the yard, such a big celebration?"

Jake didn't look at me, didn't answer. "We all used to have so much fun. When did it all fall apart? I don't remember being that kind of happy for a really long time. I feel like such a failure."

This time, he did react, his voice loud in the quiet backyard. "I think you're in shock. Give your head a shake."

When he faced me, he wore an unfamiliar expression. Jake's eyes were normally as pale as the blue sky, his attitude kind, relaxed and open. Now he glared at me, eyes angry, as he raked his hair back.

"You're freaking me out. What's wrong?" I asked.

He took my wine glass and put it on the table then took both my hands in his. His expression softened. "You can't possibly think any of his bullshit has anything to do with you. I'm angry at David, not you. He's a con; he's mortgaged our houses without us knowing for God's sake. He could have been scamming you from day one, and he's screwing his business partner. You should be screaming bloody murder, not reflecting on old memories, and questioning your own actions. What's gotten into you?"

I shook my head. "I know you're right. I've been determined for months to find answers. Now that I have them, all I have are more questions. I just feel numb."

"Well, you know what you need to do."

"Yes, unfortunately, call the cops and my lawyer. He'll get arrested. We'll get divorced. That's going to be chaos and a relief at the same time," I said.

"You'll get through it."

"I can handle all that."

"Then what is it?" he asked.

I hung my head, anger mixed with hurt causing tears to swell. He squeezed my hands, giving me courage to confess. "It's just, well, I'm having a hard time separating all those angry emotions from the humiliation that I'm the last to know he's been banging Sharlene right under my nose and frankly that she's more interesting or attractive than me. Pathetic right?"

"First of all, you're hardly the last to know. I had no idea either. And secondly, her? Seriously?"

Tears streamed down my face, landing on our linked hands. "Maybe I should go home. I'm not very good company."

He released one hand and lifted my chin to face him once again. "What I see when I look at you and what everyone else sees is an amazing, confident beauty, with long soft hair like spun gold, eyes that change like the colors of the ocean, from green to blue depending on your mood, a self-assured attitude that moves people out of your way and a compassionate perfect smile that lights up your face and says, I'm here to make things right. Sharlene has nothing on you."

"Spun gold? Where did you get that line?"

His eyes squinted and he shook his head slightly. "You are your own worst enemy sometimes."

I regretted my sarcasm. "I'm sorry. I appreciate you trying to make me feel better. You're adorable, and I love it when you say nice things; but I'm messed up, and all I can envision is blotchy red eyes, ready to punch my soon-to-be ex-husband in the face attitude, and it's going to take a long while to work my way up from this pity party to anything close to a perfect smile."

Jake didn't reply when I stood to leave. "I should get going. You need to get ready for night shift."

"Call me anytime, day or night."

"You and Courtney have wedding plans to take

care of. You don't need to babysit me." I leaned over to kiss his cheek.

He reached for my hand, not letting me leave. "Please, Christie, anytime. I'm worried about you. You've backed David into a corner, and you could be in danger if he comes back."

"He won't be back. I know him, he's a coward. He'll assume the cops are after him, and he'll likely be with his lover. And I won't be alone; Annie is probably staying over at the house. Like I said, she never leaves these days. David wouldn't start anything with her there even if he did come home." I squeezed his hand to reassure him.

"I'm not convinced. I'm going to work in about an hour, and I'll be up all night. Even if I'm out on a call, I'll have my phone. Call me if you need anything. I mean it."

"I'm leaving my evidence locked here in your house. I just need one night to think things through before I go to the police. My reputation is at stake too if I'm implicated in his fraud scam. I need to talk to my boss at the courthouse before I do anything."

"You need to take a deep breath and keep calm. Are you sure you're okay? I can call in sick if you want me to stay with you," Jake said.

"You're a good man. You've always had my back. I'll be fine."

"Call me," he repeated.

"I will, I promise. And thank you."

He held up his free hand and tilted his head, his bangs falling over his forehead once again. "Don't even start with the thank you. We've talked about this. You, Rick, and I have all had our suspicions. You knew your marriage was done. And now we have some answers. It's a start. It's going to be okay."

I groaned at the mention of my dad. "Oh please, don't bring up Dad. There's going to be a great big, I told you so waiting for me when I take this to the police station in the morning."

"Rick's your only family, and you're lucky he's your best mate. He's got your back and so do I. We'll help you through it."

"Well, thank you anyway, Jake. I don't know what I'd do without you. I'll call you soon, I promise."

Sunny and I headed home, without looking back.

Chapter 3

After a brief conversation with Annie, I bypassed the kitchen, unable to think of food. I trudged upstairs to my bedroom, welcomed by my haven of comfort with thick, soft carpet and several pillows on each side of the king-sized bed. I showered and changed into flannel shorts and a tank top, and then propped myself up in bed with a notepad and pen attempting to organize my thoughts and a timeline onto paper before I handed it over to the police.

I should have been surprised or even nervous when David walked into the bedroom just before ten o'clock, but all I felt was disdain. I should have commented on his gall at expecting to return to our bed, should have thrown things and cursed him. Instead, I simply glanced up from my notepad when he entered. "You disgust me. Get out."

"Chris, come on, it's not what you think. Let me explain; this involves you too," he pleaded.

"Of course, this involves me. This is my marriage that you've screwed up and my career that's going to be in question when yours goes down the drain. Did you really think your fraud scam wouldn't affect my life? The whole world isn't about you."

He sat on the end of the bed and begged. "Please, listen, that's not what I mean. I need to tell you the whole story. I need your help. We can work this out together. We always work things out together." His attempt to draw on my compassion irritated me more.

I stood from the bed. "I'm not helping you with anything this time. Our marriage is long over. You brought this on yourself, and you're going down one hundred percent by yourself." I pointed at the door. "We're done. I said get out."

I walked into the en suite bathroom closing and locking the door between us, dismissing any further conversation. I heard him shuffle through drawers then the bedroom door closed behind him. I wondered if he would sleep in the den or go back to his lover. I didn't want to speculate where he went or what he did anymore, and I didn't want to cry. I had cried enough over the last several months knowing in my heart things had come to an end. He didn't deserve any more waste of my emotions.

Returning to my bed after checking the room was empty, I lay awake staring at the clock, watching the digital numbers slowly mark off minutes like a Chinese water torture. I considered going downstairs to try some milk, wine, junk food, anything to distract from the turmoil in my head. Annie didn't stay overnight much anymore, certainly not since she started keeping house for only David and me a few years back. Of course, the one night I needed solitude, she had been there to greet me when I came in angry and upset. She would get up if she heard me in the kitchen and I couldn't face more questions. Near midnight I finally fell into an exhausted sleep, the kind of deep sleep that comes from relief at finally knowing the truth.

Sunny's bark seemed to come from my dream. I jolted instantly awake to the smell of smoke. Even in my panic, I remembered to feel the door before pulling it open. Sunny circled me, barking incessantly. I followed her when she ran toward the stairs. "David, Annie, fire!" I screamed. I got no reply.

Frantic, I ran through the house. "David! Annie!" I screamed out again and again. The view through the kitchen windows confirmed the source of the smoke. Flames shot and heavy smoke billowed from the carriage house in the back yard. I grabbed the phone, punched nine-one-one, and listened to the operator's calm question.

"Nine, one, one, what is your emergency? Do you need police—"

"Fire!" She asked more questions and gave directions, but I didn't remember them.

"David? Annie? Where are you?" I yelled again. Grabbing my jacket and Sunny's leash from the hook, I bolted out the sliding door into a wall of smoke that nearly knocked me to my knees. Holding my coat to shield my face, I hooked Sunny's collar and scanned the property at a distance from the fire.

The shriek of the smoke detector in the kitchen pierced the night. I stretched to close the door, then gasped when Annie appeared from behind our lilac bush. She reached her arms out. "Thank God you're okay."

"Where were you? Have you seen David?" I asked.

Sirens drowned her answer.

Jake jumped down from the first fire truck before it came to a full stop. "Christie, Annie, come and sit in the truck. Is Dave here?"

I opened my mouth to answer but nothing came out. I tried to walk toward him, but my legs wouldn't move. I stood frozen, clutching the dog to my side and shook my head.

"Marcus, get her a blanket. She's in shock." Jake held my shoulders firmly and then guided me to sit on the back of the rescue truck while firefighters donned their gear and pulled hose, calling instructions to each other.

Jake yelled over the commotion. "Chief, we may have a victim inside. David Hamilton is not accounted for."

Long hoses ran from the hydrant at the road and from the pump truck pulsing with the pressure of the water. Nozzles were aimed at the carriage house from all angles. The aerial truck extended and shot water down from the top of the ladder in a big circle like a rain spout shower. Chaos surrounded me, suffocated me. Motors and distant sirens resounded in the quiet of the night. I held one hand over my face to block out the overwhelming smoke and stench of burned possessions, while the other hand clutched Sunny's leash.

I focused on Jake. He slipped his air cylinder over his head in one swift move, adjusted his face mask, pulled on his hood and helmet, and ran toward the sweltering building, while the firefighters ahead of him forced the locked carriage house door with an ax. Illogically, I thought to offer my key. Then it dawned on me, if the door needed forcing, clearly David was still behind it.

He'd left the house after our angry words. I presumed earlier he would go back to Sharlene. I couldn't see if his car was parked in front of the house, but in my gut, I knew he'd be in that fire.

I stared in silence. Annie muttered incoherently

beside me. I didn't have the ability to comfort her. Despite the heat from the fire, the dog at my feet, and the blanket wrapped around me, I shook violently. One side of the carriage house had become completely engulfed in flames and thick smoke.

Burning branches waved to me as they flew off into the black night sky. I waited for David to rush out, or perhaps be miraculously carried out over someone's shoulder like I'd seen on television. I regretted my earlier words were likely our last.

The fire chief stood close enough for me to hear the radio messages from the firefighters inside. "Command, from interior one."

"Go ahead, interior one," he responded.

"We have a body, Chief."

Ice cold shot through me. "Jake?"

My world went black.

****

Pulling at an oxygen mask, I came to in the back of the ambulance. Jake sat facing me, holding my arm, taking my pulse. I shook off his hand and sat up. "My heart is fine. Are you okay, Jake? Did you find David?"

His eyes answered me without words as he pulled me toward him. I stretched my arms around him, clutching his coat. His gear smelled like smoke. Everything smelled like smoke. The urge to throw up burned my throat. I spoke into his chest while he rocked me. "What have I done? If I had left things alone, none of this would have happened. David's dead. You could have been hurt."

He sat back, forcing us apart and crouched to my eye-level, his hands on my shoulders. "We should take you to the hospital, check you over. You might have hit your head when you passed out. You've been unconscious for several minutes."

"I'm fine, I'll be fine. Really, help me up. This is unnecessary." I shook my head trying to gain control.

The ambulance attendant beside him glanced briefly at Jake then held out a clipboard. "Mrs. Hamilton, you'll have to sign this if you're refusing treatment."

"It's Montgomery, Christine Montgomery. Where should I sign?"

He handed me a pen and pointed to three x's where I initialed with a shaky hand. "Okay, Ms. Montgomery, you're free to go then."

Jake helped me down from the back of the ambulance never letting go of my hand. A bright light from a television camera immediately aimed at us, along with the occasional flash of a camera shutter.

A police officer stepped between us and the crowd. "Get back people. If you don't step away, I'll have you arrested for obstruction. Get back," he repeated. His arm lifted to hold onlookers back while we passed.

Jake pulled me away from the ambulance and the buzzing media, behind the fire truck out of sight of the cameras. "The coroner and the fire marshal are dispatched, but it's going to take a while for them to get here. For now, the police need to talk to you. I'll stay if you want, and I know Rick is around here somewhere. And, of course, here he is." Jake stepped back when my dad came toward me in a rush. "I'll talk to you both later," Jake said.

Rick Montgomery's face was a vision of mixed emotion, angry, worried, and relieved all at once. He shoved people aside to get to me, then grabbed me tight and hugged me like he thought he'd never see me again.

My first reaction when the ambulance doors had opened was overwhelming sadness. The carriage house had all but burned to the ground in a matter of minutes. Most of the upstairs had dropped onto the cement floor in a heap of burned furnishings and charred ruins. Only one wall stood intact. The remnants of the remaining walls made me think of a gruesome burned skeleton rising from a grave. I imagined David burned and buried among those ruins. If Jake hadn't held my hand, I might have gone down again.

Now, I felt tremendous relief at seeing my Dad. I leaned back looking into his eyes, the same blue, green of the ocean Jake had described mine to be. He clearly held back tears and I felt the same. "Hi, Dad; it's been a night."

"I noticed. Jake filled me in some. My first question is why you didn't call me after you went through David's office?"

I took a step back from his embrace. "Don't go all cop on me, I needed a night to make some notes, organize my thoughts, and figure out how to deal with David and my career. You've heard enough horror stories about him lately. Now, look what's happened."

"That's not what I meant. I would have come and stayed with you, talked things through, helped you decide what to do next, not to mention keep you safe if he came home and went off the deep end."

"I'm sorry. I needed to be alone. I knew he wouldn't hurt me." I rested my head back on his chest, glad for the support emotionally and physically.

After a moment, he pushed me back his expression

more serious. "Now we have a situation on our hands. We need to talk. You need to talk. I'm doing everything I can to keep the detectives here rather than take you down to the precinct, but it's against policy, and I can't pull the family ticket with something this big. They even put a cop on the ambulance door and wouldn't let me go in with you."

"I don't want any special treatment. David had a whole bunch of bad going on that's going to make you cringe. Your fraud squad will be busy for a good while to bury his partner, Sharlene, who it appears he had an affair with by the way. I guess that doesn't matter so much anymore. But I've got nothing to hide. If we need to go for a ride, then we'll go for a ride. Give me a few minutes to change, and make sure Annie is safely back inside."

Two officers came forward when we walked toward the house. "Relax, guys, she's changing, we'll head downtown, and then I'll get out of your way," Dad said.

One of the officers I didn't recognize grabbed my arm holding me in place as he spoke to Dad. "You know the drill, sir. I can't let her go in the house alone. The whole property is secured. This is potentially a crime scene. The housekeeper has already spoken with an officer, taken a few things, and been escorted off the property."

The second officer held Sunny's leash. "Does this retriever belong to you, miss?"

Sunny, dutifully pulled from his grasp and came to my side peering over her shoulder indicating her displeasure at the officer who detained me. "Yes, this is my dog. I need to settle her back inside."

Dad's jaw clenched, but he answered calmly. "Clearly, yes, Reynolds, as your Staff Sergeant, I'm aware of the drill at a crime scene. And although we haven't established anything beyond a drunk husband burning a pizza late at night, I will of course, follow protocol and ask that you please accompany her, us, I should say into the house to sort out her dog and get a change of clothes. She doesn't need to go downtown in pajama shorts."

As dad pulled his weight with the young officer, one ambitious reporter stepped up to us. "Why would that officer tell Sergeant Montgomery, er, ah, your Dad that this is a crime scene, Ma'am? Was David Hamilton murdered? Is someone trying to kill you both? Do they think you did it?"

Dad grabbed the unfortunate young man by the back of his jacket and tossed him away from us, cell phone and note pad flying. He then addressed one of the detectives from his unit. "If one more media person gets near my daughter, you're going to have to arrest me for assault. Get these news people behind the tape. Reynolds here has apparently established this is a crime scene, and the reporters are walking all over the damn evidence to get the best picture for the morning paper."

Chapter 4

Being escorted through the house by a uniformed officer felt surreal. I moved by some outside force, like my actions weren't my own. My mind raced with a million questions, equally angry at David, as upset at his tragic death. He couldn't have killed himself over getting caught stealing money and having an affair. Clearly there were a lot more details behind what I had found.

The officer interrupted my scattered thoughts. "Sergeant Montgomery said to tell you he'll see you at the station and Captain Anderson will deal with the dog."

"Wait, what? Why can't we go together?"

"I'm sorry, Ms. Montgomery, you have to be escorted alone until the detectives have a chance to interview you each separately."

"Jesus." The whole situation seemed so bizarre.

I spotted Dad as soon as I walked into the police station and relaxed when he smiled slightly and winked at me. People saw a handsome man, tall at six foot, four, lean and strong, with plenty of thick dark hair making him appear younger than his fifty-eight years. To me, he was simply Dad, fun, calm and loving, one of the cool dads growing up, always involved in my life, in a good way. Tonight, he had clearly rushed into jeans, a windbreaker, and running shoes.

His professional appearance portrayed something much different, always well dressed in a tailored suit, carrying out his duties with dedication and a firm command, while still maintaining an approachable demeanor. Co-workers wouldn't be used to this casual appearance, but no one would dare comment. He demanded respect and trust, and people showed it because it was an honor to gain his respect in return. I needed his advice and comfort, but he would be all professional here at the station and forced to save the consoling for later.

"Dad, I have so much to explain, I thought we could talk in the car—"

He held up his hand. "Sorry, love, we have to follow certain protocol until we have more details. You know Detectives Jennifer Scott and Nick Juzo? They're assigned. They need to take you into an interview room, audio and video are on the other side of the window. They'll read your rights, and I can't be any part of it. I'll be in my office. Come get me when you're done."

"I know how it works, but really?" I asked.

He nodded then walked away, head low, clearly upset.

I turned toward the detectives attempting a smile. I recognized Jenny Scott from high school and from a few events since. She was one of the really sweet girls growing up. What a racket she had gotten herself into, not what I would have expected for her. "Sorry, yes, hi Jenny, Nick. This is so surreal for me, please lead the way."

They both nodded at me. Walking behind them, I cringed, hoping they didn't think I expected special treatment. I accepted the rights, refused a lawyer, and started a painful, very personal story.

"What items or incidents initially made you so suspicious other than your own misgivings about your marriage? What prompted you to start your own investigating shall we call it?" Nick asked.

"David dealt with a lot of transactions through work, but he usually had staff doing that for him. He told me months ago that his company had some financial trouble but lately he seemed to have a whole lot more money to spend. He traveled on a lot of supposed business trips this summer and wore a nice new Rolex as of last week. He was super evasive, even angry when I asked about any of it.

"I've made myself crazy, running every scenario in my mind, questioning if he had a rich lover on the side or if he played me all the way from day one, knowing I had money to take. I told him recently that I had spoken to a lawyer to start negotiating a divorce, that I planned to end our marriage."

"How did Mr. Hamilton feel about you taking those steps?" Nick asked.

"He didn't want to talk about it. He would never admit any wrongdoing. He accused me of over-thinking and said we could work it out. He must have known splitting up would force his finances out into the open."

As I ended what seemed like a long story, telling the detectives what I discovered and the conversations Jake and I both had with David, I had tears in my eyes.

Jenny pushed the Kleenex box toward me. "Do you think he could have taken his own life because of the threat of financial ruin, possibly jail time based on the evidence you found coupled with an impending divorce?"

"I can't imagine he would kill himself over financial disclosure. The cat was out of the bag. If anything, he might have been relieved not having to pretend anymore. I'm sure he knew there would be grief over the mortgages, even criminal charges, but I can't imagine he would kill himself over it. No, absolutely no way."

"Where does Jake Anderson fit into all this?" Nick squinted accusingly. "Who is he to you and why was he with you after you searched your husband's office?"

I got my back up for the first time since arriving at the station. "Jake has nothing to do with anything. He's a captain on the London fire department, works full time out of station thirteen. He worked night shift tonight, actually left for work shortly after we spoke to David. Jake arrived on scene on the first truck. He's my best friend, well, our best friend, David's friend too, well until recently." My voice had become louder and more defensive.

"No one is accusing Jake of anything." Nick assured me. "We're trying to get a clear picture of where everyone fits with each other and the relevance of the conversations the three of you had directly before your husband died. If you could clarify how long you have known Mr. Anderson and the relationship you have, it might be relevant."

I reminded myself to calm down and stick to the facts. "Jake and I have been friends since we were kids. Our parents were friends. We grew up next door to each other, on the outskirts of the city, out near Llyndinshire Golf Course, close to Arva. He was a couple of years ahead of me, but essentially, he sat with me on the bus and held my hand on my first day of Kindergarten and we stayed friends all the way through school. He went off to university before I did but we kept in touch. I guess we lost some of the intensity best friends do when they part ways, but whenever we were home for holidays, we always got together with our families, that kind of thing.

"He's always been a bit of a go to guy for me, there for advice, picking up where we left off. David and I and Jake and his fiancée, Courtney hung out together many times, although not so much recently. We were all friends. We're still friends I should say."

"Seems like you two were a perfect match." Nick smirked.

"Nick! We're not here to goad her." Jenny shot him an evil glare.

I forced a smile, appreciating Jenny's defense. "It's okay, Jen. It's a reasonable assumption, one a lot of people in our neighborhood shared too. It never got like that. When David came along and charmed me off my feet, instead of Jake making David jealous with our history, Jake welcomed him and became David's friend too. Only in the last several months has Jake made negative comments about David. I'll admit I have cried on Jake's shoulder maybe a few too many times lately. I can't tell you how hard it is to be suspicious of someone every day of your life, especially for someone like you or me who spend their lives trying to figure out what people are doing illegally and take them to task for it.

"When David had extra money to spend, I told Jake something didn't add up and asked what he thought. I confided in Jake because I trust him. We put our heads together, tried to figure out David's odd behavior. Jake even followed him a few times, but David only went to his office and on his business trips to present at finance conferences, give his sales pitch to handle people's money.

"I decided the only way to find something concrete would be to search his office, check his desk, maybe find something on his work computer, gain myself some peace of mind. Jake didn't like the danger aspect of me trying to get into David's office in the city, but then I found what I needed at home."

"Were you afraid of David?" Jenny asked.

"Not afraid of him doing me physical harm; more worried he had become involved in something illegal that would be difficult for both our careers and that would put a definite end to our already failed marriage."

"Christie, last night, what happened after you searched David's office?" Jenny asked me.

I again dabbed at tears, embarrassed the detectives were privy to my distress, especially Jenny. She seemed torn between comforting me because we knew each other and sticking with the cop routine that the job required. I had nothing to hide and no one had confirmed a crime, but I still said, "sorry," for what seemed like the hundredth time.

"It's okay, really. Take your time," she reassured me.

"Thank you. Jake had called to check on me after he saw David spin out of the driveway. I told Jake I'd found something incriminating, and he came over. I showed him the mortgage papers and the picture of David and his lover and then Jake and I went to his house and phoned David. I stayed at Jake's for maybe half an hour, then went home, and he went to get ready for night shift."

"Why didn't you call us when you got home or right after you found the documents for that matter?" Nick's tone was accusing again.

"I needed time to process it and to talk to my supervisor at the courthouse. I knew once I called it in David would be arrested, there would be media and backlash on me. I was terrified and upset and relieved at the same time. I don't know how to explain it, and I realize now I didn't make the best decision, but I needed time for all of it to sink in." I slumped my shoulders and closed my eyes briefly.

"Maybe you were trying to think of a way to help him cover his tracks to keep your good reputation out of the limelight," Nick suggested.

It was a statement not a question, but I answered anyway. "Detective Juzo, when you do your job and figure out what the hell scam my soon-to-be ex-husband pulled, you will realize I had nothing to do with his finances. It's not like I found a murder weapon or a dead body. His several months of fraudulent dealings were not going to get any more fraudulent if I made some notes and slept on it for a few hours. I have nothing to hide." I glared at him.

He paused briefly before he spoke. "Well, none of this would have happened if you had called us before you called him. Your lapse in judgment may have caused your husband's death, Ms. Montgomery."

I hung my head.

"Nick, for God's sake," Jenny scolded him.

Lifting my face to him again took effort. "You think I haven't thought of that Detective Juzo? Unless you've somehow established a crime other than the fraud I've already uncovered, or you're looking at me as an arson suspect, then I think we're done here."

Jen stood. "Both of you calm down. We're collecting facts to establish a time frame for what happened on your property and to determine if the fire was somehow tangled up in the papers you found. No one has uncovered anything else, and no one is accusing you. Please, can we get back to what happened when you got home?"

She sat back down glaring at Nick then turned to me with an encouraging nod.

"I spoke to Annie for a few minutes when I walked in," I said.

"Annie?" Jen asked.

"Yes, Margaret Anne Fisher, goes by Annie. She's our housekeeper. When I walked in, I said I didn't want to talk about David. She got a little fussy earlier when she saw us in David's office."

"You never mentioned anyone else in the office. What do you mean, fussy?" Nick asked.

"She's old school, believes men can do no wrong, that women need to take care of their husbands, look the other way at affairs, what you don't know won't hurt you, kind of nonsense. She doesn't like Jake being around when David's not home, although I don't know why. She's watched us grow up together since we were kids. She walked into the office when Jake and I were talking. I told her I had found something that proved David committed fraud and she dismissed it; said we shouldn't be in his office.

"Anyway, when I came back from Jake's, I told her I didn't want to rehash details, so we talked for a few minutes about how she spent her day. Annie went to her room. I locked the door, set the security, shut the lights, and went up to our bedroom."

"Does Ms. Fisher live with you?" Nick asked.

"Not anymore. She's been with our family a long time. That is, she used to be more like a nanny years ago when my Mom had cancer. She helped me with school, helped take care of Mom, and the house. She didn't have family of her own. Her husband died at a young age in a hunting accident. Near the end, that is, when Mom became palliative, she needed help pretty much around the clock so Annie would stay over a lot of nights. That's when we made the extra room at the front into her own. After Mom died, Annie insisted on staying on with us, keeping house for Dad and me. We were happy to have her. Even Dad kept her on when I went to university. She didn't stay over then of course.

"David and I took over the house when we got married and Dad moved into the city. Since then, she's stayed over maybe once a week, if we were entertaining; or if David went away on business, and she stayed to watch a movie with me. She's always been a huge help. She had been working outside yesterday. We have a ton of leaves to rake and gardens to clear out, so I'm not surprised she tired herself out and decided to stay. I excused myself to my room and that ended our conversation. I didn't expect to see David. I presumed he would stay with *her*."

Jenny jumped in to clarify. "For the record, her refers to Sharlene Hayward, your husband's business partner?"

"Yup, that's her, business partner, slash lover, slash crook. Anyway, he did come home around ten and came up to our room, said something like ‘he needed to explain, we could work it out together’. I told him he was on his own this time, that we were done, and to get out. I went in the bathroom and he left.

“I think I fell asleep around midnight; I remember watching the clock until close to that at least. Then I woke up to Sunny barking at the bedroom door and the smell of smoke around one a.m. You know the rest.”

Nick jumped in, speaking slowly. “Soooo, you were alone from the time you and David argued in the bedroom until the fire trucks arrived?”

“We did not argue. I yelled at him on the phone earlier, and yes, I made my anger clear, and we have argued many, many times over the last year. There are a lot of witnesses to that. But last night, at home, as I told you, we spoke for less than a minute. I’m certain he knew that we were done. I told him I wanted to end our marriage even before he got caught. And Annie and the dog were there. If I had gone out the door to kill my husband, if that’s what you’re implying, Annie would have heard me or heard the dog. Sunny is a large golden retriever, she doesn’t sneak quietly around the house, and she would never let me out the door without making a commotion or coming with me, especially at night.”

Jenny glared at Nick once again and changed track. “I can’t emphasize enough, no one is accusing anyone of anything. We’re simply concerned at this point with how David came to be in the fire. Can you describe the setup of the carriage house? Why would he go out there instead of a spare room in the house?”

“Months ago, I asked the same question, why did he go out there so much? Now it makes sense that privacy likely played a part. The building itself is nothing special other than the history of it and how well it matched the house. Downstairs had a regular garage on the right side where we kept the ride on lawnmower and the usual outdoor tools; and the left side faced our pool, had a change room, little bar fridge, and then a storage closet for the pool stuff."

"Got it. Where would David have been?" she asked, keeping her eyes on her note taking.

"Upstairs. He had kind of a man cave built; had it insulated and dry walled, installed some pot lights, a big palm leaf ceiling fan and a window out the back, and two big windows facing the front driveway side. There were blinds on the windows, which would have been closed so I can't imagine anyone could have seen inside before the fire. He has, well, had, a big screen television and two recliner chairs, a big old couch, and then a little kitchen area to make snacks. There wasn't a ton of food up there, appetizer stuff in the freezer, chips and nuts in the cupboard, and beer in the fridge. Wait, he had a fryer too. He liked to make fries and wings if the guys came over. He could have been making fries and fallen asleep, although that doesn't seem like something he would do alone so late at night.

"I don't know what else to tell you. It was just an old garage with a loft for hanging out. He obviously went there after I threw him out. I don't know what happened to him. I have a lot of questions too, but I'm so tired, I'm not sure I can think straight anymore. If you don't plan to book me on something, which I presume you don't in the absence of a crime, I'd like to end my statement here and come back in the morning to see if anyone has any information for me."

Jenny glanced at Nick, but then took the lead and reassured me. “We don’t have any more questions for now. You’ve painted a clear picture and I thank you for that. We will get a search warrant and go through the main house and of course what’s left of the carriage house in coordination with the fire marshal. All we know right now is the fire marshal is holding the scene, which means he thinks there’s reason to believe the fire is suspicious, and they’re sitting on the victim.”

I cringed at the reference to David as a victim.

“Sorry, they’re not releasing your husband’s body until the coroner clears the scene. They’ll take him to the morgue and our team and the fire marshal’s group will work with forensics from there. You won’t have access to either building until we give you clearance to return. The warrant could take several hours to obtain given it’s the middle of the night; the search should start with the day shift. So, you may get back into the house by dinner time. Worst case would be tomorrow. Do you have somewhere to stay?” Jenny asked.

I nodded and she continued. “Will you be staying with Sergeant Montgomery? We’ll need to know where you are and of course, we ask that you don’t leave town. We’ll know more in the morning once the ident team gets through. And, Christine, I’m truly sorry for your loss. This can’t be easy for you. I’ll personally keep you up to date.”

I didn’t expect any special treatment, but I also knew the law and the detectives couldn’t push more questions before they had some answers from the fire investigation. As their Staff Sergeant’s daughter, I’d also be considered an unlikely flight risk. I gave Jenny my card with my cell number and asked her to call the minute she had any information. I confirmed I'd be either at Dad's or Jake's and gave her both addresses.

Dad glanced up when I walked into his office. His shoulders were slumped and his eyes bloodshot.

"You look as exhausted as I feel," I said.

"Yeah, it's been a long night."

"I can't go home for a couple of days, and I'm not sure your one-bedroom condo is going to work for me and Sunny. Can you take me to Jake's?"

"Of course, I will, sweetheart. He has the dog. I spoke to him when you were in interview."

"He's been texting me too, telling me to call or come over. Did you talk to Annie?" I asked.

"Briefly. They questioned her at the scene, took her number, and told her to go home for a couple of days. She seemed pretty broken up when I called, talking around in circles. She always stood up for David and your marriage. This must be hard for her."

"You're right. I'll call her once I've had a few hours' sleep," I promised.

"And I called Alexander for you. His wife wasn't thrilled to be woken in the middle of the night, but I assumed you needed covering in court tomorrow, well, today and there's bound to be backlash in the media. I got his usual Mr. Grumpy tone, but he said he would field it and to call him when you had more information." Dad gave me a weak smile when he came from behind his desk.

"Thanks. I couldn't deal with calling him right now. They all think I'm this kick-ass crown attorney. Right now, I feel like a bowl of Jell-O. If he raised his voice, I would break down and cry."

"Let's get you somewhere safe. We'll take one step

at a time, and we'll figure things out." He smiled down at me and put his arm around my shoulder.

Leaving Dad's office, we walked almost directly into a uniformed officer, escorting Sharlene Hayward.

"There's your murderer!" she yelled, pointing at me.

"That's enough," the officer warned.

"David told me himself. Her words were, I'll see you both hang. She threatened my life and David's. She wanted him dead. Her and her boy next door, Jake Anderson both threatened us. They killed him. I need protection not questioning," she insisted.

She had stopped in front of me now, not allowing the officer to move unless he dragged her. She wore sweatpants and a bulky sweater. Her frizzy hair flew out in every direction. Her eyes were red rimmed, and her face pale, a blatant contrast to the happy girl on the beach in my husband's embrace. I had no pity for this woman and certainly no intention of honoring her accusations with a reply.

I maintained direct eye contact while she continued her tirade. "She's been talking divorce for months. She's a stone-cold bitch, and she hated him. She wanted him out of her life, so she didn't have to fork over any of her precious trust fund. All she cares about is her money. She murdered David Hamilton, and she's got Daddy here and her fireman boyfriend to cover for her."

Dad stepped between us, forcing both Sharlene and me to take a step back. "Get her out of here," he demanded.

Now the officer did yank her forward, and she had no choice but to go with him. I watched him pull her along to the interview area I had left.

She scowled over her shoulder. "You're the one who's going to pay now, you bitch."

Jenny walked up behind me, and I jumped when she put a hand on my shoulder. "Go ahead, Christine, I'll call you in a few hours."

I took Dad's arm, and we walked toward the front door.

"Are you sure, Scott?" Nick asked Jenny.

I turned to see her glaring at him. "Seriously, Juzo, get a grip. I can tell you right now, it's not her." She flipped her hand to me in dismissal.

Having an ally in Detective Jenny Scott reassured me, but I hung my head when I realized, they were already treating David's death as a murder.

We were so exhausted heading out the front doors of the station, I wasn't sure who held up whom. "Jeez, Dad, how do you work in all this noise and bright light? My head feels like it's being squeezed in a vice. If I don't lay down somewhere soon, I might throw up."

"We'll get some rest, and you'll feel better when we have more details."

What faced us when we opened the front door had Dad pulling me back behind him. There were media people yelling questions, with cell phones pointing at us, cameras flashing, even a news van complete with a microphoned reporter and camera man, who came running.

Dad put up a hand. "Go back home people, there's no story here."

One reporter called out. "Mr. Hamilton's business partner told us, Crown Attorney Montgomery is a murderer and she's got her cop Dad and a fire fighter boyfriend to cover for her. That seems like a story to me. What's she got to say for herself?"

Dad's jaw clenched. He narrowed his eyes at me and pointed in the door. He addressed the crowd as I retreated. "No one has established anyone has been murdered and her answer is of course, no comment."

Dad followed me back inside, barking orders. "Get rid of these damn news people and get me an unmarked car." The officer jumped to do his bidding. Dad yelled after him. "Pick us up outside holding!"

I rested on Dad's shoulder in the back of the cruiser, barely able to keep my eyes open. "Tell me this. Why does the media have to pick on the good guys? I work so hard to help people, to get legitimate criminals off the streets. I've never done anything illegal in my life. But the minute something bad happens in your own yard, everyone pounces on you like you've been a murderer for years," I said.

He patted my arm. "I know what you mean, and I don't have a good answer. People tend to thrive on bad news. In fact, a lot of people find tragic events compelling. Good news doesn't sell I suppose. Even though you and I are forced to follow the rules of innocent until proven guilty, it seems the media likes to pitch things the opposite way. You've seen it all before. Cop saves a drowning kid or talks someone down from a suicide ledge, it's a heartwarming story to finish the end of the news if anyone is still watching. But when a troubled cop sells information to a drug dealer, it's a headliner for days, weeks even. People can't seem to get enough of devastating news.

"Maybe it makes people feel good about their own issues if they believe other people can screw up worse than them, especially if that someone is a person in authority like police or a crown attorney like you or a teacher or a priest, people they expect to live perfect lives. Don't you agree?" he asked.

"I don't suppose I've given it much thought before now. It's always been my job to get to the truth of an event and make sure justice is served. I'll be honest, it makes me mad I'll be front page news and strangers will sit in judgment without knowing anything about me or you or David or Jake or any of our lives, certainly not about what happened in the fire or how he invested other people's money. I don't even know the truth of all that, but everyone will jump to their own conclusions after that media frenzy. Doesn't it bother you too?"

He held my hand. "Yes, it bothers me that you will have to be victim to the press for a while. But I got over worrying about what people think of me a long time ago. In time, you will too. Be true to yourself and tell it like it is. The truth will come out soon enough."

"I hope you're right. I couldn't believe we had to be transported separately," I said.

"The hardest part for me is staying out of the investigation. I want this sorted out and quickly, so you're safe. I want updates minute by minute, but everything is completely closed off from me, and it's going to make me crazy," he admitted.

"Yeah, same for me. Did they give you grief at the station?"

"I alibied pretty quickly. They all know me, but they still have to ask. I've been working at the station every minute or at home to eat and sleep."

He paused. I glanced up and he grinned. "What's going on? What aren't you telling me?" I asked.

"Let's say, I had someone to cover for me at home tonight too." He patted my arm.

"What? Dad, honestly? You have a girlfriend, and I don't know about her?"

He skirted the conversation. "We have bigger fish to fry right now. I promise I'll tell you all about Luisa. We'll do dinner, you can be buddies, go shopping together, all that good girl stuff, but right now is not the time."

I would rather have heard about Dad's girlfriend than almost anything, but he had closed the discussion. We sat silent for several more minutes, and I struggled not to fall asleep on his shoulder. He was tall and strong and having him to lean on felt natural and loving, the security I really needed. I had that horrible trying to stay awake feeling by the time we pulled into Jake's driveway. After I thanked the officer for the ride, Dad asked him to wait to take him back to his car in the city.

Sunny and Finnegan announced my arrival before I knocked. Jake opened the door clearly having a hard time restraining both big dogs. He gave up after a few seconds and let them go. They whined and wagged their tails, wiggling around me in a sea of blond and brown fur. They were a reassuring welcome, and I bent to pat them both. "Well, this is nice you two, but I need a couple of hours sleep before I can play."

Jake pulled me away from the dogs into a hug. "Are you two okay? Never mind, stupid question." He moved the hug to an arm around my shoulder and guided me toward the kitchen. "Come on in, what can I get you both, coffee, wine, something to eat?"

Dad followed a few steps but then stopped. "Nothing for me, Jake. I'm going to get out of here and get some sleep myself. I'll be back in the morning. Well, it is morning, but I'll be back in a while. I'll see what I can find out. Everything is sealed, but I have some people who will give me something."

"Wait, take this with you." Jake retrieved a large envelope from the table at the front door, handing it to my dad. "They'll need this stuff to get the investigation going."

"From David's desk I presume?" Dad asked.

Jake nodded.

"The officer I'm with will secure it, and Jenny will see it first thing."

Dad leaned over to kiss my cheek. "I'll be back soon. Love you, get some sleep. We'll get through this, I promise. Things have a strange way of working out."

I smiled. Dad always said that, and he was usually right. "Thanks. I love you too. Don't go back to work, you need sleep."

I followed Jake to the kitchen and sat down in the closest chair. "I don't want anything either, I need to crash, I'm a walking zombie."

Jake propped himself against the kitchen counter; his long lean legs crossed at the ankle in front of him. He stared right through me, tears brimming, visibly upset. When he held his arms open, I went to him gladly accepting his comfort. He stood up full height, pulling me tightly against him, so that my face rested in the center of his chest. He smelled freshly showered, not like smoke of the fire scene or stale air of the police station. It felt secure and reassuring to hold on to him, and I was in no hurry to let go.

He spoke over me while his face lay on the top of my head. "I can't remember ever being so scared.

When dispatch said structure fire at your address, I didn't know if you were in the fire. I had trouble getting into my boots. I've experienced some crazy shit in my career, but I have never been that scared in my life."

Pulling back, I kept my hands linked behind him and gave him my best attempt at a calm smile. "We're okay and we're going to figure out what Dave had going on and how the fire started, and, well, things have a strange way of working out." It took effort not to tear up as I quoted Dad.

As I opened my mouth to say we needed to get some sleep, Courtney walked around the kitchen door from Jake's master bedroom in the back, tilted her head, and raised her eyebrows. "Well, isn't this cozy?"

Chapter 5

I immediately stepped away from Jake's embrace, feeling guilty although not sure why hugging my best friend right after my husband died, was inappropriate.

"Courtney. Hi. I didn't know you were here. It's good to see you. All this is such an unbelievable situation and Jake's been an amazing support. I'm sorry you walked into this nightmare and that we woke you. And I'm rambling because clearly, I'm drained. Really, it is nice to see you. It's been a while since we all got together. I wish it were under better circumstances." I walked over to hug her, which felt less than sincere in return.

"Nice to see you too, Christine." Her words sounded strained.

She continued talking to me, but her eyes were on Jake. "I came up to surprise my Jake for the weekend, skipped out on a big networking gig at the Tivoli and look what I walked into. I hope this news doesn't get back to Toronto. Imagine what it could do to my career prospects? Well, let's just focus on the weekend, shall we?"

She walked over and wrapped herself around Jake, gazing lovingly at him, even though her words were meant for me. "Sometimes when Jake comes off nights, I get here in time to sneak in before he gets home. He usually lets me know just how happy he is to see me."

She planted a loud kiss on his lips. “Right, my love?”

He peeled her arms off, pushed her back and stepped around her. “Courtney, really? Christie has been through a traumatic experience. David is dead, their place is half burned, and she’s been up all night being questioned by cops. Not to mention Dave was my friend, our friend and your first thought is about your career prospects? I don’t think Christie gives a rat’s ass about your social calendar or our weekend visits. You could at least offer your condolences.”

It didn’t take a rocket scientist to figure out Courtney was put out that Jake consoled me while he berated her. Clearly, she wanted to mark her territory as woman of the house, and David’s death and my emotions were low on her list of concerns.

I grabbed Sunny’s collar. “It’s okay, Jake, no worries, we’re all tired, we can talk later. I’m going to pass out for a couple of hours on your couch. Then I can get out of your hair and let you two have some alone time. Do you have a spare phone charger?”

“You’re not sleeping on the couch. The guest room is made up, and you’re welcome to it as long as you need.”

I didn’t miss the wide-eyed glare Courtney gave Jake. His open-ended invitation didn’t seem to play a part in her surprise weekend plan. Under the circumstances, I wasn’t too concerned about hurting her feelings. Overwhelmed and exhausted, I needed quiet and sleep, not more drama.

Jake pulled a charger out of his kitchen drawer and taking my hand, he led me to the guest room, even though I already knew his house like my own.

"Christie, I mean it. The bed's clean; there are towels, a new toothbrush, and everything you need in the guest bath, even a robe on the back of the door and some of my T-shirts in the drawer. Help yourself and get comfortable. Are you okay? Are you sure I can't get you something? A glass of wine, warm milk and a cookie."

I smiled, shaking my head. I started to thank him again for the offer when Sunny wiggled between us and jumped up on the bed.

"No, Sunny, get down. I'm so sorry, she's used to sleeping with me when David's out, which has been a lot lately. She must be sensing my stress or something. Honestly, dog. Get off!"

Jake laughed and turned me to face him. "Please stop. Sunny is welcome too. She's fine on the bed, I don't care. Where do you think Finnegan sleeps? Well not when Courtney's here. Really, relax, mi casa, es su casa, for both of you. Get some sleep."

He kissed my cheek, then pulled me into an embrace once again, holding me tightly. I leaned into him and closed my eyes for a few seconds welcoming his support. He stepped back gazing at me with a sympathetic smile. His compassion warmed me even though he left without any more words. He and Courtney had what sounded like angered words in the kitchen followed by a slammed door. But then things were quiet.

I washed and changed quickly into one of Jake's T-shirts and crawled under soft covers. Being in Jake's house was the closest thing to being home. We had grown up hiding on each other in these rooms, playing games, doing homework, having teenage parties when our parents were away, and later adult dinners and visits filled with laughter and friendship. Although he had renovated to keep things up to date, most of the rooms still had a familiar, relaxed retro vibe that always felt welcoming. A sudden tug at my heart made me cry, leaving me unsure if the sadness lingered for David or for me or for simpler days when Jake and I tore up the house without a care, while our Moms sat drinking coffee and laughing at us. Listening to the birds starting their predawn chatter, I closed my eyes, letting the tears fall on my pillow without any effort to wipe them away. Sunny stayed in bed with me and with one arm over her, I fell into a deep sleep.

****

I woke with a start a few hours later when Annie came into the room with a tray holding steaming coffee, waffles drowning in syrup, and a bowl of fruit big enough for four people. It took me a minute to get my bearings, especially with Annie there. She wore black jeans and a navy-blue sweater; her hair was pulled back into a small bun, with bangs and a few loose hairs perfectly straightened over the top edge of her glasses. Although she had slight bags under her eyes, she looked fresh and awake like nothing had happened.

"You need to wake up lovey. There are police outside and newspaper people all over. Your Dad and your work have called Jake's cell because you're not answering, and that Jake won't get out of my way. Mercy, I'm trying to help and get some decent food for you and there are people all over the place."

"What are you doing here? I can't eat all this, and why would Jake get out of your way? It's his house. Oh my God, Courtney must be freaking out."

"That lazy little wench isn't out of his bed yet. Let's get on with you."

"Annie, really, I can't eat anything right now. There's enough for an army here and I don't need help getting dressed. I'll just take the coffee. And get used to all the people, it's going to be chaos for a few days."

I swung my feet over the side of the bed, swatting at her nurturing hands. "Please stop fussing over me. I'll work things out." I had no idea how or when I would work things out, but knew I had no other option.

"Tell them I'll be out in ten minutes, and can you take Sunny? I'm sure she's a lot more ready for breakfast than I am." When I glanced up, I felt guilty. Annie looked hurt. Her life revolved around taking care of Dad and David, and she loved fussing over me, but sometimes, it was too much of a good thing.

I started again. "Thank you. I'm sorry, I haven't even asked if you're okay. Are you okay? This is horrible. Of course, you're not okay. I promise, Rick and I love you and I'm sure Jake appreciates that you're here and all you're doing but it's going to be a while before any of us gets back to normal, a long while. Can we talk later today maybe?"

"Oh, I'm not concerned about that. It will all sort itself." She waved her hand to the side dismissing the whole event.

"Not concerned? What do you mean by that? David is dead. It's a big deal what we all witnessed last night. It's important to talk it through. Did the police give you a hard time after the fire?"

"Nothing I can't handle," she said with a toss of her head.

I wanted to ask her more questions. She seemed

vague and unconcerned considering the circumstances, but I was too upset to process her emotion, or lack of it. Sunny continued to bark at the door, intensifying my splitting headache. I sat on the side of the bed and held my head in my hands. "We'll have to talk later, Annie, I'm not doing too well, and I need to get up and dressed. Can you take the dog and let her out or ask Jake to let her out, please? I'll be down in a few minutes." I thanked her again, and she shut the door behind them.

It took more like half an hour by the time I showered and changed. The dizzying headache persisted, despite running the hot shower on my neck for ten minutes straight. Coupled with the pile of smokey clothes nausea threatened to send me back to the bathroom.

I studied myself in the mirror noting my puffy eyes from tears the night before. The jeans and sweater I had grabbed were worn and hardly office appropriate, reminding me of Jake's description of how people see me with no-nonsense confidence and a perfect smile, the exact opposite of how I felt today. What faced me in the kitchen did nothing to improve my mood.

I had passed a uniformed officer at the front door, keeping press away. Jake tossed the newspaper on the breakfast counter, nodding to draw my attention to the front page. My story covered most of it with one large picture of me coming out of the ambulance, in my tank top pajamas, holding Jake's hand and two smaller inserts, one of the fire and one of David at the business awards last month, Sharlene grinning by his side. A long headline read, "*Prominent Mortgage Broker, David Hamilton, Husband of Crown Attorney Christine*

Montgomery, Murdered on his own Property. Is She Capable of the Perfect Crime?"

"Can't the dead guy at least get the biggest picture? And who has confirmed a murder? Perfect crime, yeah right, I wouldn't have a job if people could figure out how to commit a perfect crime. Alexander's going to go crazy over this. I guess I should say good morning before I start bitching. Jake, I'm so sorry for all this."

He smiled, his hand motioning me to sit at the breakfast counter. "Settle down. Take a breath. Drink your coffee and eat something."

His commands and comforting smile calmed me somewhat. I pulled a stool up and started to read the front-page article but jumped up again when I reached for my phone. "Shoot, my phone's still charging, and I've been missing calls. I need to call into work. It's going to be a shit show down there. I'll be right back."

As I stepped away from the counter, Courtney walked into the kitchen. When I arrived earlier, she was dressed in a long hoodie and leggings. Now she wore an almost see-through top that barely covered her top half and tiny boy shorts that covered even less of her behind. She always looked stunning to me, with a slim, almost boyish fashion model frame, delicate features like a china doll with the same pale skin, almost black eyes and long waves of dark hair that flowed naturally over her shoulders. Even without makeup and perfectly styled hair, she was classic elegance. She would likely be quite confident walking around change rooms half dressed, but Jake didn't look happy to see her walking toward us in her lingerie, at the same time as Detectives Scott and Juzo were walking in the front door of the house.

"Courtney for Christ's sake put some clothes on. We have a house full of people," he said.

Frazzled, I didn't know where to focus. Jenny couldn't have had more than four hours sleep but she appeared confident and prepared for a new day. She was a blonde haired, blue eyed beauty, but all professional. She wore dark olive slim pants and a starched white, collared shirt. Her cotton jacket covering her gun holster was deep slate gray matching her killer dark leather boots. She really presented the whole package, brains, beauty, and power. I had so much respect for this lady.

Nick, on the other hand, looked like he had slept in his clothes, or maybe not slept at all. I was certain he still wore the same shirt, jacket, and running shoes from our interview at two a.m., and he carried the biggest take-out coffee I had ever seen. He ate a breakfast sandwich that oozed grease with every bite, thankfully onto the paper that held it. I wondered how he could see what he ate with his long black bangs falling in his eyes obstructing his view of his breakfast and my view of his face. He was equally as disheveled as Jenny was put together. They were an odd couple.

"Jen, wow, am I glad to see you. Please come in. Good morning, Nick. Please sit in the kitchen. I have to grab my phone."

I shrugged at Jake and mouthed "sorry" one more time.

Back in the kitchen, I sat in front of Jenny trying to show some of my courtroom confidence, although feeling more like we were back in high school, and I needed her help in math class. "Jake, I'm sure you remember Jenny Scott from high school, and this is her partner, Nick Juzo. They're detectives on Dad's unit. Jen, Nick, this is Jake Anderson, a captain with London fire department and my neighbor, obviously."

They shook hands. Jake offered coffee which Jenny declined, and Nick answered by lifting his giant cardboard cup, not taking his eyes of his notebook.

"Okay then, I'll leave you alone." Jake nodded.

"Do you mind if he stays? Jake, will you sit?" I asked.

Jenny smiled at me, then glanced up at Jake. "Of course, he can stay. Christine, I know this is agony for you so I want to keep you updated and make it as easy as I can. I'm here because we're lead detectives. We all go way back, but I need to keep things professional. There will be questions while the investigation progresses, and you need to answer without reading too much into the why.

"And don't start your own investigation. You amaze all of us with your reputation for putting the puzzle together and making it stick, after we arrest the bad guy, but this time, you need to stay out of it. There's something off here and you could be in danger, so could your Dad or Jake." She eyed Annie, rattling dishes in the sink. "Or anyone else living in your house."

I tried not to show my annoyance at the racket she made. "I should also introduce you to Annie. I told you about her last night."

Annie smiled at the detectives. Jenny nodded briefly seeming anxious to move on. Nick didn't acknowledge her at all.

"Annie, really, the dishes can wait. We can do that later, please," I said.

She didn't hide her irritation at being dismissed, huffing loudly as she retreated to the family room.

Jenny continued. "As I was saying, we need a whole lot more answers, and it's sticky right now because I face reprimand if I'm giving information to your dad. But, since you're the wife of the deceased, it's also appropriate for us to report to you and to get details about what's been going on the last few months. I can't tell you not to tell Rick, but, well, you get it."

"I'll do anything you say," I promised.

"Sergeant Montgomery's back at the office going crazy. It's difficult since he's my superior. I'm used to us brainstorming together but I simply can't involve him. It's hard on all of us. So please, I know you want information, but I can only offer bits and pieces when they become facts, no speculation."

"I get it. We appreciate what you're doing more than you know. We'll take any update, whenever you're allowed to tell us and answer anything you need to know," I said.

"The thing is, after the interview last night, no one suspects any of you are involved. My gut tells me there's something tied up in all the mortgage fraud, but there's more emotion to this than several hundred thousand worth. He didn't steal enough from any one person to get himself murdered and there's no indication of mental illness to suggest suicide," she explained.

"Please, Jen, everyone keeps talking around murder like it's a given. The fact your team is investigating tells me that's what you think too. Did someone kill David?" I winced.

"I can't confirm that. Truly, I wish I could. The

coroner cleared to have the body removed while we were asleep. Mr. Hamilton is at the morgue now. Gavin is working on him and you know he's the best. The fire marshal secured the scene even before our team had a warrant, so they knew things were fishy from the get-go. I'm sorry. The vic…that is, we recovered Mr. Hamilton from a face-down position on the couch. There's nothing to suggest he was attempting to get out the front door because he left a pot on and the smoke woke him up. It's going to take time, but first indications point to a struggle and the preliminary fire report points to arson. So, although we can't confirm murder, the sweepers and the fire marshal are already handling it like a suspicious cause of death."

I nodded, expecting the answer. "Thank you, I understand."

She continued. "That's why the major crimes unit is assigned, so there's a big team getting all the answers as quickly as possible. You are all spoken for. Certainly, Captain Anderson arrived directly from station thirteen. Staff Sergeant Montgomery worked until eight at the precinct and then had company at home. I can't see motive for you, Christine. I believe your story, and I believe you too may be in danger if there is a killer and he thinks you're tied into the fraud. You need to help us. Did David have a history of gambling? Drugs? Did he owe someone money? It seems he and Sharlene were involved romantically, there are a lot of questions there too."

I shook my head. "I never saw anything leaning toward addiction of any kind. I told you last night, Jake and I explored that possibility. I wish I had asked more questions when I had suspicions about him and a lover.

Now, more than ever, I want to know what the heck he did at his office. Start with Sharlene. They spent more time together than we did in the last several months. And, by that I mean, at the office, but that's true in all aspects it seems. She's got to know more than he ever told me.

"I had no access to any of his home electronics. His computer, emails and phone were all protected, and he changed the passwords regularly. Like I told you in interview, there were so many other things that made me suspicious that led to what I found last night. I had a tough time trying to figure him out even when he was alive."

Jenny nodded. "I can appreciate your frustration. We'll get to the bottom of it. We've secured all his electronics from home and at the office, and we have the mortgage papers you sent back to the precinct with Sergeant Montgomery last night. We've had Sharlene in and she's co-operating. The fraud team is really working her, but she's genuinely grieving, and she had an alibi. She went to her sister's after David told her you knew about the two of them and what you and Jake said to him. That's where they picked her up in the middle of the night. She seems in the dark about the mortgage papers also. Either she's a good actress or he really kept everything secret even from his own colleagues. We do have her electronics, and we'll make sure she's not involved before we let her off the hook.

"They did the warrant early this morning, before the sun came up, so things are really moving over at the house. Hopefully, they won't be too long in there. They've also taken David's BMW downtown. The coroner has signed off. Fire investigators will be at the scene for a few days, maybe a good part of the week. That takes a lot longer than searching the house. And the insurance people and media will get in the way too.

"There is something else that I can tell you we're checking. When we played the dashcam from the fire truck, we saw someone in the crowd who was kind of mesmerized by the fire and a little too calm for the situation, never making eye contact with any of the essential services. Wayne Duncan, do you remember him from high school?" Jenny asked.

"I sure do; creepy, skinny guy. I've seen him in the courthouse a few times too. He lives around here somewhere, although I'm not sure where exactly," I said.

"Yes, that's him. It may be nothing, could be a nosy neighbor, but we're looking for him to ask a few questions."

"The door was locked," Jake said out of the blue.

"What's that?" Nick finally spoke. His voice startled me.

"I said the door was locked. When we got to the fire, we had to force the front door. It will all come out with the fire marshal's investigation, but whoever killed David, if that's the case, won't have walked right onto center stage of the driveway cam. Unless he stopped to lock the door behind him, the killer went down the pool slide," Jake said.

"Pool slide?" Nick lifted his head from his notebook and squinted at Jake.

I answered for him. "Like I told you, the carriage house was old, maybe close to a hundred years. The big room above the garage side of the building, had solid walls, but bare bones, maybe for hired help way back in the day or even heavy storage. It had only the one exit through the garage and out the front door at the bottom of the steps. When we renovated it into Dave's man cave, we knocked a door out the back to make a skinny set of stairs that curved down to the pool area. The guys used to say they were going to grab a cardboard box and make the stairs into a pool slide." I recalled laughing about that with David and Jake and it made me sad.

Jenny brought me back. "Christine, stay with me. And Jake, thank you. We do have the films from the driveway cam since they transmitted to David's computer, at least up until the fire took out the camera. Of course, that's where they looked first along with the fire truck dashcam, but there's nothing out front so you're probably right about the back door. If another person got up there when the fire started, he likely knew the lay of the land. That's the kind of thing I need you two to think about, small details. It all helps. I have to get back, but keep thinking, and write things down. Call me, text me, email, anything no matter how unimportant it seems, details are what count.

"And, be warned, when the fire marshal is investigating, they'll bring in a backhoe and pull it all apart. It's going to be hard to watch, be ready for that. Hopefully, the police ident will be done with the main house by later today. We don't expect a smoking gun, so I can't imagine they will have disrupted your things. There will be a uniformed officer outside for a while, to keep the fire scene secure and keep reporters away from your property. Will you both be here today?" she asked, glancing from Jake to me.

"I'm going to try to go to work for a while. There

are tons of cases in limbo. I've never left without organizing my office and leaving instructions and they're already calling with questions. Obviously, the press is all over them too; one of their own, a potential murderer, honestly," I said, shaking my head.

Jenny pointed her finger at me. "You could be in danger. I know your Dad and Jake will keep an eye on things, but even when you're in the city and in your car, watch yourself. We don't have enough manpower to keep a cop on you. You need to be more careful than usual."

"I'm used to the bad guys and I have my trusty Range Rover with tinted windows so no one can see me, practically indestructible. Just about everyone thinks I'm a murderer right now anyway so maybe they'll keep a distance." I shrugged.

"That's what I'm worried about. You are not indestructible and no matter how big and elegant your SUV is, it's not bullet proof. People around here know your car and media will be on you. You won't be able to tell a reporter from a stalker in a crowd and you have a lot to distract you. Maybe some gossipy folks think you had something to do with David's death and they'll snub you for a while, but if there is a murderer out there, and he wants to get near you, your vehicle isn't going to protect you," she warned.

I shook off a shiver and faced Jenny and Nick with a smile that took effort. "I promise I'll be careful. Please call me when you know more and when I can get back into my own place please. I made a rushed exit last night, with only a change of clothes, my briefcase and my purse. I didn't get to pack appropriate work clothes or necessities. It's not a priority, but I need to get at my stuff. Going to work in jeans and a T-shirt is not going to go over well."

I walked them to the front door, shook both their hands, and thanked them again.

"I've probably got something you can wear, Christine," Courtney said from the kitchen.

Surprised by her voice, I wondered if she'd been eavesdropping the whole time or had just surfaced from her morning routine.

"Who are you?" Nick called out before I answered her.

Jake held her hand and pulled her toward us at the front door, speaking for her. "This is my fiancée, Courtney Kalder. Courtney, these are Detectives Scott and Juzo from the major crimes unit."

She slowly offered her hand to shake theirs, not saying a word in reply to the introduction. She had paled like she'd seen a ghost.

"Courtney, are you all right?" I asked.

It didn't help that Nick replaced the civil introductions with demanding questions. "Where were you last night? Do you live here with Mr. Anderson?"

She kept hold of Jake's hand, pinning herself against his arm. "I live in the city, in Toronto that is. I didn't get here until after, well before…that is, I didn't get here for the fire, you can check. I left Planet Night Club on Steeles Ave in Toronto after two a.m. I had people there with me who can vouch for me. I drove here to surprise Jake. I do that sometimes when he comes off nights. Usually, he comes in around eight in the morning after I've had a few hours' sleep. But, last night, well, I got here after four and he came in right after. He said the fire chief sent him home. I got the surprise this time when I drove up and saw police cars and giant bright lights and tape marking off Chris and Dave's place. Then Christine and her dad, well, Rick, you know him, well yeah, they showed up at like five. We hadn't even got any sleep yet and well, it's been crazy, but I didn't have anything to do with anything."

Jenny thankfully jumped in to stop Courtney's rambling and calm the growing tense moment. "It's fine Ms. Kalder. Detective Juzo is not accusing you of anything. We've been asking neighbors if they saw or heard anything before the fire. I'm sure Mr. Anderson can vouch for your arrival time. Perhaps, just in case we need to check, you could write down the name of the club and a couple of the people you—"

"No!" Courtney screamed at Jenny.

Jake spun Courtney toward him, holding her shoulders, and crouching to her eye level. "What's gotten into you? Why are you acting so weird?"

Jenny frowned at them. "Perhaps we could sit in the kitchen again for a few minutes."

"No, I'm sorry, I didn't mean to yell. And I don't want to sit down for questioning. There's nothing to say. The thing is, my job, that is, I model and do commercials and, well other things, and I'm trying to network into some more serious gigs. You know what I mean?"

"Ah…no, I'm sorry I don't. Where are you going with this Ms. Kalder?" Jenny asked.

"It's just that it's really tough competition. That is, trying to get into the screen business. If cops start sniffing around like I'm involved, especially in something big like a murder, sorry, Chris." She half-smiled with a tilt of her head in my direction then kept talking. “Well, it’s just, bad for business. Don’t you have highway cams or something that you can check my license passing like they do on that *Manhunt* or *Hunted*, whatever that show is? Can’t you find something that gives me a time frame without asking my people?”

“Unbelievable,” Jake muttered. He rolled his eyes then went back to the kitchen leaving Courtney alone with the rest of us at the front door.

“That won’t be necessary for now, Ms. Kalder. We’ll be in touch if we have any more questions.”

Jenny glanced at me, eyes wide. “Christine, I’ll call you.” She shook her head slowly as she and Nick walked out the door.

“Oh, thank God.” Courtney sighed. “I thought they might take me in. Imagine if my photo landed in the news alongside you two?”

I wasn’t sure if she directed her question to me or if she was thinking out loud, so I didn’t answer. Her behavior shocked me, and the answer that immediately came to my mind didn’t seem appropriate even if she expected one.

She gave another half-smile in my direction, then strutted back to the kitchen. “Is there coffee?”

Jake pulled a mug from the cupboard without answering her. Their silence felt like my cue to get out of the way. I spoke from the doorway of the kitchen. “I’m going to get ready for work and see if I can accomplish anything positive today.”

“I’ve got a couple of skirts if you need to borrow something Chris,” Courtney offered again.

“I think jeans will have to work for today but thank you.”

Courtney's elegant style of glamour and glitz rivaled my business casual and weekend converse runners. She might have something to loan me in a pinch, but it didn't seem the time to start a riff over fashion. Getting between these two and dealing with Jen and Nick zapped all the emotional strength I had left. Courtney seemed so nervous and self-absorbed, even distant to me, making me question if she had something to hide or if she was jealous, or sadly if she was really concerned with only her career?

Maybe she felt threatened since her fiancé's best friend had become single overnight. What a morbid thought. We all used to be such good friends. A lot had changed over the last few months and it annoyed me that I hadn't taken more notice. If I had to admit it, I was better friends with Jake than I had been with David. In Courtney's shoes perhaps I would be clingy too. Maybe Courtney had changed for the worse before now and I hadn't noticed that either.

I packed up my few things and straightened the bed, hoping to be clear to go home after work. Entering the kitchen a few minutes later, carrying my briefcase, purse, and my bag of smoky clothes, I sensed tension. Jake and Courtney were silent and to make things worse, Annie had reappeared underfoot. "I'm taking my stuff so if they clear the house, I'll go straight home tonight. Annie, you need to take a couple of days off; go home and stay home and keep the doors locked. I promise I'll call and let you know when I can get back in the house. If it's tonight, you can come by tomorrow for a while if you really need to, but please, you've had a huge shock, take some time to recover. It's only me now, I can manage."

Annie nodded but didn't reply. "Jake, Courtney, thank you again. Have a nice weekend together, get outside, enjoy the beautiful warm fall weather. I'll be fine, and I will text you the minute I hear anything. Can I trouble you to keep Sunny for today until the police are done? You can take her over later, maybe by dinner time. I hope they won't take longer than that."

Annie smiled and blew me a kiss. Courtney smiled but didn't say a word returning to the paper and her coffee.

Jake came forward and wrapped me in a hug. I felt like Courtney's eyes bored holes into his back. I couldn't hug him back with my hands full, but I melted against him. It took everything in me to act a degree of normal when I stepped away. Facing the reporters outside and the focus the office would demand didn't intimidate me, but in the big picture, my insides screamed help!

Jake's hug told me he sensed my despair despite my cheery departing words. He whispered against my ear like he had read my thoughts. "You have a friend here who knows you and has your back no matter what."

I stepped back from the security of his embrace, gazing into his compassionate eyes. "Thank you," I whispered, turning away before tears fell. Reaching for my keys in my purse, I realized my car wasn't outside his house. "Ah, Jake, could I have a ride over to my car?"

Chapter 6

Getting out of Jake's house had been bad enough. While the officer kept the few reporters at bay, they still took pictures and yelled out questions. "Why did I stay at Jake's house? Were Jake and I lovers? Did I kill David? Was David having an affair?"

"Why are people always so interested in other people's sex lives?" I stared at Jake when he pulled into my driveway.

He laughed and leaned over for another hug.

I backed away and he jolted up. "Please, no more fuel for the fire. Ugh, why do I say things like that? No pun intended. There's probably a damn reporter in the bushes waiting to take our picture. I'll call you later," I said.

"I don't think anyone can see inside my truck, but fine, I'll keep my distance. Are you sure you're up to this?"

"I have to keep moving or I'm going to crumble."

"Text me when you get to work," he said.

I gave him a thumbs up, jumped down from his truck, shut the door, and ran up the driveway to my SUV scrambling in like I was being chased. I did feel more secure, locked in, hiding behind my tinted windows.

I stared at the front of my house, now surrounded by ugly, yellow police tape. My mind spun with questions and sadness and guilt. The day of my wedding flashed back to me, bright and vivid like it was happening all over. The big tent filled the side yard under the warm August sun. The house was surrounded at a distance by huge maples and grand oak trees with mature flowering bushes perfectly placed closer to the house so there were different colored vibrant blooms at intervals all the warm months of the year. The view from the front boasted a picture-perfect two-story century old home. It had been power washed so many times and faded from the sun that the soft yellow brick appeared almost white. There were full story windows in the front downstairs and up. Large round white pillars held up the roof over the full-length porch while the small white spindle railing and the big porch swing completed the impression of a beautiful southern estate.

Dad had walked me from that front door, through a path of flowers leading to a handsome, smiling David at the makeshift altar. Later, he had carried me over the same threshold to mark our possession of the house Dad had gifted for a wedding present. My happiness marrying David filled me. My excitement to take over my childhood home and fill it with lifelong memories and a family of our own equaled my pain at missing my Mom so much it hurt my chest. It was a bittersweet day.

I shook my head quickly, erasing the day, knowing my dreams were no longer remotely possible and once again feeling that too familiar chest pain. I avoided even a glance at the carriage house, wasn't ready to go there again. I backed out of the driveway, determined to focus on the work ahead of me and take everything else one step at a time.

Getting to work proved ridiculously worse than

expected. The drive into London was uneventful, the usual fifteen minutes. With no police protection this time, I had second thoughts the minute I pulled into the parking lot across from the courthouse. There were several people pacing out front, a few with signs, reading "murderer" in red paint that had drips like blood gushing down from a wound, adding affect to their message.

"Why would people protest me? They don't even know me. Don't they have anything better to do?" I muttered reaching for my briefcase.

Jenny was right; people knew my car. A reporter with a camera on his shoulder bombarded me the moment I stepped out, followed by a microphone shoved in my face so close it almost hit me.

"How will the Crown's office feel about putting one of their own in jail, Ms. Montgomery? Do you think you'll get special treatment once you're in the slammer with all those crooks you put away?" the reporter demanded.

I said "no comment" repeatedly. Advancing slowly to my office building, people were shoving at me, a second reporter shouting absurd questions over the chanting protesters. Panic overwhelmed me. Focusing on taking short, deep breaths, I tried to ignore the small crowd and push forward to the front door.

The first bold reporter pulled at my sleeve, so that I lost my balance against a woman with a sign who pushed me roughly upright again. She shoved her sign in my face as I stood straight, so I had to back up to see what hit me. "Justice for David" the sign read, to match their chant. Jenny's warning replayed in my mind making me jumpy. Already regretting my decision to come to the office, I gasped when a reporter spun me toward him.

I twisted from his grasp. “Get your hands off me or you’ll be sorry.” Of course, someone snapped a picture of my vicious face, which I had no doubt would be on the front page of the London Free Press in the morning.

I made my breakaway to the door several feet ahead, wondering why this handful of people felt like a swarm of a hundred. Mitch and Ed, two of our court room security officers shoved people aside to come to my aid.

“I’ve never been so happy to see you two. I’ll buy you coffee, no make it lunch, maybe even dinner, I promise. Thank you so much for the rescue.” I smiled but received no reply. They each grabbed an arm like they were escorting a criminal from a prison cell and dumped me in the front door returning to their stations without a word.

“Jeez, tough crowd, this may take a little more effort than I thought,” I said.

I rounded the corner relieved to see my assistant, Karen at her desk. She had been my right hand since I started several years before. Almost a generation older than me, she had worked at the Crown Attorneys’ office for many years before I got there. She had grown kids and spent more hours working than she got paid for, making me think she preferred the office over spending time at home with her retired husband. Consequently, she knew how everything functioned and made a point of making sure everyone else knew that she did. She had a slim build, straight hair cut in a bob, dyed dark to cover occasional sprouting grays. She was always well dressed but plain and unassuming. Her personality was much more outgoing than her attire suggested. She demanded respect from her colleagues and had little tolerance for ignorance, making her a bit of a go to for the other staff. She also kept them in line with experienced advice for both the office and their families. I often called her the mother hen, especially when she told me stories about some of the younger staff.

“What are you doing here?” she hissed at me.

“Well, good morning to you too. I just got beaten up trying to get out of my car, Mike and Ike dumped me in the door like a convict and wouldn’t even talk to me. Oh yeah, and my husband is dead, everyone thinks I killed him and I’m banging the boy next door in my spare time. Now I have to answer to you?” I raised my eyebrows, inviting another snide remark.

“I’m sorry, truly my condolences, but you have no idea. Mitch and Ed have been working their butts off since we opened trying to keep reporters and nosy locals out the door, while keeping the criminals in. There are threatening people out there. Some staff are ready to leave because they’re scared to be here. Not to mention the phone calls. I can’t get anything done. You haven’t made anyone’s job any easier. And don’t call them Mike and Ike. Mitch and Ed are decent guys.”

“I know, I’d still be out there bouncing off reporters if they hadn’t come to my rescue. I’ll buy them lunch. Remind me, would you? Maybe they’ll forgive me for causing so much trouble. I’m not sure why I expected my own colleagues to give me the benefit of the doubt. This has always been the one place I felt most appreciated. I thought all of you might be sympathetic and maybe I could hide away here and make things right with the world again. I guess I didn't think did I. I'm kind of lost today to tell you the truth."

Karen stared at me without saying anything.

"What? Why are you staring?"

"I've never seen you like this, so, I don't know, normal. You never say anything about how you feel, and you always dress so, so…"

"So, what? Really, what are you saying? Next time your husband dies in a fire and everyone thinks you murdered him, let's see how put together you show up at the office the next day. Jeez, I tried to help by coming in here to organize some cases so everyone wouldn't be in a panic and all I'm getting is grief."

Slowly enunciating her words, like she was explaining to a child, she answered in a quiet voice. "Calm down, Christine, that's not what I meant. What I'm trying to say is you look really good, like relaxed and well, natural or something. I mean, under the circumstances. Can I just say, your hair is amazing? I had no idea it was so long. And how do you get those golden highlights? You've got to be what five, eight, five, nine? And it's still almost to your waist. You must have a few feet of hair. And I've never noticed how blue your eyes are. Are they contacts?"

I didn't answer her, standing dumbfounded while she continued. "Usually, you walk in here with an attitude telling everyone what to do, decked out like you stepped out of a dressed for success magazine with your hair pulled back so tightly, it pulls your face, and your glasses cover your eyes. Your suits are all the same and so pressed and perfect, and frankly, they cover these nice curves you've got going on there, girl."

She waved her hand in an S shape from top to

bottom, and it made me chuckle despite my distress.

"I know you have to present that uptight image in court to show your authority and all that, but, well, your weekend-wear and this frazzled attitude are um, I don't know, refreshing. It's a way better you in my opinion." She smirked and tipped her head.

"Thanks, I think. And sorry I jumped all over you. I'm in a bad place, Karen, but I'm glad someone thinks it looks refreshing. And no, I don't wear contacts, and this is my natural hair color and I'm five, ten, not that any of that seems relevant to anything. This is the real me, how I dress when cops are dragging me out the door and I don't have time to grab my glasses or makeup or clothes for work."

"You might want to do that more often, well minus the cops," Karen said, returning to her screen when I walked away. My office was a disaster, at least a disaster by my standards. Normally, I would have my files organized and my desktop would be completely clear before eight and I'd be ready to appear in court for the day by eight-thirty. I dumped my bags on my desk and sat for a minute wondering where to start. I didn't like being late, I was uncomfortable wearing jeans to the office, despite Karen's flattering words and my mind raced with a hundred things, none to do with courtroom procedures. I stood without starting my computer and headed back toward Karen who appeared to be taking a call from another inquiring mind. She shook her head with a scowl on her face.

"Is he in?" I whispered, pointing down the hall.

She nodded to me. "Of course, I have nothing to confirm." She spoke firmly into the phone.

Without waiting to talk to her, I went down the hall

to see my boss, a man I admired and respected more than most people I knew. Alexander Walker had been in charge at the Crown Attorneys' office since my articling student days. He was an attractive man in his early sixties, with the distinguished air that came from expensive suits, a full head of salt and pepper hair, and an ever-present sun touched complexion indicating his time on the golf course or out on his sailboat. He had trained me to be a top-notch Crown Attorney, and he assured me that he respected me and all the work I did. He was tough, though, and exceptionally private. No one shortened Alexander to Al or Alex or Andy. In fact, most called him Mr. Walker or sir and not many colleagues were welcome in his social circle. He believed in the justice system and never bent the rules. I didn't know the policy for a Crown Attorney with a recently murdered husband. He liked me, but I didn't know how much he could have my back under the circumstances.

I stuck my head around the door before entering. "Alexander, good morning."

His brows raised when he glanced over my attire, but he'd be too polite to comment. He gestured for me to come in and sit. His office represented him well, tastefully decorated with dark green walls, dark brown wood blinds, a large mahogany desk and soft brown leather chairs. His shelves covered one whole wall beside me and were lined with the typical hard cover volumes of criminal law outlining jury addresses, courtroom procedures and precedents by the hundreds.

On the corner of his desk sat a picture in an antique gold frame of himself and his wife alongside a more modern frame showing his daughter at her graduation from the police academy. They were displayed at an angle so he and any visitors could see them. Other than the photos, the huge desktop was clear of personal effects. The most recent edition of the Criminal Code of Canada lay open beside a standard legal pad of yellow lined paper with his scribbled notes for the day's cases, his expensive silver pen lying on top. The desk lamp in standard green with the gold cord shone down on the paper.

The only modern item was a large screen Mac computer, currently depicting a screen saver of a large sailboat slicing the waves. I smiled at the picture, remembering the last time we spoke in his office, and he excitedly explained his most recent regatta, with terms like tacking upwind and mark rounding. I didn't know much about sailing or racecourses, but I felt privileged he considered me close enough to share his experience. The sailboat picture only added to the rest of the office decor to perfectly denote his masculine, distinguished persona. Despite the precision of his office, it calmed me compared to the overwhelming confusion that waited at my desk. I was temporarily relieved to step away from making decisions and talk things through with Alexander, confident he would be able to see my situation from a legal angle that no one else could.

"I'm surprised you made it in today." His tone didn't tell me if surprised meant impressed or annoyed that I had made the effort. "Firstly, my sincere condolences and I truly mean it. I know things were dicey with you and David the last few months, but this is a shock."

"Thank you. We've never had to deal with

anything like this in the office. I'm not sure there's a protocol, but I appreciate you talking to me. I need someone who knows the real me and the affect this kind of scandal can have on my career. I'm not getting the welcome mat out there, that's for sure." I waved my hand in the direction of his door and forced a smile.

He folded his hands together on his desk before he spoke. "I'm not going to sugar coat. I can't be that person for you today. If you need a lawyer, I'm happy to help you find one, but I can't be your confidante. This is a serious situation, and the press is implying that we are trying to cover something for you in collusion with the homicide department and even the fire department. It's a zoo down here on regular days, without all this extra nonsense. You're going to have to pack up for a while until all this blows over. You can't be here."

"I have work to do, Alexander, cases to complete. I can't leave. It usually takes me weeks to review and summarize and remand my cases so I can take a week holiday. I've never got up and left everything without planning ahead. That's why I'm here to make some sense of things so I can take a few days off. And for the record, it's not nonsense and I'm not asking anyone to cover for me. I didn't kill him, and I'm not going to act like I did. Running away with my tail tucked between my legs looks like I have something to hide. If I can't come in, people will think I've been suspended. I didn't do anything wrong."

To my surprise, he didn't confirm or deny his belief in me right away. He sat staring at me like he expected me to say something else.

"Seriously, Alexander, you can't possibly think

I'm a murderer. You know me better than that. It's my life to put those people away."

He made a downward motion with his hand. "Calm down, of course I don't think you're a murderer. Part of the problem, part of the reason the damn media are all over you, all over all of us, is that it is your life to handle these cases. You have the ability to plan a crime based on the cases you've handled, opportunity to conceal your actions, and you have colleagues and, frankly, family to help you cover said actions. And, given the information in the local paper, it sounds like you had motive. It doesn't matter what I think. I certainly trust you, but this is an unprecedented predicament and it's in our face. I'm happy to stand up for you and I will in my comments to the press through our liaison, but the whole courthouse can't be disrupted day after day like this. It's my job to keep things in order and running smoothly in your absence. It could take weeks or months to figure out what happened to David. You can do some work on the cases from home, but Fenwick will take over your court appearances until the investigation settles down. Once the police and fire marshal gather their evidence, you'll come out like the hero you always are, and everything will be fine again."

"But wait, really? Not Fenwick. Please, no, all the work I've done, he's going to blow half my cases." I protested but Alexander held up his hand and shook his head. No one argued with my boss. He assigned the cases and I likely wouldn't be in line for anything good for a long while.

"I'll give you a few hours in your office, Christine and I mean it, make it brief. You'll have to do the rest from home or from wherever you're staying.

Summarize what you've got and report to Fenwick. I'll see you briefly before you go."

He glanced at his watch, indicating my dismissal.

"Thank you, sir. I'll keep you up to date on the investigation."

I didn't get a reply. He had already returned to his work before I walked out the door.

****

I sent Jake and my dad the same text message, outlining my disaster morning. I declined Jake's offer to meet for lunch then buried myself in my court files for a few hours, declining calls, and visitors, keeping my office door locked.

By noon, my neck hurt, and my stomach protested my lack of food over the last twenty-four hours.

"Get you guys a sandwich for rescuing a damsel in distress?" I smiled when I reached the security desk where Mitch laughed at something he showed Ed on his cell.

Their faces lost expression and they straightened when I leaned on the counter.

"I'm good," Mitch said focusing on his security screens.

"Me too, Ms. Montgomery."

"Ms. Montgomery? Come on Ed, give me a break. Let me buy you guys' lunch."

"We ate already," Ed said firmly, walking away to the front door. Mitch concentrated on his screens. I walked away feeling incredibly alone.

"Hey, Rose, please tell me you have a joke for me. You always have a good story."

"Ah, Bella, don't be so glum. Let me think. Okay, I got it, my kid came home with this one from school.

Why does a seagull fly over the sea?"

I finally smiled. It felt so good to see a friendly face, I almost cried. I answered with a tired grin. "I don't know Rose, why does a seagull fly over the sea?"

"If he flew over the bay, you'd have to call him a bay gull, haaa, get it a bay gull, like a bagel! That's like a lunch counter joke. You can use it if you want."

"You're the best, Rose, you always make me smile. Give me a special would you." I chuckled. Others near the counter averted their stare when I made eye contact. People sitting at the few small tables whispered and pointed. I held my head high and kept my cool, paid for my wrap and a coffee, and walked back to my office to lock myself in again.

By four o'clock I was exhausted. I'd done a lot without having interruptions. For a few minutes, every now and then, I almost forgot about the disaster that had taken over my life. Working longer wasn't an option, having long overstayed Alexander's demand of a few hours, but thinking about what faced me at home, caused panic to rise. I closed my office door behind me with the distinct feeling I may never be back.

"Karen, I'm reachable any time of day on my cell. Give Fenwick my number because he'll have questions. I'll email the rest of the summaries soon if I can. It's going to have to be in bits and pieces, but I'll do the most urgent stuff first. Tell him to remand everything. Don't let him go to trial with any of my cases. And don't let him near my stuff. I don't want him in my office touching my stuff."

She nodded but kept her eyes on her computer.

Just thinking about Fenwick irritated me. He was a nerdy wanna be, lanky and unprofessional. He always wore a suit that didn't fit and had a weak, sticky handshake. As one of the judge's nephews he was expected to instantly morph into a good officer of the court. No matter how much we tried to help him, his record stood at two of every ten. He simply couldn't be taught. I had no idea how he had managed to pass high school, let alone university, and law school.

I shook my head thinking of the mess my office would be by the time this ended. I tried to speak to Alexander again before I left but he hadn't returned from court, and I was too tired to wait.

"One more thing," I said to Karen after locking my office.

She rolled her eyes.

"Really, Karen, really? Do I deserve that look? Come on. You know what, forget it. Please tell Alexander I'll call him tomorrow."

Once again, she nodded, but didn't speak. I had never felt so alienated. Thank goodness it had started to storm when I left. The protesting crowd and their precious artwork seemed to have been rained out. I also had the forethought to head out the lunch counter back door with a hood pulled over my head and an umbrella carried low. I walked a full two blocks out away from the courthouse parking lot and circled back on the other side of the block. Reaching my car, one die hard reporter yelled from the front door. "There she is!"

Chapter 7

Safely inside my car, I was already backing away by the time his camera had a chance to get near me. My miserable mood matched the lousy wet weather and made the evening commute gloomier.

Jenny had sent a message to say they had cleared the house for me to go home. I welcomed being alone tonight to think things through, but it seemed strange to accept that from now on I would arrive to an empty house every night.

I stopped at the roadside diner to get soup and a salad. The young man at the drive-thru window stared. "Do I know you? You look familiar."

"I think you're mistaken." I rushed to take my food and get away before he remembered where he'd seen my story.

Reaching home, I ran for the front door. Across the yard trees bent and bright colored leaves came off in droves with the wind. Sunny barked her welcome when I stepped inside.

"Hey, girl, I'm glad Jake brought you home. At least you're one friend I can always count on. Did he feed you?"

She barked once more and led me to the kitchen.

"I'm guessing that's a no." Wind whistled through the windows like something from a horror movie. The picture out the back door was bleak. Working spotlights shone through heavy rain pouring down taped off remains of the carriage house. I away. The investigation scene was shocking and made me nauseous all over again.

"David, what the hell happened to you?" I closed the blinds over the sliding glass doors and sat to eat my food alone at the kitchen island.

I walked to my bedroom to change into flannel pants and my favorite hoodie, the Chicago Bears. I never thought about it any other time I grabbed it off the hook, but now I remembered our weekend in Chicago almost three years ago. We took selfies in front of that giant bean, kissed under the sparkling lights of the night skyline, walking hand in hand along the water's edge. The next day at the game, we cheered for the Bears like it was Superbowl Sunday. People said they didn't win much, but they won that day. We attributed it to our cheering. Things were good once.

It felt strange coming back into our bedroom, thinking of the last conversation I had with David, and knowing investigators had been through our personal effects. It had been only twenty-four hours since I'd seen him alive. It felt like a week. David's wedding ring sat in a dish on top of his dresser where he always left it at night, with change from his pocket and little bits of things like paper clips and receipts. I needed to stop asking myself when everything changed. It didn't matter anymore.

I started a fire in my study with the easy start, paper covered log, adding a few kindling sticks to give it some fuel. While it crackled and sparked to life, I poured a glass of wine from my sidebar cabinet then sat at my desk to attempt some work. Rain pelted the windows as I fought to concentrate. I got up to shut heavy curtains over the inside shutters. Feeling the fabric made me think back to the day I chose from so many bolts to have them made.

"*Navy? Does everything have to be blue? And why do you need curtains when you already have shutters*?" David had asked.

"*It's my workspace. I like blue. And the shutters match the other windows from the outside, but sometimes I need to shut out the weather, so I need both.*" My choices rarely made sense to him and his modern, less is more taste. I only wanted a room of my own, to do my work, relax, shut him and the rest of the world out. Surrounded by ceiling high dark shelves covering most of three walls, they encircled me, like a hug from my favorite books. Some were filled with stories Mom used to read over and over, others were antique literary classics. Dad and I had such fun scouting those treasures on the fifty cent tables at flea markets. Other people never realizing their worth, called them old books.

Comfortable in my flannels, I carried my laptop and my wine to the overstuffed fireside chair. Kicking off hot slippers, I rubbed my bare feet on Sunny's soft fur using her as a foot stool. The thick burgundy carpet made me think once again of David's voice. *"Merlot?"* He had screwed up his face. *"Why do women always name colors after food? It's red and it's going to be a big mess when that mutt of yours rolls all over it."* I had laughed back a reply. *"At least it's not blue."* He hadn't laughed.

I wanted to have positive memories of David, but for now, his negative comments repeatedly invaded my thoughts. He used to be teasing, but in the end, he seemed insulting and impatient with almost everything I did. How many times had I asked myself in the last year, *did he ever really love me? Maybe he needed money all along.* Now I sat wondering, *what did he need the money for? We had everything and he threw it all away for more money than he would ever need. What could possibly be going on in his life that was worth dying for?* These questions were pounding in my head like a jack hammer. I got up to add a small log to the fire. Sitting back, I took a deep breath, and a sip of my wine and tried to let my quiet surroundings calm me.

"Okay, David got one thing right. Wine colored carpet with you around was a mistake, you big hairball." Sunny replied with a heavy sigh and a one-eyed glance.

My open laptop reminded me I should be accomplishing something. Ignoring it on the table beside me, I leaned my head onto the high back of my chair, staring at the flames coming to life and watching small pieces of ember drop from the burning logs. Strange, how fire could be so relaxing, when it had brought such destruction to my life less than a day ago.

The telephone's ring startled me causing Sunny to bark and leap up from her resting spot, narrowly missing spilling my wine onto the top of her head.

"Jeez, girl, easy."

She sat down in front of me staring like she questioned my next move. I hesitated, unable to face another reporter or work colleague. The phone didn't stop ringing. I finally stretched behind me to the corner of my huge oak desk, another flea market treasure, and greeted my caller with silence.

"Are you okay?" a familiar voice asked.

"Oh, Dad, I'm glad it's you. Sunny and I were a little jumpy when the landline rang. It's so loud. She almost wore a glass of wine. She must sense my nerves."

"No doubt you're nervous out there. I wish you had stayed downtown until I finished work. I sent you a text just now, but you didn't answer. We could have grabbed a bite and gone home together. This is quite a storm."

"I'm okay. Sorry, I plugged my phone in to charge over by the bookcase, didn't hear a text. I'll turn it up. I drove through Ruby's on the way home, and I'm hiding here in my den with my tough dog, my glass of wine, and my damn work files."

"You shouldn't be out there alone."

"You're probably right, but I doubt anyone expects me to be at home. Seems like reporters have given up hiding in my bushes at least. They've probably seen investigators around all day, and I'm sure the weather will keep them at bay at least for the night. I'm trying to find the energy to finish some of these outlines to email over to that simpleton Arnold Fenwick to deal with until they let me back in the office. It's more work to tell someone what needs doing than to do it yourself, especially him. It's like I'm trying to simplify case investigations for a student to present. No, scratch that, our students are brighter than him."

"He'll be fine. You shouldn't be at work anyway in the middle of that media circus. At least take a few days for yourself," he suggested.

"It was horrible. Other than Rose at the lunch

counter, no one cared. They treated me like a freaking convict. So much for innocent until proven guilty. Even Alexander didn't want to hear my side of the story, like I might confide something he would have to cover up. He pretty much insisted I not come back until the papers make me out to be a star again."

"It's probably not a bad idea."

"Not like I have a choice. I'll have to do what I can from here for now," I said.

"They can manage a few days without you, remand stuff and deal with it later," he said.

"I'm having a hard time letting go. When I stop working, I think about tougher stuff and the tough stuff is making me crazy. Work is all I've focused on for a long time. Not saying that's a good thing but I'll feel better if I can at least do some summaries and pass them over to that…kid." I hesitated to ask. "Has the verdict come in from Gavin?"

His pause told me to expect bad news. I prompted him again. "Dad?"

"I'm sorry honey; the only thing they could tell me is that it's now officially a homicide. If I even told you who gave me the information, he would lose his job. They found David face down on the couch with no evidence of smoke inside his esophagus, so they know he stopped breathing before the fire started. He didn't inhale anything that killed him. And it's likely he had something around his neck indicating strangulation. In other words, he was definitely dead before the fire started. That's all we know right now."

I expected murder would be the answer. Jenny had spelled it out this morning and everyone had spoken that way almost from the get-go, but it was still a shock when Dad confirmed the violent nature of David's death.

He stayed silent for a few seconds, then continued. "It's up to the pathologist to get more details, figure out the why and how. You know how it works. Whoever did this needs to go away a long time. David was an ass, but he had a lot of life ahead of him. He didn't deserve this.

"I've also been told they need to get out a press release tomorrow. This is big news given your position. It might be best if you're there. Field a few questions if you're allowed, at least be visible so no one thinks you're hiding anything. I'm sure that's not what you need right now."

"Not really, but I get it. Anything that might help get the reporters out of my face," I said.

"I can be there in twenty minutes, keep you company for a while, go over what you might need to say and what not to say."

"It's so hard to wait and not know anything about what he got himself into," I said so quietly, I didn't know if Dad heard me.

"What I'm worried about is you, out there alone with a killer on the loose and a whole lot of crap going on in your head, in a damn storm to boot. Why don't you go back to Jake's?" His voice was more forceful.

I shivered and tried to sound calmer than I felt. "Really, I'm a big girl, and I don't need to get in the middle of Jake and Courtney again. You're almost done with your shift. Come out when you can if you feel up to it. I'd like that. I'm locked in, and I've been home alone a million times. No reporters are stupid enough to be out in this weather. I'll call Jake if I need something urgently, and I have other neighbors near enough. I'm going to let you go so you can get done."

"Remember if the storm gets rough, sometimes you have to—"

The phone went dead. The hairs on my neck prickled. I sat alone surrounded by darkness but for the few embers in the fireplace.

"Sunny?"

Chapter 8

Sunny jumped to attention, a low growl aimed in the direction of the door.

"Easy, girl; it's just the power out."

I searched with trembling hands for matches in the drawer. My cell phone lit up when it rang. Seeing the number on the display, I answered. "Dad I'm good. Well, I'm okay. I'm lighting a candle. The power cut out, so my cordless phone went dead."

"As I started to say, when there's a storm sometimes you need to fire up the generator. I'm on my way right now." Dad sounded panicked.

"It will be back on soon I'm sure. It's just super windy. But I would feel better if you came out, maybe for tonight. Hang on, stay with me, someone's pounding on my door. It's got to be Jake. His power will be out too."

I peeked through the side panel of the front door and saw Jake, flashlight in hand reaching to knock on the door again.

"Okay, okay, I'm coming. Hang on."

"Jeez, you scared the heck out of me. I didn't think you were going to answer." Jake pulled me to him.

"You scared the heck out of me, more like. And you're all wet," I said.

"What? Oh, sorry." He took a step back.

"Give me one second, Dad's on the phone."

“Sure thing,” Jake came in, his coat dripping on the front mat.

“All good now, Jake’s here. Take your time please, the roads are terrible.”

“Your dad on his way?”

“Yeah, please, come in. I presume your power’s out too?”

“It is, but my generator kicked in so it’s all bright and cozy. Never could have left Finnegan otherwise. He’s a big chicken in a storm. I was watching one of the trees out the front afraid it might come down in this wind. I saw your car in the drive and a few work lights from the investigation past the trees, then nothing, pitch black, kind of creepy. If my power hadn’t gone out too, I would have had nine-one-one on the phone. You really shouldn’t be here alone.”

“I’ve heard that already. Trust me; I’m starting to feel the same way. I kind of freaked when I was sitting alone, and everything went dark. Dad is on his way. He’ll stay the night, and I’m sure the power will be back on soon. Always seems to do this when it storms.”

“Want to grab Sunny and come over to my place?” he asked.

“Not sure I’m up to it. The fireplace in the den is so cozy on a night like this. The thought of going out in the dark and the rain past the burned-up carriage house, I don’t think I can do it. Would you mind coming in for a drink, maybe just until Dad gets here? Where’s Courtney? You didn’t leave her alone did you?” I asked.

“Of course, I don’t mind keeping you company. Lead the way. And, no, Courtney’s worse than Finnegan when it comes to storms. She left before noon," he explained.

"Beer from the kitchen or wine's open in the den. What's your taste?"

"Wine's good," he said.

I lit more candles and poured wine for Jake while he stoked the fire. It felt comfortable, and I relaxed for the first time in twenty-four hours.

"Her early departure is my fault. Sorry I ruined your weekend together." I handed Jake his wine and sat down in the chair beside him, opposite the fire.

"No, it's not your fault. And please stop apologizing. I had to sleep for a while today, coming off nights, especially after last night and she, well, she, that is, we…this isn't the time to talk about it. Let's just say, things aren't what they once were for any of us."

"I'm sorry to hear that. I thought the wedding plans were coming along and you guys were doing great."

"For the first time in weeks, we didn't even talk about the wedding. And we really haven't been great since at least summer if not before. This long-distance relationship is hard, and she keeps talking about us moving to the city, and I mean Toronto, not even London. We had always planned to live here in Arva. And why wouldn't we? She loved Mom and Dad's idea to sell me the house when they moved to the lake. She helped renovate, picked the colors, and we designed the two back rooms into one big master bedroom for both of us. I built her a giant bathroom and walk-in closets like she wanted. Now, I'm getting the impression there's change in the wind and I'm not sure what to do about it. She doesn't seem happy out here anymore. She really doesn't seem happy with much to do with me. Honestly, I'm not sure I want to do anything about it," he said, shoulders slumped.

It felt good to focus on something other than my problems, at least for a few minutes. "I don't like the sound of that. Maybe give her some time. She expected a fun surprise weekend, to relax and kick some fall leaves and what faced her when she got here was the complete opposite. She's bound to be a little out of sorts."

"It has nothing to do with the fire or the weekend. Every conversation is all about her career, her damn agent has her convinced she's going to make it big. You saw her today when Jenny and Nick questioned her. She's panicked that something might threaten her next audition. How about what's going on here? You're living a nightmare; we're all going through hell, and it's not even fazing her. That attitude is so different from the Courtney I met a few years ago.

"Even if we were both living in the city, I don't think we would spend much time together. We're growing apart before we've had a chance to be together. I can't say anything that pleases her. Every wedding conversation has been more about how good she will look in pictures instead of how meaningful it will be to get married. We got in a big blowup last time we talked about plans, and I said that to her. She's out of sorts a lot more than in sorts these days."

I chuckled. "I'm not sure in sorts is a thing. I wish I knew what to say."

We sat silent for a few minutes staring at the fire. When he spoke again, his voice was low. "All things considered; this feels really good."

"I know what you mean. Thanks for staying with me," I said.

Our eyes met and I found myself flustered and lost for words something I never felt with Jake. I quickly turned back to the fire.

"Oh, I can stay for hours if you like, I slept all afternoon. Now I have to stay up late and sleep in enough to get me back in day shift mode," he said.

"Well, I'm not sure I can stay up all night to keep you company. I feel like I've been up for days. Hard to believe the fire, well, everything changed twenty-four hours ago after I went through his office."

"I intended to keep us off that topic, but since we're back to it, is there any update since your text this afternoon?" he asked.

"Dad called right before the power went out. He said Gavin, well, he didn't say who, but someone at the morgue confirmed murder. Seems like that's been apparent from the start but hearing it out loud was hard. He said David hadn't taken in any smoke and had some marks that indicated something around his neck. So, they know he died before the fire started and likely someone tried to cover his tracks. But as you know, that's pretty much impossible."

"I'm so sorry. This still seems so unreal." He shook his head.

Sunny jumped up and barked. "That will be Dad."

"I'll get going and let you two hang out," he said.

I walked Jake to the door. Dad was already in the hallway. "Hey, Dad, I'm glad you're here."

"Hi, honey, I'm glad I'm here too. Jake, you don't have to go. Stay and have a drink."

"It's okay, Finnegan will be sucky in this weather, and I should check on things, put away patio chairs or something useful."

Jake seemed flustered, fumbling with the zipper on his coat, like he couldn't get out the door fast enough. "You okay?" I asked.

He didn't answer, just smiled and pulled me into a tight hug. Again, I leaned into Jake, feeling a sense of wellbeing I couldn't seem to get anywhere else. He kissed the top of my head and pulled away what seemed a little abruptly. "I should go."

"Thanks again, Jake, really. I'd be lost without you." He smiled but didn't reply, closing the door on his way out.

Dad shook off his coat and put it on the hook behind the door. "I can leave and let him stay. You two seem pretty cozy."

"Don't be ridiculous, he's being a good friend," I defended.

Dad put his arm around my shoulders. We walked toward the den, the only room with light other than my flashlight. "Mmm hmmm, whatever you say."

I elbowed him, causing a chuckle in reply. The lights flickered, once, twice, then back on full.

"Apparently, I know how to light up a room," Dad said, with a smile.

"Well, aren't you Mr. Charming tonight. I'll say it again, I'm glad you're here." I leaned into him.

"I wouldn't be anywhere else. We're going to get through this, you'll see. And you're going to be okay. I'll be sure of it."

"I know you're right. But is it okay to admit I feel like absolute shit for right now?"

"Me too, sweetheart, big time. Let's have a nightcap, then we can get some good sleep and things will feel better in the morning," he said.

I made sure Dad had some food, and we sat in front of the fire and talked while I finished my wine and he had pint of Guinness. By about nine we were both having trouble keeping awake.

"I've got to go to bed," I said, standing and stretching. "The spare room is all made up. And Annie left tons of stuff in the kitchen for morning. Push the middle button on the coffee maker if you get moving before me. I already loaded it."

"Stop, would you, I know my way around the kitchen. Go on up, I'll let the fire burn out and lock up. I'm exhausted too, I'm right behind you, I promise." He squeezed my hand when I walked by him.

****

I fell asleep within minutes of hitting the pillow, falling into a dream I hadn't had in years. *"Don't you care, Dad? Fight for her, please, make her do something. Please! Dad!"*

I woke with a start to Dad sitting on my bed. "Wake up, it's only a dream. I'm here, you're okay."

"Oh, Dad, the nightmare's back. I haven't had the dream about Mom for years. I can't go back there." I sat up, shaking my head to erase the vision of my dream.

He wiped my tears with the back of his hand. "You've had a huge shock, sweetheart. It's bound to bring up old stuff, scary stuff. I promise I'll keep you safe."

I hugged him, feeling like a teenager again. "It wasn't supposed to be like this."

"I know, it's okay. Everything is going to be okay," he reassured me, patting my back while he held me close.

Chapter 9

Not long after my nightmare, I managed to convince Dad to go back to the guest room and I eventually fell back into a fitful sleep. Waking earlier than expected, I ignored the groggy feeling, determined to follow my morning routine. It was a perfect sunny fall day after last night's storm. At least the rain kept reporters from my door, that and the on and off investigations bringing lots of uniformed personnel around the property to further deter the bold paparazzi.

Dressed in bright colored tights and my jogging tank and zip up, I pulled my hair into a ponytail and fed it through the hole in the back of my favorite London Fire Department cap. A few stretches later, I grabbed the leash, whistled for Sunny, and stepped out into the cool, fresh morning air. Within minutes the exertion of my run increased my breathing and heart rate and kept me warm. The trees and scattered homes on either side of the road soothed me. I hated the crowded city, all the tall buildings, traffic, and people on top of people in elevators and shops. I felt claustrophobic just thinking about it.

It crossed my mind; Dad would say I shouldn't jog in isolated places under the circumstances. *If it doesn't feel right, it's probably not right.* I laughed at his voice in my head. Most of my neighbors knew me enough to help if needed, even though the houses were spaced apart by trees and large properties. I needed so badly to get some fresh air away from the phone calls and investigators and newspapers, but I still felt a little paranoid.

My thoughts wandered to simpler days when no one paid much attention to my comings and goings. *Who would have thought, news media would ever be interested in me? In a matter of forty-eight hours, everything in my life had changed. Sure, my name came up occasionally when I succeeded at putting away particularly newsworthy criminals. How long would it take before people stopped gawking at me like I had become one of those criminals. I believed David to be loving and genuine. I should have known that charm would eventually be aimed at another woman, should have seen him sooner for what he really was.*

"You tried to warn me, Sunny."

The dog answered with a glance up at me.

"You never did like David much, did you, girl? Dad tried to warn me too. I should have listened. How could I have been so blind?"

Expecting to be alone to berate myself at this early hour, I jumped when Sunny abruptly stopped and turned to growl. "What is it, girl?"

I gasped, raising my hand to my chest when Wayne Duncan ran up behind me.

"A little jumpy?" Wayne smirked when he stopped within a few feet of me. He was wiry and malnourished, with dark bags under sunken eyes and dirty spaces between not enough teeth. His greasy, dark hair stuck flat against his head, like he had neglected to wash it any time recently or like he regularly wore a ball cap to cover it. He was definitely out of place on an early morning jog, especially dressed in jeans and a turtleneck sweater, chomping on a bag of tortilla chips.

Like I told Jenny, I remembered Wayne from early high school. I also knew he had a rap sheet full of petty, cowardly crimes dating back to those juvenile days. "What are you doing here, Wayne?"

"Nice you remember me, Chrissy. Is there a law against early morning exercise?"

"Try again. You've never jogged a day in your life and who the hell exercises with a bag of nacho chips in his hand?"

"Maybe it's a good time to start. I like the scenery." His eyes wandered slowly from my head to my toes. I shivered despite the sweat pouring down my back.

"How's the fire investigation going? Any suspects yet? Word around town is you off'd your old man, Chrissy," he said with a sneer.

I hated that *Chrissy*, and the way he said it made me want to punch him. "I'm telling you Wayne, back off."

"What'd it set you back to get that bastard out of your life?"

I had no intention of answering any of his questions, and I certainly didn't want him to detect my irritation or nervousness. Knowing Jenny had Wayne on her list of people to be questioned, I decided to try a bit of investigating myself. "What do you know about the night of the fire? Where were you in the early hours of Friday morning?"

"Ha, nice try, Chrissy. You can't catch me, I'm the gingerbread man! I'll be *seeing* you." The creep winked at me, blew a kiss, and ran back in the direction he had come.

I was beyond annoyed, and I sure didn't like the emphasis on his *I'll be seeing you* comment. I worried he had been seeing me a little more than I already knew.

"What was that all about? Gingerbread man, what the hell?"

Sunny answered me with a solid bark and a glance to make sure our stalker had disappeared before we continued.

I dealt with some bad-ass criminals at work. Thanks to my training and Dad's help, I read body language better than most and easily deciphered a truth from a lie. Unfortunately, when it came to the truly psychotic types, like Wayne Duncan, I occasionally came up short. He had always been one of a few people who really gave me the creeps.

I stepped up the pace for the last stretch of my run and shortened the distance I planned to be out, continuously checking over my shoulder. Once home, I hung up my hat and the leash, filled Sunny's bowl at the sink, then filled my own water. I punched the speed dial for Jake and bypassed formalities when he answered. "You won't believe what happened."

"Well, good morning to you too."

I jumped right into the story of my encounter with Wayne.

"I'll kill him," he stated.

"It's not that bad, he maybe startled me a little, but I'm good," I said.

"Startled you, how about terrified you? You didn't even catch your breath before you called me. And it's barely light out, why the hell are you out alone this early?" he demanded.

Jake was right. Wayne had me rattled, but I couldn't tell him that. The whole incident made me want to shower off more than the usual after jogging sweat.

"It's not that early and I needed air. I can't stay a prisoner in my own house. Oh, crap, I forgot you needed to sleep in to get back on schedule. Did I wake you? You stayed up all night, didn't you?" I asked.

"It's okay I have to get up anyway. Does your dad know about this?"

"Not yet. Jenny said they're looking into Wayne's alibi. Remember she asked about him, said they saw him on the dashcam in the crowd. I told Dad last night what she said about Wayne, but I better call her too."

"I remember all right. And yes, you should be letting them both know, especially since the cops want Wayne for questioning. Jeez, you can't be out alone like that," he scolded.

"I know, I know. I promise, no more. I'll stay where there are cops around or you or Dad. I agree I'm kind of jumpy. Dad left before I got up this morning or he probably would have come out for a run with me. I'll call him after I shower. He'll want to go out and strangle the guy for coming near me."

"Well, I'll be right along for the ride if he does. Wayne could be dangerous. He could even be their guy. They may not have the manpower for a bodyguard, but I'm sure Rick will make sure they hunt a little harder for our Mr. Duncan now. Even if he had nothing to do with the fire, he'll want to know why he came to your property that night and how he happened to show up when you jogged by today," Jake said.

"You think I would know if he'd been stalking me. I agree, Dad will have questions, but he's not allowed in on the investigation. That means he can't tell his team where to look and he can't harass suspects or take extra measures because I'm family."

"You know you're more than family; you're Rick's life. If he wants to be protective, let him. And it's hardly extra measures when Jenny already wants Wayne for questioning. You think that weasel torched your garage with Dave in it?" he asked.

"I'm not sure what to think. He's half Dave's size; I can't imagine he'd have the ability. And more importantly, why? What would a guy like Wayne have to do with a bunch of bogus mortgages?"

"I don't know either," Jake said.

"I do know they won't be able to put Wayne Duncan's sorry butt or anyone else anywhere near a jail cell until someone gets the proof we need from forensics and from what's left of the carriage house."

"They're working on it, Ms. Crown Attorney, but you just said you want it by the book and that takes time. I need to be hands off just like Rick. The whole conflict aspect is making us all a bit crazy. Meantime, I'm going to say it again to drill it in your head. You can't be out jogging alone even around our own neighborhood. Until they have answers, keep your doors locked and don't go out without letting Rick or me know."

"I know, I promise, I just said that. Close to cops and away from isolated areas, I got it. At least I have Sunny to scare off intruders."

"Oh, yeah, she's vicious. What can she do, slobber the guy to death?"

I chuckled. “She did manage to growl at Wayne. Anyway, I can’t sit around here. Like Jenny warned me, they brought in a backhoe early this morning and started pulling the carriage house apart. They go so slowly and keep stopping. It’s not easy, it’s like watching a building autopsy, it seems so invasive to pull at it.”

“That’s messed up. You know it has to be done for them to figure things out?”

“I know, but I can’t stick around and watch. I’m going to hang out at Dad’s apartment or maybe take my work to the station, use one of his spare desks. I still have so much to do, but I can’t go to the office. At least I won’t get beaten up by media or stalked by crazy neighbors if I’m at the precinct.”

“True.”

“Thanks for listening. Should you be going back to sleep or something?” I asked.

“No, I’m good. I’ll get back to normal now that I stayed up. I’m going to the fire hall and I’ll see if I can get a few details without getting myself in trouble. I have an appointment with the chief and the fire marshal at ten-thirty. They have to interview all of us who were on scene, reconstruct the specifics of the fire before they discovered David, and then after we knocked the fire down, before they moved him,” he explained.

“Don’t they take pictures of all that?”

“Sure, but reconstruction is a big part of the investigation. Firefighters take things apart when fighting the fire, then we need to hypothetically put it back together for the fire marshal. Then the investigators come in and take it all apart again to find the arson version of the smoking gun. I would have been working tonight again and been off tomorrow and Monday, but I've asked for some personal time. I don't have to go back in at all really, until I'm ready. This kind of thing can be hard on first responders. They need us to go through counseling and all the right steps. Besides, I want to be here for you and Rick. I need to help."

"You don't have to do that. I'm taking one day at a time and we'll get through it."

"I know I don't have to; I want to. You and Rick are family to me, and I'm going to be around to help get us all through. You want to walk the boardwalk later or tomorrow maybe? It's supposed to be unseasonably warm." He chuckled.

"Fancy words for nice out. I'm not sure I'm up to it yet. And I don't think Courtney would be happy to have us seen together. Not to mention the gossip about our relationship already. We don't need any more pictures of us together on the front page of the news."

"Courtney left, like I told you, said she'll be traveling again for a bit, however long that means. She does that a lot these days and it's not a date. We've been walking that strip since we were kids. I'm trying to help take your mind off things."

"No, what I think is you're trying to be my bodyguard. I won't be jogging my usual stretch alone anytime soon but going out in public is a little risky. I'll see how I feel, but thanks. Thanks for everything. Talk to you soon."

"Watch your back, Christie."

"I will," I promised.

Still jumpy even as I headed to the shower, I screamed when Annie came around the corner. "Jesus, you scared me to death. Why are you here so early; and why on a Saturday and why at all for that matter?" She usually didn't come to clean until nine or ten when I had already left for the day and she was even less likely to come on a Saturday.

"Oh, sorry, darling, didn't mean to frighten you. I've been cleaning the bathroom. I heard you on the phone. What's going on now?"

"I told you to stay home and relax for a few days, that I would call you."

"Sitting home and worrying about you doesn't do either of us any good. It's easier to busy myself here. I went to the farmers' market early this morning, then I came straight here. Now, what was all that about on the phone?" she asked again.

"Well, okay, don't go overboard; it's only me and I can clean up for myself. Market already, really? What time does that open?"

"I get there when the farmers make their deliveries right after dawn, get the freshest stuff then. Really, why all the fuss this morning, you haven't answered me, and I won't be put off," she demanded.

"Okay, relax; I called Jake to tell him I ran into that squirrelly Wayne Duncan when I went out jogging. He kind of gives me the creeps."

"You need to be doing your jogging on that dusty treadmill downstairs. Keep those types away until all this business is over. And you shouldn't be running to that Jake Anderson every time you get annoyed. Stick closer to home, Christine. I'll be sure no harm gets in the door."

She loved nurturing me, but Annie's commands seemed a little out of place, and she called me Christine only when she got upset with me. I didn't need her beating me up for running to Jake; I already did enough of that myself. "Thanks for the offer; I've got a lot of people wanting to protect me today. Trust me, I'm watching over my shoulder, especially after running into Wayne. But I do have to work, and I need to call the police station to see if there are any updates so I'm going to get moving. You look tense, are you okay?"

She smiled, but it didn't seem sincere. "I'm fine. Never you mind about me. Get on your way. I've got a few more things to do here. Then I'll sit down for my tea."

****

I took my time getting ready, showered, and dressed in jeans and a sweater, packed up my laptop and briefcase, dreading doing more work, but at a loss what to do instead. I got only one step out the front door when my neighbor Agnes came up my driveway. My first thought was to retreat and hide, have Annie tell her I wasn't well. She had seen me though and greeted me with a smile and a wave. I had no choice but to welcome her. "Hi, Agnes; what brings you over so early?"

"Well, hi yourself." She reached over for a brief hug which I obligingly returned. "I brought you some cookies, wanted to make sure you were okay and offer our deepest condolences. This is horrible. You must be feeling terribly." She glanced at my briefcase. "You can't be going to work?"

"Thank you for the cookies, that's really nice. I'd invite you in, but things are kind of, well, to be honest, I'm not up for a coffee date right now."

"Nonsense, don't you worry. I totally get it, under

the circumstances; you're not up to neighbors dropping in. I don't want to intrude."

Yes, you do. "That's kind, really. We'll get together soon, when all this is sorted out."

Standing like her shoes were glued to my walkway, she didn't take my hint.

"Of course, we will. Andy and I were saying over the morning paper how impossible it must be for you. People accusing you of murder and having Rick to cover for you and our dear Jake involved. And, murdering your own sweet husband, unbelievable."

"If you think I'm a murderer, why come across the street with cookies?" I asked, feeling long past polite formalities.

"Oh, heavens no, I didn't mean *we* thought you were. Just that people are saying. What do you suppose really happened?" She tipped her head, smiling with a curious glare like we were gossiping about a celebrity social media post.

"If I knew that, I'd be in a much better place right now. I really have to go," I insisted.

"Of course, you do, so many details to sort through I'd imagine. Call on us anytime if there's anything we can do to help. We'd be thrilled to lend a hand." She handed me the cookie plate which thankfully presented an excuse to go back inside.

"Thank you again. I'll go put these inside. I'll see you both soon." I nodded in dismissal.

She had no option but to leave when I closed the door behind me and leaned against it. "How could a two-minute encounter with the neighbor leave me so drained?" I asked.

"What's that, dear?" Annie called from the kitchen.

"Did you forget something?"

"No, I almost got out the door when Agnes came up the drive with these." I put the cookie plate on the counter. "Of course, she put them on a fancy plate so now she has an excuse to come over again to collect it."

"Oh, that's harsh; she's only trying to be a nice neighbor. People are bound to come and offer sympathies. That's what's appropriate."

"That's appropriate in normal losses. This seemed more like she wanted some juicy gossip to take back home and tell her friends. She even asked what really happened. Of course, we don't know and if I did, does she think they'd be the first ones I'd run to with details. I'm not good with all this invasion of my privacy."

"No one is, dear. Things will get better soon." She smiled sympathetically.

"I've got to get out of here. Help yourself to the cookies with your tea. Then, can you put them in the cupboard or fridge so Sunny doesn't finish the whole plate."

I checked through the window before I opened the door this time, dashing for my car while the coast was clear. I expected the media to stay away from me at home, but in town I wasn't so sure. Intending to head to the station to see Dad and Jenny and Nick, knowing I would be safe there, I found myself instead driving toward the cemetery. I pulled up to Mom's grave site, pain clutching my chest and tears flowing. One of the awful protester signs from the day before leaned against her stone, large letters spelling "murderer" dripped down like blood onto her grave. Anger surged like never before. I ran from the car and kicked the sign away, falling to my knees in front of her grave.

"Oh, Mom, I can't believe anyone would be so cruel. I wish so much that you were here. I can't do this alone. You always knew what to say to make things better." I had one knee on the ground, facing the stone, when a twig cracked behind me. I spun quickly, startled to find a man approaching me for the second time this morning. It wasn't scrawny Wayne but a bigger man, perhaps mid-forties, with graying hair, a beard to match and brown eyes. He had a smirk on his face and a camera in his hand. He snapped a picture of me in tears, one of many I'm sure he had in my various vulnerable states over the last couple of days.

"What do you mean, you can't do it alone? What did you do that she needs to make better? Did you kill your husband Ms. Montgomery? People are entitled to the truth."

I didn't like being stuck in the awkward position with him between me and my car. Jumping out of the car so quickly in my rage, I hadn't grabbed my keys or my phone. I stood, wiped my face with my sleeve, and stared directly at my intruder, intent on hiding my fear. This man was no Wayne Duncan. I easily perceived him to be the nervous one, a jerk hoping for a good story and I'd had enough of these people. Finding the protester sign on my mother's grave hit my final nerve.

I made a mental picture to describe him to police. "You would be well served to get out of my personal space before I have you arrested," I said in a clear voice.

He gazed around the empty graveyard then shrugged. "Who's going to arrest me here?" He stared like he was trying to intimidate me. I'd seen his type many times in court and the best reaction to them was no reaction. I started to walk around him, and he sidestepped to block my progress. “You don’t know who I am do you?”

“No, and I don’t care to. Step out of my way,” I demanded.

“You don’t care about the people you put in jail? I told you I’d be back to find you one day. Now see how our roles have reversed. I get to be the reporter of the truth while you get to feel how it is to be accused and tried for something you maybe did or didn’t do.” He wiggled his head looking satisfied with himself.

I wracked my memory trying to recall his face from any recent trials. “Who are you?”

“The name’s Jordan, Alistair Jordan. You put me in jail six years ago for doing nothing,” he admitted.

The name didn’t help; I still couldn’t place him or his trial. Six years ago, would have been one of my earliest cases. I should have been able to remember him. Maybe the beard and the gray hair weren’t there back then. “I don’t put people in jail Mr. Jordan. People’s actions put them in jail. Our justice system is thorough, and I’m merely an officer of the court who makes sure people reap the consequences of their criminal actions. You are, however, committing a crime by detaining me against my will, and if you don’t let me pass, I’ll be sure you are charged once again and you will return to jail, I’ll see to it.”

“Well, aren’t you all fancy legal talk. There’s no camera here like last time. I made sure to meet you somewhere that wouldn’t have any witnesses. Last time you took my old lady’s word for it that I slapped her around. A different camera angle in that apartment lobby and I had a defense. Truth is she tried to kill me, like you killed your old man. I'm probably better off in jail. You bitches be crazy. And now it's time for payback. I'm going to make sure people know you killed your old man. You're going to be front page news from now until you're in jail. Payback is due and you owe me plenty." His voice had escalated as he spoke.

His story rang some bells now and his warning sent chills up my spine. I remembered the bitches be crazy comment. He had been charged with assault with a weapon, one of many in his life if I remembered correctly. His only plea had been self-defense. He swore his wife had come at him with a knife, not the other way around. I didn't remember his face though and doubted he had become a legitimate reporter if he got out of jail just recently.

A calm approach was my only option. He was right, I did have a huge disadvantage in such a deserted place without witnesses or cameras or even my phone or keys in hand to use for a weapon. I wanted to keep him talking, get his story, while I figured out how to get past him.

"Mr. Jordan, I'm sorry for what you went through. And I'm sorry you're not familiar to me. But this conversation is getting neither of us anywhere. There is no law against printing whatever you like if your publication allows it, but you cannot threaten me nor detain me. And if I find out you had anything to do with my husband's death or the fire on my property, you will suffer the consequences accordingly and to the full extent of the law."

"Whoa, whoa, whoa, I didn't say I had anything to do with that." He held up his hands and took a step back.

"Your words were you have been planning revenge on me for quite some time. That could certainly be interpreted to mean you had something to do with the current crimes at issue, in which case you will spend much more than a few years in jail." I took a chance goading him, especially given his history of assault, but he struck me as nervous and unsure of himself, and I wanted him to know his threats couldn't affect me.

"Easy, lady, save that court lingo for someone who really did something to you and your old man. You're barking up the wrong tree."

"I'll ask you once again to step out of my path, Mr. Jordan. We're done here."

I took a step past him, attempting to appear confident. Just when I thought I was out of his reach, he grabbed my coat and pulled me back against him. With his arm around my neck and the side of his face touching mine, I smelled his bad breath and felt the heat of it when he whispered in my ear.

"Look, lady, you've done enough damage to my life. This meeting never happened. If anyone comes after me, I'll make sure Daddy dear and your firefighter lover pay for your mistake. I know you wanted your old man out of your face. I can read between the lines, you and the boy next door probably scorched him so you could have at each other. I'm going to make it my mission to lead the public against you, and I'll be sitting front row at your trial with a big smile on my face."

I lifted my leg and stomped hard on the top of his shoe causing him to scream out. He loosened his grip when he grabbed his foot, giving me space to pull my elbow forward and force it back into his belly. He let go of my neck and bent over, allowing me to bring the back of my fist up into his face with a loud crack.

I bolted to my car leaving him yelling behind me. "You fucking crazy bitch!"

I reached my car by the time he recovered himself enough to chase me. With trembling hands, I turned the key I had left in the ignition. Once the car started and my doors were locked, I pulled my phone from my purse and snapped several pictures of him coming at me, then spun my tires on the gravel as I sped out of the cemetery.

"No time for sentimental with you, Mom," I said. "Go see your cops and let them protect you and stop being your own worst enemy," I scolded myself.

****

I circled the police station four times looking for street parking close enough to beeline the front door. Wayne had rattled me, but the cemetery guy really set me into a panic. It had been bad enough getting threats from ex-cons in the past, but now, with all these people around me, accusing me, and a murderer on the loose, I had nowhere safe to go. Anxiety rising while I circled the block, I finally parked around the corner from the police station, grabbed my purse, kept my head down, and ran for the front door. As I entered the precinct, someone across the street yelled, "there."

Once inside the doors, I took a deep breath to steady myself, relieved that I finally reached a safe place. Tami Riley sat at the front desk. I recognized her from court where she'd testified a few years back. There was a story as to why she couldn't work the beat anymore, but at the moment, it didn't come to me. She was a fit woman but had a masculine stocky appearance, due in part to her brown hair cropped short in a manly cut above her ears. She had pock scars on her face and neck, a pointy nose, and a generally miserable demeanor. She certainly didn't make any move to welcome me. I waited but she continued to glance alternately at her computer screen then down at her notepad, all the while chewing her gum with her mouth open. I approached. "Hi. Tami, right?"

"Constable Riley is my name. Christine, right? Staff Sergeant Montgomery's girl?"

Okay, so she wanted a little power trip. I'd give her that provided she let me past her desk to sit with my dad and calm my nerves or at least get my story to Jenny about my day of stalkers.

I gave my best effort at a polite smile. "That's correct. Could you buzz me in to see him, please?"

"Not here," she said, without taking her eyes off the screen.

"Not here? You mean I can't pass through right here or Sergeant Montgomery's not here?"

"Both. Staff Sergeant Montgomery is signed out, and you can't pass here without a visitor's pass." She huffed loudly.

"Damn it. How about Jen, I mean, Detective Scott. Is Detective Scott here?" I winced.

"Is she expecting you?"

"Well, no, but I really need—"

"Doesn't matter, she ain't here either," she cut in.

"Look, Tami, sorry, Constable Riley, I'm really in a bit of a panic here. Do you know when either will be back or where they went?"

"Look, Christine, sorry, Crown Attorney Montgomery." She imitated me with a smirk and a cock of her head, finally acknowledging me with a piercing glare. "All I got is the sign out board. They sign out when they leave, they sign in when they come back. I'm not exactly in charge of all the directions they take and the like. That's pretty much your Dad's job. So, since he's not here either, I'm at a bit of a loss how to direct you. You're welcome to sit and wait." She pointed a pencil to the waiting area behind me.

The ancient wooden bench in the front lobby was currently occupied on one side by an elderly lady wearing crooked red lipstick and a large, white furry coat. She clutched a tiny dog whose hair matched the dreadlock weave of her coat. It sat up and wagged its tail when I glanced at them. I gave them a brief nod and a half smile, turning back to the desk before encouraging any conversation. Clearly hanging out waiting in Dad's office wasn't an offered option. Doubting I would get anywhere asking Constable Grumpy to pass on a message, I had no choice but to leave.

I opened the door in a hurry, heading to my right while glancing over my left shoulder where the reporter had been when I came in, only to stumble straight into a young man with a full tray of coffees. He grabbed me likely to avoid a collision. I straightened and shook his hand off my arm. "Sorry, miss, just trying to stop you from falling. Are you okay?"

I glanced up to apologize. "No, please excuse me; my fault, for not watching."

He pointed one finger and started to speak. "Aren't you—?"

I took off running, started my car, and once again squealed my tires out onto the street, something I had done only a handful of times in my life, and now, I had done it twice in one day. Professional, confident Crown Attorney Montgomery had vanished today, replaced by what felt like a fugitive with nowhere to hide. Repeatedly checking my rearview mirror, I drove back toward home, panic and paranoia overwhelming me. Instead of pulling into my driveway, I drove on into Jake's, going all the way around behind the back of his shed so no one could see my car. I sat there for a few minutes to catch my breath.

Finnegan barked when I approached the house. Stopping to retrieve the spare key under the fake poop in the garden, I used it to let myself in through the mud room, bringing the key inside and locking the door behind me, patting Finnegan as I did. "Can I hang out with you for a while, buddy? Will you protect me from all the creeps out there?"

He wagged his tail and rubbed against me for more attention, certainly much more welcoming than anyone else I had encountered.

The silence in Jake's house embraced me in contrast to the turmoil I left outside. My heart rate and breathing slowly returned to normal. I punched Dad's contact on my cell but got his voice mail. I tried Jenny next and got a rushed "hello."

"Jen, it's Christine. I'm sorry to bother you, I know you're super busy, but I've had a couple of odd encounters today, and I'm a bit rattled." She listened to my shortened versions of encounters with Wayne and then the guy at the cemetery. I even told her about my nosy neighbor coming around with questions and about the guy outside the station who had grabbed my arm, adding in fairness, he was likely a decent dude delivering coffees, maybe even one of their own.

She initially sounded rushed, occasionally speaking to someone else while I relayed my encounters. She was interested in the story about Wayne, but when I told her about Alistair Jordan grabbing and threatening me, that really got her undivided attention.

"For the love of…what the hell? You can't be out alone; I've told you that."

"I swear I intended to come and hang out at the precinct because it seemed like a nicely crowded and safe place to work. I didn't think I'd be in danger stopping at the damn cemetery. It usually brings me some peace to sit there and talk to Mom for a while."

"Listen to me and listen carefully. I'm aware your dad told you that someone murdered David. Things are coming along, but we don't have anyone arrested yet which means you could be in grave danger. Not like the usual, I'm coming after you because you put me in jail types. I'm talking about a legit murderer who came on your property two days ago and killed your husband and is currently at large. Are you hearing me? Lock yourself in and don't move unless someone is with you. We're out on a lead right now, but I'm going to send Juzo back to investigate this Jordan character and bring him in, charge his sorry ass with threatening an officer of the court and assault and kidnapping and anything else I can think of and interrogate the crap out of him to make sure he has nothing to do with David."

"I didn't get that impression. He seemed nervous, like he wanted to get back at someone for having to spend time inside, but I don't know if it was anything more than that. Like I said, I roughed him up a bit by catching him off guard. David knew all those self-defense moves too, so if they struggled, this Jordan guy would have got the worst of it. When I suggested that he had anything to do with the fire, he got all defensive on me. I'm trying to say; he didn't seem capable of murder for revenge. How bright can he be when he gave me his name? Doesn't seem like a think-things-through kind of guy, and I'm usually a pretty good judge of character," I said.

"Yes, you are, and I trust your instinct, but you're making me nervous. We've also tried to catch up with Wayne Duncan only to find an empty house at his last known address, and I mean empty, nothing but walls and floorboards. It was creepy. I can't believe he stood right in front of you this morning after being there at the fire. That's real stupid on his part. If he comes anywhere near you again, don't engage in conversation. In fact, don't even open the door to anyone anymore and stop going out alone. Send me the pictures you took at the cemetery, and I'll bring this Jordan guy in. I'm sorry, but I have to go. I promise I'll check back with you from the office before the end of the day. Please be careful."

I couldn't go home. There were investigators all over, yelling to each other over the machinery, dragging apart burned ruins. I also wasn't in the mood for Annie treating me like a teenager. I felt guilty getting comfort from Finnegan while my own Sunny sat at home without me. I knew Jake wouldn't mind if I made myself at home, and the peace and quiet was too tempting to leave. I had locked myself in like they all told me. Since my bodyguards were all busy, it would have to do. I grabbed a bag of my favorite salt and vinegar chips out of his pantry and curled up in his overstuffed chair patting the dog who now drooled on my lap.

Feeling exhausted and beat up, I hadn't meant to sleep but noticed two hours had passed when the phone's ring jolted me out of a deep, dreamless nap. "Dad, hey."

"What's going on? Where are you? Jenny said you were upset, and you'd run into some trouble at the station. What does that mean? I called the house and Annie said she hasn't seen you all day. And what the hell is the story about Wayne Duncan, that fuck up?"

"Easy, one question at a time," I said with a stretch and a yawn.

"Were you sleeping? Damn it, where are you?" he demanded.

"Okay, okay, I'm awake now. I'm over at Jake's, and—"

"Is he right there? Put him on would you."

"He's not here. He doesn't even know I'm here," I said.

Dad lost it. He didn't yell at me often, but when he did, it meant he was damn mad, or in this case, damn scared. "What the hell are you doing? You have criminals following you all over town. There's a murderer out there. You haven't told anyone where you are and you're hanging out at the neighbor's having a wee nap?"

"Please, calm down. It's been a difficult day. Wayne the creep got up my ass when I went jogging. I know, I know I shouldn't have been out alone; I get it before you go crazy on me too. Then Agnes the annoying got in my face when I tried to get out the door. I wanted to visit Mom on my way to see you and some asshole put a murderer sign on her grave and then when I sat there crying, trying to talk to her, another jerk came right up behind me with a camera in my face. Then he grabbed me, and I had to punch him to get away." I hardly got my words out between sobs, partly because it was Dad and mostly because I had reached the end of my rope.

I continued my rant without giving him the opportunity to jump in. "I needed somewhere to hide. I couldn't go home, and you weren't around and clearly the office is out of the question. That Constable Riley wicked witch on the front desk wouldn't let me take a step toward your office."

"Oh, honey, that's the rules. I wish you had—"

"You don't get it, Dad. No one will talk to me and I mean no one. My secretary rolls her eyes at me, my boss doesn't trust me, and everyone treats me like I'm a murderer. I can't even get take-out food or walk down the street without someone pouncing on me. Unless it's a reporter or a nosy neighbor looking for gossip or Annie who's frankly all weird and annoying right now, I have no one to talk to. And Jake's at the hall so I hid my car and locked myself in and crashed here where no one would harass me. And I didn't mean to have a nap, but I'm exhausted, so, I don't know, ease up, seriously." I broke down on the last few words, trying to stop crying at my pathetic life summary, but finishing with a loud sob and a hiccough despite my best efforts.

"I didn't mean to make you cry. Damn it, I'm so worried about you, and I can't get out of here. You're right, it's a good place to hide for now. But can you please call Jake?" Dad's voice had softened.

"I'm sure he'll be home soon. He's not on shift. He had to go in for an interview this morning, but otherwise he took some time off to help us. He wanted to see if they had any information from the fire marshal. I didn't want to take him away from that. He's done enough for me, for us. Once he's home, I'll stay with him until you get done. Can you meet me later at home?"

"Of course, I will. I'll call on my way, and I'll be there in time for dinner or a nightcap at the latest, I promise," he said.

He hesitated.

"You can hang up, Dad. I'm locked in and my car is hidden. I'll be fine. Call me later. I'm going to go make some cookies or take something out for dinner, do something useful for a change."

Dad chuckled. "Well, if you want to say thank you to Jake, don't make him eat anything you're cooking. I love you, please be safe."

"Thanks a lot. Love you too. I'll see you soon and I'll save you a cookie."

I tossed my phone on the coffee table and walked toward the kitchen, then froze when a shadow passed the window.

Chapter 10

Following my gaze, Finnegan growled toward the window, then barked continuously, while he ran to the back door, then across to the front like he followed our intruder. I dove to the ground, crouching behind the counter out of sight of the kitchen window. After a few minutes, Finnegan quieted and came back to sit in front of me, licking my face. Short of someone breaking in a door, I knew I was safe and locked in, but that didn't help me feel any less terrified. I grabbed the dog and hugged him close. He seemed content to stay close and be my protector.

I stayed on the floor, frozen in fear for the longest half hour of my life, questioning what or who had been out there. *Had someone seen my car, watched me sleep? Was he still out there? Was he peeping in the window?* I stared at the clock on the wall, willing Jake to come home, trying to calm myself. *Maybe my imagination created a bigger shadow out of an animal, a bird, or a giant leaf. Yeah right,* I argued. *More than likely a damn reporter lurked or that psychopath Wayne again. Or maybe cemetery guy or a freaking murderer. Calm down, take a breath, calm down.* Finnegan relaxed with his head on my lap while I sat trembling.

This is how Jake found me after he came whistling through the front door. Finnegan ran to him, barking. "What is it boy? What has you dancing around in circles?"

Jake gasped and clutched his chest. "Jesus, you scared me. What are you doing down there? What's wrong?"

I glanced up and shook my head quickly but didn't answer. He dropped down in front of me, grabbing under my arms and lifting me to my feet. I twisted, checking quickly over my shoulder for my peeping Tom.

He put his finger on my chin, pulling my face back to him.

"When did you get here? What were you doing on the floor? And what has you spooked about the window? Talk to me."

It took me a few seconds to gain my voice, and I teared up when I once again summarized the details of my awful day. "I thought I'd be so smart hiding my car and taking refuge in your nice quiet house, with your big brave dog. I fell asleep after I talked to Jenny and then Dad called and woke me up and he laughed at me when I said I'd go make cookies for you and then there was someone at the window and I couldn't reach my phone without going out in view and I didn't know when you'd be home. God, I'm a train wreck, Jake." My voice had become squeaky through my sobbing.

He pulled me to him, one arm holding me tight while the other hand stroked my hair. Again, I allowed him to console me, feeling like I'd been lost in a desert and found a lake. I hated that damsel in distress feeling of needing a guy to make things right, but maybe just this once I would make an exception. I had made a lot of this same exception in the last couple of days, it seemed.

A moment later, Jake set me at arms distance rather abruptly like he had last night. I had wondered if my affection made him uncomfortable but, in my current state, I worried he saw something behind me. "What is it? Did you see something?" I spun around but didn't see anyone outside.

He shook his head, which brought me back to my original assessment that I was taking advantage of his offered comfort. "I'm so sorry to interfere like this. I'm sure you have better things to do. I didn't know where else to go."

"Don't be ridiculous and I told you, stop apologizing. Of course, you should come here. Sit down. On a chair. I'll get us a drink. Probably better than the cookies you were heading to make."

His joke about my cooking seemed forced. He was short with me which was rare. I sensed it had something to do with me overstepping the boundaries of our friendship.

"I should go. I need to feed Sunny. You seem preoccupied and I ought to get out of your way. I'm sure whatever was there is gone and besides, I need to get a grip and stop running to you."

"Sit down," he repeated, pointing at the kitchen chair.

He crossed to the table with wine and two glasses, opening the bottle and pouring in silence. I knew Jake better than I had known David. We had seen each other in every situation from embarrassment to celebration, from the time we were kids. This expression, I had not seen. He clenched his jaw like I'd made him mad, but his eyes were staring right through me.

"I can't read your mind. What the hell's going on?

We're best friends, you can tell me anything. This whole situation has us both upset, but there's something else. Is it Courtney? Am I in your way, overstepping our friendship? Did the fire marshal tell you something?"

He got up and went to stare out the window, pausing several seconds before he finally spoke. "You're right. David's death and all the circumstances around it does have us rattled. No, the fire marshal has nothing conclusive yet."

"Then, what the hell?" I prodded.

He looked down at his hands like he weighed his reply, then turned back to me, but didn't smile. "Nothing, really, it's nothing, let's get some food and go feed Sunny and then take one day at a time."

My glass of wine felt rushed, and I was relieved when Jake offered to walk me home. Walking the path between our houses, we chatted about the weather and the dogs, while Finnegan ran off zigzagging ahead of us. Jake seemed distracted but it didn't feel like the right time to press him. It also didn't help that Annie appeared out of nowhere the minute we walked in the door. "What's he doing here again?" she asked.

He crouched down to ruffle Sunny's ears while I hung up our coats. "Currently patting the dog," I said.

"Don't be flip with me. It's not appropriate for you to be out with another man when your husband is not even buried in the ground. Rick called, and I didn't know where you were and obviously you've been out with this one here all day with no concern for letting either of us know."

"Don't talk about Jake like he's not here and don't call him another man. He's my friend, and he's been welcome in this house all our lives. And I haven't been out with him all day, I've been running from intrusive, possibly threatening people if you must know, and I don't need to be disciplined like a teenager. What the hell has gotten into you?" I asked.

"Finnegan and I should go now."

"Yes, you should," Annie said.

"Annie, stop it. No, Jake, you're staying. I'm cooking and you and Dad are damn well going to eat it," I insisted.

I stormed off into the kitchen as Annie stormed into her front room, slamming the door behind her.

I walked back to Jake when he didn't follow. "Please, will you stay? I will be really, really happy if you stay and Dad will be glad to see you, compare notes, relax over some food. I promised him I would hang with you until he got here. I'll get heck from him too if you don't wait for him. I'm honestly expecting one of these two to tell me I'm grounded."

He tilted his head with a smirk and pointed a thumb toward Annie's room.

"Ignore her. I don't know what's gotten into her. I'll let Dad barbecue, so you won't get food poisoning, I promise. Please stay?"

"Well, okay, if he's cooking." He grinned.

"Ha, ha, I can cook, damn it. Get in here and make us a drink," I demanded with a smile.

We couldn't sit on the back deck with the carriage house ruins staring at us. The front porch was also off limits with nosy neighbors and passers by slowing to stare.

"Big screen? Should be some football on," I offered.

"Not in the mood for TV to be honest." He leaned over to whisper. "And I feel like Annie is watching us or listening from her room."

We took our drinks and a bowl of nuts and bolts and again sat back in my den in the big fireside chairs.

"Okay, now this is one thing you make that I love," Jake said.

"Great, a bunch of cereal and nuts baked together for a couple of hours. I have a long way to go to gourmet dinner. Maybe I should take a cooking class, learn to be a bit more domestic."

Jake raised his eyebrows, pinching his lips in a tight line.

"Seriously, stop it. It's time I took a step back from the office grind, rethink things, experience life around me. Yesterday and today were a shamble and I felt alone. There's a lot missing from my life. I expected to be building sandcastles with kids and being the fun mom on school trips by now, with a bunch of cocktail couple friends like our parents had. Instead, I bust my ass every day for a job where no one knows me or cares what happens in my life other than how it affects them. If it had been me in that fire, they would replace me in a week with a loser like Fenwick and no one would ever look back."

Jake reached for my hand and stared through me again. "You are amazing. You are accomplished and brilliant and beautiful inside and out. And you have so much life ahead of you." He came to crouch in front of me and put one hand on either side of my face. "Don't ever let me hear you say that your life means nothing. No one would replace you in a week or ever."

He stared into my eyes, his tender words causing

me to tear up. It seemed like one of those movie moments when you know the couple will kiss. I glanced down at his mouth then leaned in when he came toward me. Reaching one hand behind his head to pull him closer, our lips barely touched when my cell phone rang in my lap, making me jolt back.

"Sweet Jesus." Jake jumped away from me standing and raking his hand through his hair.

I cleared my throat. "Hi, Dad."

"Hi, honey, just checking in. Is Jake with you?"

"Yup, he's here, everything is fine now. I'm back home, we're having a drink."

"What do you mean, now?" He sounded uneasy.

"Not sure, I think someone was lurking around Jake's after I hung up from you. It scared the heck out of me. I'll tell you about it when you get here; could have been something or nothing."

"Make sure he stays until I get there. I should be out of here in a few minutes."

"No worries, he's not going anywhere. I have steaks for you to barbecue," I said.

"Perfect, I'll be there shortly. Do you need anything else on my way?"

"No, no, don't need anything, thanks. We'll see you soon."

I punched off the call and dropped my head, focusing on my hands, embarrassed to look at Jake. "He's on his way."

"Yeah, I got that. Listen, I'm sorry, I overstepped. Please don't think I would ever take advantage. I don't know what got into me. Emotions are high and when you said no one would miss you. Jeez, girl; you have to know how much we all care about you," he said.

"You have nothing to apologize for. I keep leaning on you, and I don't want to make things bad for you and Courtney. I need to get my act together on my own. I appreciate what you do for me more than I can ever say. But if I'm the one overstepping the boundaries of our friendship, you need to tell me. I can't ruin what we have; I'd be lost without you."

He shook his head, not responding or meeting my eyes. I wasn't sure how to interpret his reaction.

"I'm sorry too for that little moment. Let's pretend it never happened, shall we? Dad's on his way, and we can have a nice dinner and take one day at time, just like you said before, okay?" I asked.

He looked up smiled. "How about those Buffalo Bills?"

We both laughed and the tension seemed to disappear, getting us back to silly banter until Dad arrived.

"I'm going to make sure the barbecue is going, I'm starving. Do you want another beer or ready for wine, or maybe a whiskey?"

"So many choices; a beer would be great, thanks," he said.

Jake picked up his cell and started scrolling as I walked out of the den. Annie's angry voice startled me when I got to the hall. I backed against the wall eavesdropping, like a spy.

"Relax," Dad said. "They've been hanging out since they were kids. He's harmless."

"You didn't see them, Rick. He's always got his arm around her, they're walking the dogs and smiling, side-by-side, like school kids in love, as if nothing ever happened. David's been murdered. It's not right. She went over there this afternoon with him, alone. She keeps going over there unchaperoned. One minute he's in bed with that model, actress person, the next he's hitting on our girl. God knows what moves he's making in her vulnerable state. You need to watch him, have your cop Jenny follow him; see what he's up to. I don't trust him. He could be our killer. Poor David. That Jake has always been jealous. He's trying to make his move now David is out of the way," Annie said.

"Unchaperoned, honestly? We're not in the eighteenth century. And he's engaged to that actress person. And my cop Jenny is a detective in our major crimes unit who is working on several serious investigations. I'll certainly not be assigning her to spy on the neighbor because he's holding my daughter's hand. You need to accept that Christie is an adult, and *that* Jake has been a friend of both hers and mine and David's for that matter for many years. You're way out of line."

"Of course, you'd say that. You men all stick together. I figured I'd have to do some digging myself to convince you."

"Us men? What the hell are you on about and what digging?" Dad demanded.

"I tried to go around to his place today, press him with a few questions of my own, maybe have a peek inside if he wasn't home. He had the place locked up like a prison, so I got nowhere but trust me, I'm going to find something on him, and you'll all see I'm right," Annie said.

I spun from my hiding spot, dropping the empty beer can with my rushed entrance to the kitchen. They both jumped at my sudden appearance and the clanking can on the tile floor.

"How dare you? You were lurking around at Jake's? You scared the life out of me. I've had psychos following me around for two days, jumping out of bushes, taking photos, threatening me, and assaulting me. I should be safe in my own house and at Jake's without you sneaking around scaring the heck out of me too. What the hell has gotten into you? You can't go wandering around people's properties and you sure can't go into someone else's house. That's against the damn law. Do you know something you need to tell us?" I glared at Annie, my voice louder with each question.

"You don't understand." Her voice gentle now, she walked toward me with arms outstretched. "Darling, I'm only watching out for you. You can't trust him. I'm sorry I gave you a fright."

"A fright? No, it went way beyond a fright. I thought I'd be next in line to be murdered. Don't darling me and stop picking on Jake. There is no reason in the world to doubt his intentions." I pushed her hands away.

Jake walked in the kitchen behind me. "What the hell is going on in here?"

"Annie was the shadow that passed your window today and scared the life out of me. It seems it's not appropriate that we're spending so much time together, unchaperoned!" I said with a huff.

"I've had enough of your accusations. Rick and Christie and Dave have been family to me and my parents since we were kids, and I would never hurt any of them. Further, to be clear, you're not welcome on my property when I'm not home."

Dad held his hands up, commanding a stop. "Okay, everyone let's take a step back please. We don't need to gang up on Annie. She's trying to help in her own way. We're all on edge and we all have different ways of dealing with grief. Annie, listen, Christie and I have both suggested you take some time away. You're always welcome here, but maybe this situation is getting the best of you. Would you like to go see your sister for a few days? I'm happy to pay for a flight and I can personally commit to keep you updated," he offered.

"Oh, you'd all like that wouldn't you, get me out of here, fly me out of your lives for good, after all I've done for you?" She stormed from the kitchen.

"Annie, wait," I called.

She ignored my plea, grabbed her jacket and purse from the bench, and slammed the front door on her way out. The three of us stood dumbfounded in the kitchen staring after her.

"What the hell was that all about?" Dad asked. He reached in the fridge, handed a beer to Jake, and opened one for himself.

"I told you. She's been all over me since the fire. Maybe she's scared something will happen again, or she's upset about David, or she's losing her marbles. I don't know. I can't deal with her emotions right now. I'm losing my own marbles trying to get through each day. I can't believe she went to question Jake."

"Let it go for now, I'll call her tomorrow after she has some time to cool off. I really wish she would go home and stay there for a while or go to her sister's, give us all space to do our own grieving," Dad said.

It seemed strange being with only Dad and Jake at

the kitchen table. Our usual Saturday barbecues included David and Courtney for as long as I remembered. The absence of both our partners felt like a bit of an elephant in the room. Despite the change, I enjoyed our night and felt calmer by the time Jake left with Finnegan. I tried to get Dad to go home too, assuring him I would be fine behind locked doors.

"Until there's a murderer in jail and until your nightmares are a thing of the past, you're stuck with me. I'll be gone early though. I have a few issues to sort out at the office, then I'll be at my place for a while. I need to see to a few things there too, but I'll be back here tomorrow night."

"Would the lovely Luisa be one of those few things that needs your attention?" I crossed my arms waiting for an answer.

He grinned. "Luisa is lovely and yes, I would love to give her some attention. And like I already told you, once we're past the next few days of hell, I will be happy to introduce you. Until then, we both need some sleep and that's all I'm going to say."

"Daaaadd, come on, tell me something. Is she tall, short, fat, skinny, old, young? Where did you meet her? Is she a cop? Please say no."

Dad paused, glancing up to the ceiling, then answered, counting off one hand with his other index finger. "Yes, no, no, no, no, and no; at a baseball game and no. Now go to bed."

"You're impossible. Hey, wait. Get back here. We're not done." I called after him, but he walked out of the kitchen.

"Goodnight, my love. Call me if you need me."

He went up the stairs laughing leaving me to talk to

myself while I cleaned up the last of our dishes. "Tall, great, his girlfriend is tall, and she likes baseball. That tells me a whole lot."

It didn't take long to get to sleep after the crazy day I'd had.

Sitting at the kitchen table reaching for my hot chocolate, my hands trembled. Instead of feeling the usual ease, with Dad on one side and Mom on the other, this felt more like a trip to the principal's office. Even at sixteen, I recognized tension on my dad's face. That could only mean bad news. Mom tried to smile, but her eyes were tortured. It was the kind of smile she used to reassure me, when all it made me want to do was hug her and say, it's okay to cry, Mom.

"Okay, I can handle whatever you've got to say. Whatever it is, we're the three musketeers, we can work it out, right? You always say that," I said, with a calmness I didn't feel.

"Sweetheart, we've got some bad news. There's no easy way to tell you. Julie, that is... Mom..." Dad rose from the table and walked away.

Mom had reached for my hand. I looked down now at our linked fingers, then up to her beautiful deep blue eyes. "What is it Mom?"

She spoke softly. "My sweet pea." She paused for a breath. "Today the doctor said there's nothing else he can do."

It was clear what she meant. She'd been sick off and on over the last year, endless appointments, runs of chemo and radiation for weeks, sometimes staying in her bed for days. Up to that point, it had never occurred to me that she wouldn't get better one day. "Dad?" I prompted.

"I'm sorry, Christie. You know Dr. Levine is good. He has some suggestions. We won't give up. There are other specialists, new treatments—"

Mom interrupted and spoke with a tone I would never forget. She was calm, but decisive and so factual, I wondered if we were talking about the same thing. "There will be no more treatments and it's not a matter of giving up Rick." He reached for her other hand. She let him hold it. Her exhaustion forced a rare show of weakness. She lay her head down on their linked hands. "I've had it. I can't take anymore appointments. There will be no more specialists or tests or new treatments."

Dad stroked Mom's hair. He and I exchanged glances over her head, tears in both our eyes. "We'll be okay, honey. I promise you," Dad reassured me.

Mom raised her head when I jumped up. "How can you say that Dad? How can you be so calm, both of you? What do you mean, no more, Mom? You need to keep trying. You have to stay with me."

"Trust me, love, if I could do more, I would. Dr. Levine says the disease is too advanced, too far spread. I don't want to spend my last few weeks plugged into a machine. I want to be with you two." Mom had tears on her cheeks. I knew she was sad for me, not for herself.

I was desperate. "Don't you care, Dad? Fight for her, please Dad, make her do something. Dad, please!"

I woke again to Dad sitting on the bed beside me. He pulled me to him and we both held on tightly. Neither of us had anything to say to make things better.

Chapter 11

"Hey, I got past the front desk this time, and I brought treats. I can always get a smile when I bring you sugar." I smiled triumphantly walking into Dad's office.

"I read Riley the riot act for not letting you into my office yesterday. Her little power trip could have put you in danger. You'll be getting the royal treatment when you walk in that door from now on no matter who's on the desk. If you don't, I need to know. And you are what makes me smile, sweetheart, but I'll take the Krispy Kreme doughnut any day. Come in. Sit. I have a solid eight minutes for you. I need to get out of here by noon. Are you okay? I thought you were going walking with Jake today."

Dad hadn't slept much in the last few days. He'd been up twice in the night and his car pulled out of the driveway before six a.m. His eyes were glossy, and his suit wasn't its usual crisp collar and pressed pants he prided himself on.

"I'm fine, but you look like hell." I told him. "You need to let your team do this. Go off on your date with Luisa or whatever your top-secret plan is for today and leave this place for now."

"You don't look much better. Did you get back to sleep last night? Dream again?" he asked.

"Thank you for getting up with me. I can't believe

I scream out like that. The dream is so real, like I'm sixteen and living it all again. Maybe having Annie so upset is making me relive what we all went through with Mom. Anyway, yes, I got through the night okay after that. I got up again later because you were up."

He waved his hand dismissing an explanation for his restless night.

"Okay, let's not dwell on it. Did you ask Jenny if they've got anything on Wayne Duncan yet or what happened with my friend Mr. Alistair Jordan?" I asked.

He shook his head. We were laughing off the absurdity of Wayne jogging with tortilla chips when Jenny stuck her head in the door.

"Sorry to interrupt, Sir. Hey, Christine, how are you holding up?" Her smile showed genuine concern.

Dad broke in before I answered. "No time for a tea party, Scott, what can I do for you?"

I knew part of the bark resulted from his lack of sleep, followed a close second by his lack of involvement in the case.

"Sorry, Jenny; he's grumpy. I was about to come talk to you. Anything new?" I asked.

"No worries. Nothing concrete to report, but we're onto some good leads. I'll feel better when we get our hands on that Wayne character. I'll call you about Mr. Jordan probably later today. He's a nut all right and you did convict him way back. I'm still working his angle before we get him a bail hearing. But I'm pretty sure your instincts were right. It doesn't seem like he had anything to do with the fire."

Dad stood abruptly. "Can you please take this conversation to Detective Scott's office?"

"No, my apologies, Sergeant, I'll catch up with

Christine later. I came to tell you, there's a gentleman requesting to speak to you personally. It may be nothing, but he said he knows you. Bruce Elroy drives a cab."

Dad dropped his head to his chest.

Jenny cringed when he looked up to her again. "Sorry for asking. I know you want to get out of here, but he says it's urgent."

"Everyone thinks they have something to solve a case. Usually, they're just being nosy. I'm off limits in the investigation," he said.

"Of course, Sir. I didn't get the impression it had anything to do with the Hamilton murder. I'll come with you so there's nothing improper if you think that's why he's here."

Dad walked toward the door. "Sorry, Scott, didn't mean to snap at you. Bruce is a decent guy. We used to play baseball together if you can feature that. I'll go see what he wants." He turned to me. "We'll have to catch up later."

"I hadn't planned to leave yet. I wanted to work in your office for a while. Surely Bruce the cabbie can't be a suspect in the murder. Call me nosy, I'll come too." He didn't answer, nodded his head in the direction of the door, so both Jenny and I went ahead of him.

Bruce appeared several years older than Dad, with short cut gray hair on the sides of an otherwise bald head. He stood no more than an inch taller than my five, ten and wore a flannel checked jacket, jeans and runners that had seen better days. He twisted his baseball cap in his hands, jumping up from his seat a little too quickly when we approached.

Dad shook his hand. "Nice to see you again Bruce,

come on into my office, take a seat and relax. Want some terrible coffee?"

Jenny and I followed to the door.

"No, no, Ricky, don't go to any trouble. Sorry, I mean officer, sorry Ricky, I'm not sure what to call you." Bruce sat down taking a deep breath he seemed to need to steady himself.

I raised my eyebrows and smirked at Jenny in reference to Dad's high school name.

"Bruce Elroy, you remember my daughter, Christine and Detective Jennifer Scott is also here. Maybe you remember her too? And relax, I said, and call me Rick for Christ's sake. You didn't commit any crimes, did you? Everything okay at home? Stella, the kids?"

"Of course, wee Christine and Jennifer what good girls you've become. Your mamas must be so proud. Oh, Lordy Lord, Christine, I'm so sorry, I didn't mean ta offend, God rest her soul." He made a sign of the cross and pointed upward but kept talking. "I'm such an idiot. And I'm sorry too for all your trouble."

I shook his hand and took in his sincerity. He seemed like a real genuine guy you could count on. "Thanks, Mr. Elroy we're working things through."

He smiled and shook Jenny's hand next before speaking to Dad. "No, no, of course not, no criminal here, I'm hoping maybe I have a tip for y'all."

"Bruce, for obvious reasons, I can't be part of an investigation into my son-in-law's death. If you know something about the fire, you'll have to speak to Detective Scott."

Jenny winced looking torn. "It's okay Sergeant, I'm not sure Mr. Elroy would be comfortable talking to me. You two seem to go back some."

She smiled at Bruce. "We'd love to hear what you have to say Mr. Elroy. Do you mind if I sit in, maybe take some notes?"

"Right, right, sorry, don't mean to take up time. Y'all are so busy. So, here's the thing. Last night, I'm doing my usual Saturday night run, you know, downtown folk, getting them all home safe and the like. These two young lads come along, hoodies, and ball caps like they wear y'know so's I couldn't see too well who I'd be getting. Apparently, they didn't get the gist of my flat rate fee, pay-up-front kinda rules for late at night. Those darn fools bashed their way right inta my cab at ten minutes afore midnight, that's ten minutes till I usually call it a night. One big guy spilled his fat self right inta my front seat and said "drive" while the other skinny guy crunching on a bag of something, poured his self inta the back.

"What the hell could I do? Big guy in the front didn't strike me like a rules kinda guy. I had to drive. All the while, I kept thinkin' of my wee wife at home and how she'd have my hide if I kept her up worryin' and waitin' late for me again. But then, I'd heard a lotta bad stories 'bout guys like me who tried to argue with guys like these, ended up with their heads busted up. So, I kept real quiet like, didn't bother with my usual small talk.

"Damned if the big guy in the front didn't start singin' to the Keith Urban tunes I had playing. Blue Ain't Your Color, you know the one? He was drawing out the bluuuuuue part. He finally took a breath, when skinny guy from the back seat told me 'down old Townline Road.' I prit near wet my own drawers, somethin' I ain't done since being a wee un when I got my tongue stuck to the frozen fence post at recess. Old Donny Harman dared me, member that Ricky?

"Anyhow, I knew old Townline Road would be pitch dark and darn near nothin' lived down there, but some critters and a couple a ancient redneck types. I did like he said though, and soon we were pullin' up to a real shady old farmhouse. I wouldna even known it existed but for one lone light hanging down on the porch and a couple hounds barkin' their stupid heads off. Skinny guy in the back seat snored so loud, he almost drowned out them dogs. I saw him in my rear mirror, his head lolled back, mouth open with a bunch of rotten teeth. His singin' buddy had to belt him four times afore he budged enough to roll outta the car.

"It took me all I had to muster enough nerve to ask for the fare, knowin' full well I'd be more likely in for a whack upside the head or maybe a slashed tire and a real long walk home. I got a grunt and a slammed door instead. I figured that was better than what coulda been."

At this point, Dad jumped in. "Bruce, you and I go way back to grade school and I'm sorry you got stuck with a lousy fare, but couldn't our nice Detective Scott or better yet one of the officers at the front have filed a report for you? You told her you had some urgent information?"

Dad took a deep breath and shook his head slowly, his impatience and his exhaustion showing, and I sure knew how he felt. I put a hand on Dad's arm and smiled at Bruce. "Please, Mr. Elroy, we're all really on edge, if you could get to the point."

His hands waved us to sit, not that we were getting

up. "No, no, listen, then, then, imagine my bad luck when next this crazy lady, hair in some curlers and then a weird net thing over top, wearing a bumpy pink robe like my own mama used to wear about a hundred years ago; she comes right out onta the porch dressed like that and swinging a rifle round. 'Frank, Wayne, that you?' She yelled louder than the singin' and snorin' guys put together. She held up that dang gun, so's I figured one of us would be meeting our maker. I was so scared I couldna even get the car in gear, wasn't even thinkin' straight. 'Yeah, Ma,' the snorin' guy hollers back, like this crazy situation weren't nothin' new for him."

Bruce's eyes were huge. I nodded for him to continue.

"Then she says, 'You get in the house, you good for nothing drunks. Did you pay the poor cabbie for bringing you bums all the way out here to the end of the earth?' Skinny guy from the back just grunted, only right at his mama. I wondered if that guy had two words inside his head, or iffen he only snored and grunted like that every day of his life. Damn me, if she didn't point her gun right at those two young lads and shoe the fat, singin' Frank guy right back to my car door.

"I real slow like leaned outta my winda and said, 'Evening ma'am. It's okay, this one's on the house,' I said, real polite like, so's not to piss him off or worse the gun lady. Good idea, right?"

He seemed to be asking me directly, so again I smiled and nodded so he would get on with it.

"Then that big Frank guy, he looked back at that crazy old lady, her gun pointed right at them, then back at me. Darndest thing, if he didn't open his wallet and toss me a hundred bucks and say, 'Sorry buddy; thanks for the ride, keep the change.' A course my wee Stella at home sure got over her naggin' bout the one a.m. home time when I told her that story and tossed the hundred buck bill right onta the kitchen table. Go figure, that's a night I won't forget no time soon." Bruce smirked and wiggled his whole body back and forth, clearly proud of himself.

Then he flinched when dad yelled. "Bruce, what the hell? Nice, story, and I'm sorry they scared you—"

Bruce waved his hands for us to sit. "No, no, jeezus, sorry Ricky, I'm so excited and nervous like being in here with y'all. I ain't never been involved with police business afore. Of course, the thing I came to say, so's when crazy lady goes to drag skinny grunt guy back in the house, she grabs him and jerks that hoodie and hat right off his head and pulls his head round by the ear. I saw him for a minute with the headlight of my car, wish I coulda seen more of him, but then I had a pretty good view in my mirror when he was sleepin' too.

"So's anyway, they started to go in, but I heard clearly 'cause my winda stayed open still and there was nothing making noise out there but a few crickets and bull frogs. She said, 'why did you go anywhere near her, you imbecile? I told you to keep away.' That's what she called him, an imbecile.

"And then skinny guy, her boy I'm guessin' 'cause he called her Ma, well, he's awake all of a sudden and says, 'what the fuck, get off me, you crazy woman. They're pinnin' it all on her, there's nothing they got on me. No one even knows where to find me out here in this fucking hole.' Pardon my language ladies; I wanted to say, word for word, y'know.

"So's, like I said, she yelled back, 'Pinnin' it on her? No, they're not, they're getting close to pinnin' it on you, you fool standing right there on camera watching the fire. You want crazy? I'll show you fuckin' crazy'. Then skinny guy shoved her off him like a nasty fly and then walked inta the house, her still waving that damn gun around like she aimed to shoot them both. Then I skedaddled it out of there, some quick.

"Like I said, I got all excited about the hundred buck drive and getting back to my wee Stella in one piece, so's I never thought much about what they were saying until today, when I read the Sunday news about the latest on Christine here. She's big news around these parts. So, sorry again, miss, for all your dealings and how they trying to make you look bad. Those of us know Ricky here, know your family never coulda done somethin' like they all sayin'. But, the thing is how, it struck me right then, 'cause the paper used them exact words 'pinnin' it on her' and then I thought, maybe this kid had somethin' to do with somethin', 'cause he said 'pinnin' it on her' too, right like the papers, so's I'm thinkin' maybe he meant pinnin' on you like, 'cause the Mama said somethin' about watching a fire and then asking why'd y'all go near "her"?"

He put his fingers up in quotation marks to emphasize the "her" in case we hadn't understood his meaning, then continued his lengthy story. "Then I remembered the crazy lady said how they were goin' to pin it on her boy, the snoring skinny guy, musta been Wayne 'cause she said Frank and Wayne and the fat singin' guy who paid me was the Frank one. So's I thought maybe y'all might wanna know about it in case somethin' had to do with somethin', ya get me?"

Now Rick stood looking a whole lot more interested in what his old baseball buddy had to say. "I can't hear any more of this. You need Nick and you need to get Clancy in here, now," he said to Jenny.

Clancy Parry had been a dear friend of our family for years and was by far the best sketch artist in the province. At Mom's funeral he sketched a small portrait of her, gave it to me and told me Mom had the kindest heart of anyone he had the pleasure to know. I kept that picture in my wallet since that day. When it came down to the business of finding criminals, no one could get descriptions out of a witness and draw an ident photo the way Clancy could.

I'd been tense listening to Bruce's story, knowing who he had driven last night. The idea they now had something to pin on Wayne, made things real and brought on panic. I picked up my purse and excused myself. "Mr. Elroy, I'm really glad you came to see Dad, but I'm going to leave you to chat with him and Detective Scott now. Here's my personal card. If you or your family ever need anything that I can help with, please call me anytime, truly anytime. My cell number is right there on the card."

Bruce stood, took the card, and nodded. "Thank you."

Dad reached for my hand and held up a finger to Bruce. "I'll be right back, see if you can remember some details for our friend Clancy here."

I squeezed Dad's hand to reassure him as I too called back to Bruce. "Thank you again, Mr. Elroy, you've been such a huge help, more than you know. You're in good hands with Detective Scott."

He sat up taller in his chair and beamed back at me with a proud smile. "My pleasure, miss, glad to be of service to you and your daddy. And it's Bruce, people call me Bruce."

"Well, thanks again, Bruce. Oh, one more thing, the skinny guy in the back, you said he crunched on something in your car, did you happen to notice what he ate?"

"Well, yeah, I sure did. I had me a mess of leftover crumbs and an empty bag to clean up first thing this morning and the whole darn car stunk from those two."

"The bag. What was he eating?" I asked.

"Oh, right. Tortilla chips, miss, stinky nacho cheese tortilla chips."

Dad and I shared a knowing look. I nodded to him, then tilted my head toward Jenny.

She nodded too and gave me a thumbs up. "I get it and I'm on it."

"I know what you're thinking; we're on the same page. I jog right past old Townline Road. When can they bring him in?" I asked.

We stopped in the hallway. Dad faced me. "I'm sure Jenny will use Bruce's info and whatever Clancy can get to at least question Wayne. They can't bring him in for eating smelly chips in a cab or watching a fire, but what he said in front of Bruce, to his mother or whoever that woman was, along with stalking you on your jog, will sure give them something to talk to him about. They need enough to keep him here or he'll come bother you more when they're obligated to let him go. If he got in Bruce's cab last night, chances are he's still hanging out with his hillbilly friend or brother, Frank and whoever the old lady is. I'd really like to know who she is and what she knows, especially where she got the information something is getting pinned on Wayne and how she knew he had come near you."

"Yeah, I was wondering that too," I agreed.

"They'll find him and get him off the street, at least for a while until they figure out who knows what. If you're going to do work, and that's a big if, I don't see why you should even try on a Sunday. But if you are, I need you to wait for me to take you home myself," Dad insisted.

"Dad, I have to do some of it, there's so much just in limbo. I planned to work at your desk or in a spare room, but there's too much going on here. It's suffocating. Maybe you're right and I should stop killing myself for people who don't even want me at the office anymore." I was exhausted and whining like a cranky kid.

"You do it for the vulnerable and they value you more than anyone else in their lives. When you put the bad people in jail, the victims can get on with their lives. You know how that feels now. Without what you do, what we do, they have no hope for a normal future. You are everything to them. Forget about those idiots at the office who don't know you."

I nodded. "You're right, Dad. I'm having a pity party, again. What Bruce said has really thrown me. I don't like Wayne being out there, but I can't stay here. I'm sure I'll be fine at home. There are backhoe dudes still picking things apart and fire marshal investigators around. Their presence and the fact some are in uniform seems enough to keep media people away. Surely that's enough to keep Wayne away too. It's not ideal, but at least there are still other people who can be trusted.

They won't let anything happen." I paused. "Maybe, I'll quit my job and go work at Ruby's Diner, five minutes from home. Maybe I'll go sit on Jake's porch for a bit."

Dad stared, wide-eyed.

"Right, rambling again," I said.

"Work will wait or someone less compromised will deal with it. And don't trade in your briefcase for a waitress apron yet. It's not the time to be making any major life decisions. Please text me when you get home and when you're going to Jake's and when you're leaving Jake's."

I rolled my eyes in reply.

"I mean it, I'll send an officer to stand guard if you don't keep me up to date." He pulled me in for a hug and kissed the top of my head.

I smiled up at him. "Okay, okay, I promise I'll text. No more cops, please."

I blew him a kiss before I walked out the back exit, knowing he would be leaning against the door frame until I left.

****

I arrived in my driveway, calmer now that I had seen Dad and knew Jenny was working things through. Bruce's information had been the huge break they needed. I shook my head thinking, what are the chances Wayne happened to take a cab with someone Dad knew. I sat with the engine off, staring at the remains of the carriage house for several minutes. The pile of rubble had been strewn several feet out from what remained of the building. Apparently, they were in the tearing it apart again stage.

I closed my eyes and felt like life flashed before

me. Visuals of his man cave renovations, picking wood panels and old antique signs, moving furniture and appliances, Dave with his big smile, the guys yelling woohoo while they pretended to slide down to the pool where we girls were lounging, laughing at them. Had I been happy then or only playing the part? I didn't know anymore. I remembered events, remembered that I loved David or at least loved the idea of a life with him. I did things to make him happy and somehow that seemed enough.

Then I pictured Jake, earlier in the summer, behind our Tiki hut by the pool, making a jug of Margaritas, affecting a Spanish accent, only to come around with the tray wiggling his hips, wearing a grass skirt. We girls laughed and adored him while David hung back and said "no thanks" without lifting his eyes from his phone. I had laughed too at the time, presuming David was in a bad mood, now realizing those moods were more often than not, certainly in the last year.

I tried to shake the image from my mind but couldn't help the nagging feeling I was jealous that Courtney got the fun guy, my best friend Jake, my guy, who never really had been my guy. Dave would never have stooped to serve us, let alone entertain us with silly words or a grass skirt. *Had he been thinking of Sharlene that day? Had he been texting her while he sat with all of us? Did it matter to me? Would it have mattered in all of this?*

Who did you run home to tell your news of the day? I asked myself. Dad and Jake came to mind. *Who seemed to care more about your day, and that's why you went there?* Dad and Jake came to mind again. "Stop it," I scolded myself. I got out of the car.

"Daddy's not here anymore and Jake is getting married." I stood in the driveway to stare once again before unlocking the door. "You're looking at your husband's murdered ashes and thinking about the boy next door. Get a grip."

My phone rang in my purse before I opened the door.

"Whatcha doin', babe?" Jake asked.

"Why do you call me that? Courtney's your babe and I shouldn't rely on you so much."

"Whoa, where did that come from? I've called you babe since eighth grade. I'm just checking in, seeing if you're ready for my awesomeness of barbecue ribs for dinner tonight. Bring Rick, we'll have a brew. I owe you guys dinner. You know you want to." He sounded excited and happy to talk to me.

I didn't know what to say. My thoughts from the car were so fresh in my mind. Here he was being my fun guy again to ease the awkwardness between us and I continued to beat myself up with guilt for enjoying his company; but I ached to see him at the same time. My husband just died, of course he would cook for us, be friendly, what was wrong with me?

I guessed he took my silence for a negative reply. "I'm sorry if it's not appropriate, I'll call you something else, ahh, let me think, honey? Sugar pie? Okay, what the hell? You always laugh at my teasing crap. I'm trying to lighten things up. We did fine eating together last night. You guys need to eat. What's going on? Where have you been this morning? What's your game plan for today?"

I had teared up again and couldn't get my words out to stop his string of questions, without him knowing

I was crying. "I need a minute to regroup or something."

"What the hell? Why are you crying?"

"Damn it." I reached for a Kleenex, as Annie walked around the corner from the kitchen. Not expecting her back after last night's angry departure, I let out a scream.

"What is it? Talk to me. I'm on my way." Jake sounded panicked.

"No, wait. It's okay, I just walked in the door and ah Annie is here. I didn't expect anyone, and she startled me. I was a little upset when I came in. Can I call you back in a minute? I'll call Dad and ask him about dinner. No, wait, he's trying to get done with work. He's got a date this afternoon. Barbecue would be amazing, but you don't owe us anything and I'm not sure when Dad will be back."

"You sure you're okay over there? You're talking around in circles. What's going on?" His voice was demanding.

"I'll have to get back to you on that. Can I call you back in a few minutes? Annie is here and I've had a day and a half already and its barely noon. I have an interesting story to tell you from a cab driver Dad knows. I also need somewhere to work in quiet if I can have a piece of your porch for a couple of hours and I'll bring the wine or brew or whatever you want. I'll be there shortly if it's okay. No, I'll call you back. Just, give me a minute, I'll call you back and thank you."

Annie looked ready to pounce, like I had snuck in the back door after my curfew or eaten the last cookie without asking.

She laced into me the minute I hung up the phone.

"Why are you spending so much time with that boy? Your murdered husband's not even in the ground yet. You're obviously devastated at his loss; you can't even stop crying."

If only she knew what was upsetting me. I didn't reply and she continued. "It's not appropriate for you to be running off with the boy next door, for, for, God knows what he's after. You're vulnerable and lonely without David and that Jake is likely to take advantage. You should reconsider and stay put here where you belong. And Rick has a date? What's that about? Doesn't anyone have any respect for the dead?"

I hadn't expected her back and certainly didn't anticipate the accusations again. After her repeated tirade, my turmoil of emotions and guilt over David and Jake were quickly replaced by anger. "That's enough, Annie. Like Dad said, you're way out of line. I don't want to hear anymore judgments. I get it, you loved David and I know you want to protect me and Dad, but this has to stop. Jake is not a boy looking for a booty call. And certainly, Dad is way beyond reproach. He should have someone to share his life. Mom has been gone for almost fifteen years. And even if either of us was seeking well, comfort, we're adults now. I can make my own decisions based on my own feelings."

"Fine job you've done so far," she said with a sneer.

"How dare you say that? That's completely uncalled for. I'm not sixteen anymore and I won't take any nonsense from you. Jake is an amazing man who has been hugely supportive, professionally, and personally through all of this to both Dad and me. We have grown up together, that's like almost thirty years we've been friends. You need to accept that he's part of our lives." I glared at her.

"I don't trust him, and you shouldn't either. He's after something, I can tell. That boy has always been trouble," she huffed.

"You're wrong and you're upsetting me. I've had enough to deal with today. Sunny and I are going over to Jake's for a few hours. Dad will be here later tonight. I really wish you would take some time at home or with your sister. We have been through this; you don't need to be fussing over me or the house. This isn't like you. I know this has been tough, but you need to—"

"Don't tell me what I need to do. You don't know your mind, you or Rick. You're all muddled. David was murdered and you're acting like it's a Sunday in the park."

"Okay, that's enough. Sit down right now and tell me what the hell's going on. I've tried to be patient and understanding. I get that this is difficult for you too. You must know that we love you and we've said you're always welcome and I mean it. You can stay or go, but you can't cross the line about Jake. You have never treated me like this before. I don't know where your attitude is coming from. You aren't making any sense," I said.

"I don't want to tell you anything. You tell me what's going on. What happened today that had you tearing up when you came in the door; that you have to run over and tell him about? What did you mean when you said a cab driver told your Dad a story? You used to tell me everything. Now, you go running to that Jake or to Daddy." She waved her hand dismissively.

I didn't want to tell her about Bruce's revelation.

She had been acting bizarre enough and that story would give her more reason to want to lock me up. I wanted to tear a strip off her about the "running to" comment when I realized maybe all the fuss might be because she felt left out. David had always taken the time to invite her into his office, ask her about her day, offered to help her carry groceries or laundry. There were times I came home, and they would be chatting over a glass of wine together. She really did have a soft spot for him.

I took a deep breath to steady myself, sat at the kitchen counter and softened my voice hoping she would calm down too. "Please stop with the "that" Jake and believe me, I'm not running to anyone. Dad and Jake and I are all involved in this investigation. It's important we keep each other up to date, that's all there is to it. And of course, I'm tearing up when I pull in the driveway and they're ripping the carriage house apart. This is tough for all of us, including you. I know you miss David, but tell me, what else has gotten into you?"

She didn't answer, just stared trance-like. I waved my hand in front of her face. "Hello, where are you? What are you thinking about? I swear, I'm not keeping anything from you. I don't know anything. The police don't know anything."

She stared directly at me like she was trying to figure out which way to go, soft or angry. When she finally spoke, she sounded worn down. "I wish we could go back to the way things were years ago. Remember when your friends teased you and Rick for keeping me around after your mom died. We were good back then remember. Things have changed so much."

I reached for her hand, but she pulled away. "Oh,

Annie, I've grown up."

"I know, I know. But remember when you and David were married; remember they used to say you couldn't live without my cook pot? Remember, you defended me, saying we were family. You told me it was worth it to take the teasing about your lousy cooking to have me around. You said I was like a second mother. Remember?"

"Of course, you were like family. You still are. And I'm not trying to stifle any good memories. You were always a huge help to me and Dad, and David too. His death is upsetting you; I get it. I'm only asking that you appreciate it's difficult for me too."

"Please let me stay." She pleaded, but her expression didn't match her tone.

"Of course," I said, with as much compassion as I could, although wondering what my invitation would mean in the long run. "You are always welcome, and I want you to be wherever you feel most comfortable until all this blows over."

"Well, staying right here is the best thing for both of us. Now what shall we have while you tell me about this cab driver? Can I get you some tea or a cold drink?" she offered.

"I'm sorry, I just…It's just…I told Jake I'd go over for a bit and I have some work to do. It's easier away from the excavation and noise. It's nothing to do with you. I need to be away from the house right now—"

"Right, there it is again. Never mind then. Don't let me add to your issues, heaven forbid. Go sort your problems out with that boy and tell him all about the investigation while you leave me out of it." She walked toward her room. "I'll be fine."

"Annie, wait." I followed her stopping the door with my foot before she slammed it.

She spun around and the angry, trance-like face returned. "You said I'm like a mother to you and you welcome me here, but the minute you walk in the door, it's Dad this and Jake that. I know where I stand and it's not with you. Go, be off with you. I'll not hold you back from that…from your friends." She said "friends" with a smirk.

There would be no use belaboring the point for now. "We are all working through our grief and need to focus on getting through one day at a time. I meant it when I said you are welcome to stay here if it makes you feel better. I'm happy to have you, but the attitude needs to go. Can we please call a truce? It's not helping to argue about who I hang out with or talk to. You respected my adult choices up to about three days ago before anything happened. If we're sharing space, that respectful adult relationship needs to continue, or we're done sharing space."

She stared at me and didn't reply, so I asked again. "Deal?"

It seemed like minutes later when she finally flipped her hand in dismissal walking away, but at least she answered. "Fine, truce, deal, whatever you want to hear. Be off with you. It's time for *The Price is Right*."

I went to my room to change, shaking my head and questioning, what I had offered. Her appearance and repeated accusations had shocked me. When I came back down, she had closed herself in her room. I whistled for Sunny, grabbed her leash, and a bottle of wine, threw my briefcase strap over my shoulder and headed out the door locking it behind me. "What the hell was all that, girl?"

I went through our backyard path, hoping the air might help clear that ugly meeting and my mixed-up feelings about Jake. It didn't. I knocked on his back door as I walked through it. "I should probably wait until you answer before I walk in."

"Why would you start now?" He smiled.

"I also said I'd call you back. Can I come in and hide here for a while, like maybe a month? And can Sunny and I accept your kind dinner invite? Please say yes. I have so much to tell you."

"Sunny has already left with Finnegan, so I'll leave it up to him if he invites her to stay for the day, but for you, hmm, let me think, yes, it would be my pleasure." He gestured me into the kitchen with a bow.

There was some element of truth to Annie's accusations. I always came to Jake when I really needed to talk. Damn it.

"Okay, talk. Why the hell is *she* back in the house?" he asked.

"She said the same things all over again and again and again. She went on about your motives and why did I keep running to you and telling you about the investigation but leaving her out. It was like she hadn't just run off on all that last night. She even complained about Dad having a date. Apparently, it's disrespectful that he's seeing Luisa. Mom's been gone for fifteen years. It's about time he found some happiness again. She started reminiscing about the old days, saying we were all family. She seemed to calm down at the end, but I don't know. I told her she could stay if she wanted, provided she loses the attitude."

"Really? Was that the best idea?" he asked.

"I'm not so sure. She and David were always thick as thieves, having their drinks together and their own private jokes. She probably misses him and feels left out. She's done a lot for us and I feel sorry for her, even if she is pissing me off."

"You're being a lot more understanding and considerate than she is. It's your husband who died and you're stuck in the middle of all the media fiasco. They hardly asked her three questions. She's not all over the news being accused of murder and trying to work full time. She needs to cut you some slack," Jake said.

"Let's see how the next couple of days go. I'll try to spend some time with her and maybe that will be enough. There is some element of truth to what she says. I do need to stop relying on you and Dad, and I do need to get back to routine and make some decisions about work. But first, let me tell you about Bruce in Dad's office. Then I really have to get some files over to the office if I can park myself on your deck for a bit."

We had a reasonable afternoon under the circumstances, each working on our own laptops, but chatting and snacking while we did. Jake loved Bruce's story and the huge lead it gave Jenny. We both agreed it could be the answer they needed to get at David's murderer. Dad called around five to say he wouldn't make it for dinner. I made him promise to stay and spend his evening with Luisa. I told him I'd be safe with Jake and that Annie had unfortunately come back to the house, but I would be fine alone even if she hadn't.

Our day and dinner together felt friendly and comfortable, no pressure and no drama. By evening, I felt more relaxed than I had been since the fire.

Jake insisted on walking me to the door. "Home again," he said bending to hug me. He didn't let go right away, and we again, had that awkward moment gazing into each other's eyes. I was thinking too much about almost kissing him yesterday in the den, but after our companionable afternoon, and struggling with Annie's accusations, I mustered all my discipline and stepped away.

"I need to go in, Jake. This feels too right and so wrong at the same time. Thank you again for another fabulous dinner."

He smiled and nodded before he turned for home without a reply.

I opened the back door and hung up Sunny's leash. Annie's bedroom door clicked to close. She had been watching again while I stood with Jake, I was sure of it. She had really started to freak me out. I had no idea what would make her act this way. I decided I would have it out with her in the morning and establish a truce once and for all or I would ask her to leave. In the meantime, sleep would be the best cure to my anxieties.

Chapter 12

I woke again to the phone ringing. I let the call go to voice mail struggling to wake up and figure out what day it was. Usually I had been up, gone jogging, and showered by now. The kitchen table with Mom nightmare had come back and I had trouble getting back to sleep. I dragged myself to the bathroom, then went downstairs in my robe and slippers, Sunny wagging along behind me. Annie was down in the basement, doing laundry or something else I hadn't asked for.

I picked up the morning paper and poured coffee from the pot she had made. My life story had moved on to page four, a small quarter page article about an ongoing investigation and no one really had anything solid. What else could they report?

Noting the missed call had been from the office, I punched in Karen's number and greeted her chipper, "good morning" with a half asleep, "good morning yourself."

"Things have settled down over the weekend. The press must be on to someone else's news. I'm sorry we were rough on you last week. It just got difficult for all of us to keep the office normal and rolling," she explained.

"I'm sure you guys had a really rough time. I should have put aside my feelings about my recently murdered husband and been more sympathetic to the feelings of all my hard-working colleagues." Aware my sarcasm wouldn't help, accepting false congeniality from them this late in the game wasn't an option.

"I'm sorry, really that's not what I meant. We all feel horrible for what you are going through. I wanted to tell you that and assure you we got most of the case files. Thank you for sending all that over the weekend. Things are pretty much covered."

"Great, once again, that's my first priority in the midst of being investigated for murder and hounded by strangers," I said, sarcastically once again, suspecting her sympathy had an ulterior motive.

She paused, then switched the conversation. "Are you going to have a funeral this week?"

"We have to go to the funeral home this morning. They haven't released his body yet, so if we do anything, it will be later in the week. We may cremate and wait to have a memorial when all the press dies down. We don't need idiots snapping photos, making things into a circus."

"Wow don't you think a cremation might make you look more guilty?"

"Jesus Karen, I can't believe you said that. Nothing will make me appear guilty or more guilty because I'm not guilty. And I don't give a damn anymore what the papers say or what people think. We will put a murderer in jail and soon. In the meantime, get your head out of the gossip rags and let me know if there is a legitimate reason for your call."

"Again, really, I'm sorry. Listen, if you don't need to deal with funeral preparations right away and maybe you feel up to it, we could use you back here, maybe for a couple of days to start. Mr. Walker is okay with it, I checked. But only what you feel up to."

"What are you getting at? I'm so tired I can hardly hold my head up. Do you need something specific?"

"Well, I hate to ask, but can you message me where the remand list is stored. Fenwick seems to have lost it. Oh, and if you're not going to be back anytime soon, can you send the rest of the files. He's so slow and well, sorry, like I said, I really hate to ask."

"The show must go on. I get it. I'll email you the remand list and the backup file it's stored under for when he loses it again, and I'll try to get you everything else by tomorrow. I may even try to get into the office but don't make any promises to Alexander. I have to go now, someone else is trying to call me."

I hung up, cursing everyone in the office and took a call from Jenny. "Hey there. I'm really tired and I just got pissy with my assistant so please tell me you have something concrete for me."

"Not so much. We followed up on Bruce Elroy's story. Wayne Duncan definitely rode in the cab, got his greasy fingerprints all over the place and Mr. Elroy picked him out of a photo lineup without any hesitation. And Clancy's sketch matches him exactly. We went to the house on Townline if you could call it a house. It's lived in, but no one was there. We can't find him at all or any big Frank guy or a lady with a gun. Wayne's gone into thin air."

"Thanks. That's a bit of good news, bad news, I guess. And David?"

"I do have some information from the morgue but would rather go over it with you and your dad in person. They should be able to release the body tomorrow or Wednesday so if you want to make some burial plans, feel free to make arrangements for the end of the week."

"We're going to Patterson Funeral Home today, over on Waterloo Street, Dad knows a guy there. We may have his remains cremated and deal with a service or memorial later. I'm not up to any more invasion of my privacy right now," I said.

"That's reasonable. I know where it is, I can meet you later this morning in one of their private rooms to go over the details."

"Thank you. Around eleven be okay?" I asked.

"Perfect. I can't say it enough Christine, Wayne's still out there and he's definitely involved in this. You need to watch your back."

We signed off as Dad walked in. "Why are you still in pajamas? This isn't like you."

"I can't wake up today. The nightmare came back last night. Then I couldn't sleep. Karen and Jenny both called this morning. I have so much running around in my brain and I just want to go back to bed," I whined to him, stifling a yawn.

He poured himself a coffee and sat across from me at the kitchen table. "I should have come back last night."

"No, Dad, it's not that. I wasn't nervous. Jake saw me home and Annie was here, and I set the security. I don't need a babysitter every minute and you need to deal with your own life too. I'm happy you had some time with Luisa. That's one thing in my life right now that makes me feel good. The thought of you with someone who makes you happy is a really good thing, so let it go please."

I dropped my voice to a whisper. “I have a live-in bodyguard already trust me. Annie and I had it out again yesterday. I can’t believe she even came back. She keeps saying the same things over and over and it’s making me nuts. I told her she could stay but if she can’t show me some respect, she’s going to have to go. I’m emotional enough without her upsetting me more. She was peeking through her door when Jake walked me home. It’s weird.”

“I’ll talk to her,” Dad said.

“Leave it for now. We’ve called a truce, and I can’t handle any more tantrums today.”

Annie came thumping up the stairs, obviously carrying a bucket of wash. I made a slashing motion across my throat to drop the conversation.

“Good morning you two, get you some breakfast?” she offered.

And so, apparently everything was back to normal.

“Morning. No thanks, we need to be on our way soon,” Dad said.

“What were the phone calls about?” he asked me.

I picked up my coffee and tilted my head toward the family room. “I don’t feel like answering all her questions when she joins our conversation.”

“What’s going on?” he asked again.

“Maybe nothing. Karen called because she wanted the damn remand list. They really didn’t care how things were or what the truth is. She said that the press has settled down over the weekend, so I’m allowed to be part of them again, now that I’m not an inconvenience. I guess the paparazzi are onto ruining someone else’s life.”

“Awe, sweetheart, give it time,” he said.

"No, you had to hear her. She said like, sorry we were so miserable last week, but you really put us out. And then, sorry you have to go bury your murdered husband, but could you hurry it up so you can get the remand list ready. This has been a real eye opener. I'm thinking maybe my talent would be more appreciated doing something else and it makes me sad. I put my heart and soul into that office. Maybe I should have focused some of that energy closer to home and none of this would have happened."

"Everything is bound to make you sad this week, and probably for the next several weeks. I don't want to hear you blame yourself for any of this ever again. There's a whole lot we don't know yet, but I guarantee none of what happened to David is because of anything you've done. Send what they need to the office and tell them you're taking some time off," Dad suggested.

"Jenny called too, said they checked that house on Townline Road and there's no sign of Wayne or anyone there. She also said she has some details from forensics, and she can meet us at the funeral home."

"Are you going to change, or do you think we should make funeral arrangements in your robe and slippers?" Dad asked with a grin.

"I don't know about a full funeral right now, maybe just cremation and figure it out later. I certainly don't need a casket at the front of a room and a bunch of smelly flowers and nosy strangers coming in to pay respects."

"Cremation? Do you think that's a good idea? Kind of officially puts all the evidence to rest."

"Jesus Dad, you too? I didn't kill him; I'm not trying to cover any evidence. I'm sure Gavin has done a thorough job gathering every tiny detail and frankly I don't have it in me right now to go through all the motions."

He patted my hand. "I didn't say evidence against you. I meant, once the body's cremated, there's no going back if they missed something. But you're right, Gavin is the best. Go get dressed sweetheart and let's get this over with."

****

The funeral home was horrible. They were professional and compassionate, but I still felt like I had to defend every decision. Being there also reminded me of Mom. Even though, she died so long ago, my chest burned, and my head spun every time I had to go in a funeral home. I was miserable by the time we met with Jenny.

We had been escorted to a private area meant for grieving families. Like stepping back into a different century, the room was full of stiff antique furniture and the walls were covered in pale green paisley wallpaper. Thick curtains in the same putrid green tone draped over three tall windows. Hung equally distanced were framed pictures of doves flying off and butterflies meant to represent after life. Adding to the unsettling decor, was a smell of mold mixed with death that caused my head to pound the minute I walked in.

Dad held my hand. When we sat down on the offered settee, he pulled me to lean on him. Jenny sat opposite us and supplied details without wasting time on formalities. She explained that David had been strangled with his own tie, the murderer coming from behind him. He had fallen forward, his hands under him and landed on the couch.

"How can you possibly figure these things out from his charred remains?" I asked.

"As you know, they found no smoke in his esophagus or his lungs. He didn't have the chance to breathe in any smoke. We knew early on that he died before the fire started, which confirmed we were dealing with a homicide. From there, we got lucky with a few factors that allowed Gavin to be so precise." Jenny consulted her notebook briefly, and then continued. "Because he had an old couch, the fibers burned more slowly than some of the newer more synthetic furniture, making almost an insulation to the front of David's body against the fire. Also, because David stayed fit and trim, his body burned more slowly. Fat burns faster than muscle."

"Go figure." I smirked.

Dad glared at me. "Cool it."

"I don't mean to be rude. This is so detailed, it's hard to take in. Please go on. Is that it?" I asked.

"No, most importantly, because he landed face down with his hands under him, coupled with the slower burn and the couch acting as insulation, enough of his hands were maintained to get a sample from under his nails and enough of his neck to provide fibers. Gavin confirmed David struggled prior to the fire being set, based on tissue under his nails. He also confirmed David had been strangled with his own tie based on the fibers found along the line of strangulation. We have Wayne Duncan's DNA from his previous arrests that matched the fingernail sample. There's no doubt Wayne was the last one to see David alive."

"That's impossible. David and I took a self-defense course together. Wayne's a skinny runt and, like you said, David stayed in good shape."

"That's the only piece we're waiting on, the drug tox report. We think David must have been given something to slow him down. If that's the case, Wayne would have to get it from someone a lot more intelligent than he is. He may have done the dirty work, but the someone with the drugs, if that's the case, is likely the one with the motive. That's who we really want. When we get the drug report back, we should have more answers."

"Answers, yes, but I still have a whole lot more questions. Why drug him? Does that mean he intended to murder him from the start, or did Wayne just try to slow him down and assault him and then things went wrong? And why come after him at all? That's my biggest question."

"We're not sure yet, but we're getting close." Jenny tilted her head apologetically.

"I didn't really expect an answer. I was only thinking out loud," I said.

"That bastard," Dad stood and began to pace. "We need to get this kid off the street Scott."

It was my turn to give Dad the "cool it" stare. Jenny also stood. "Well aware, sir, we're on it. We have several investigators specifically assigned to locating him. It would also help if we could find the woman with the gun who clearly knows he had something to do with it or the big guy Frank. That shack where Bruce dropped Wayne off is an old hunting lodge registered to a numbered company that went bankrupt years ago. There's no owner, no tax roll number, it's primitive and a smart place to hide way off the grid. I can't believe it's never come up on our radar before now. We can't get a warrant for a search or prints until we at least talk to these people. We have a unit staking out there, but it seems they've all disappeared into thin air, part of the reason I keep telling Christie to watch her back.

"The other issue, sir is we may need to speak to the press. We've held them off so far, but Wayne could be a danger to the public. If he goes off on some wild tangent, and something happens to a civilian and we didn't put out a warning, well, you know."

"Do you really think he's a random killer?" I asked.

"We just don't know I'm afraid," Jenny replied.

"If he were a killer, wouldn't he have taken me when he followed me the other day? I believe you that he's responsible for David's death and likely the fire, but he doesn't fit the serial killer profile," I said.

"I agree, he doesn't seem the type to kill at random. I believe something connected him to David, or that Wayne was working for somebody who had a connection and David was likely the only target," Jenny said.

"What connection could David possibly have to that little weasel?" I asked.

"We have detectives working that angle too. There may have been nothing. He had a rap sheet going back to high school, and he certainly didn't work for a living or maintain a fixed address. He likely got offered a chunk of cash to maybe rough up David, to send him a message and Wayne got carried away. Trust me, we're getting there. It seems like forever but we're getting close," she explained.

"Thank you again." I nodded.

"I'll talk to you later about the press release, see if

we can come up with something to buy us another day to hunt this guy down," Jenny said.

"I'll be downtown after I sort out Christie. Can you mark me out for a few more hours, please?" he asked.

Jenny nodded. "Of course."

Dad and I both shook her hand and thanked her again. My cell rang again. Seeing Jake's number, I took the call.

"What's up? I'm just leaving the funeral home with Dad."

"Perfect, can you guys swing by? I've got some information for you. I can throw on a burger," he offered.

"Sure, we can come by, but you don't need to keep feeding us."

"We all have to eat," he stated.

"Well, thank you again. We're twenty minutes out. See you then."

****

It was a warm fall day. The house sheltered Jake's back deck from the wind and with the sun shining on us, it felt more like summer than late fall. Jake had set up the patio table with plates and all the fixings for lunch, a welcome sight when I realized I hadn't eaten all day.

As we sat with a beer watching Jake barbecue for us once again, we told him everything Jenny had said.

"Well, I also have information. I pulled some strings to get the initial fire marshal's report. You're not going to believe it." Jake grinned.

"What is it?" Dad asked.

"Tortilla chips. A bag of freaking nacho cheese tortilla chips. That loser Wayne started a fire using his own favorite snack for lighter fuel after he strangled Dave with his own tie. They've been barking up the genius tree, expecting some high tech, home-made, pyro cocktail and Wayne faked us all over with a greasy bag of chips."

Rick chuckled. "Now we know it's Wayne, and how things went down, but where the hell is he, and why did he go after Dave? And by the way, you, young lady are not staying alone until he's off the street. You're stuck to me or Jake. Annie doesn't cover it. She's losing it and she'd be no help if Wayne showed up at the door," he demanded.

"I hate to bring it up, but Courtney's wondering if she should come back up for the funeral," Jake winced.

"I'm sure everyone thinks I'm a stone-cold bitch, but I've decided not to have a funeral. We're having what's left of his body cremated, and we can do what seems right when all this is over. I can't be bothered right now."

"Pardon me?" Dad's eyes widened.

"I don't mean I can't be bothered, like it's something trivial. That came out wrong. I can't take the invasion of doing what you're supposed to do to make other people feel better when everyone is treating us like criminals. If he had family, it might be different, but Sharlene is the only person close to him and she's the last person I want to see right now.

"I have to finish my damn work and get them off my back, and oh yes, we need to trap a murderer, find out why the hell he did it and who hired him and catch that guy too and then, maybe then, I'll feel like dealing with flowers from random acquaintances and church and scattering sacred ashes. I'm sorry guys, I'm worn out."

We finished our visit and barbecue without talking any more about what I now considered another case to solve. We talked about football and the weather and a bit about Courtney and Annie and nothing that would cause any of us stress.

When I left later that afternoon, Jake leaned in to kiss me goodbye and I stepped back, squeezing his hand instead. I couldn't think about what had been going on between us either.

When we got home, Dad went to do some work in the study, and I went straight to my bedroom. I had planned to get up after a nap and get some work done. Instead, I fell asleep while it was still light out, sleeping soundly for several hours, waking in the dark, once again to the sound of my phone ringing. "Jake? Is everything okay?"

"I'm sorry to call so late, this time I'm the one who needs to talk." He sounded defeated.

"It's okay. It's only, ahh, oh, eleven. I fell asleep hours ago, but I'm awake now. What's wrong? What's going on?" I urged.

"I just hung up from Courtney," he said, and then paused.

"And?"

"It's not good, we're not good. People at her work saw the picture in the paper of me holding your hand when you came out of the ambulance. Like everyone else, they all think there's something going on with us and her friends are doing a good job convincing her she can't trust me," he explained.

"Courtney should know better, and that's what matters. We've been friends forever. Obviously, something like this makes friends watch out for each other a bit more. We keep saying this, but emotions are high. This is a bad time for you two to be deciding on your future."

"It's not that. I feel like she used the picture in the paper to bring up the subject. She said she's worried for her career, that if word gets back that her fiancé is tied to a murder investigation, no one will hire her. She's not concerned about how this is affecting you and Rick or me for that matter. She said I have to deny that you and I are even friends if anyone asks. I honestly think she may have told the people at work that she's done with me, so I'm the bad guy and she comes off like the smart one for not being involved in anything untoward. All she can talk about is her people, her career, her apartment. Like I told you before, even when we have talked about the wedding, it was all about how she would look walking up the aisle, how the pictures could be used in a magazine to help her career. I asked if she remembered I would be at the wedding too."

"Aww, Jake. Wedding days are like that. We girls tend to take center stage. That's our thing. It's our day to shine. A lot of girls spend their lives planning their wedding day. It's kind of inbred or something." I chuckled, but he didn't.

"I'm not trying to take away from her being center of attention on her wedding day. I'm not telling it right. I sound like a spoiled brat asking for attention. The truth is lately I feel like she wants to live her life in the city, and I want to live mine in the country and we can't seem to meet in the middle anymore. I'm not sure either of us wants to make the effort to make it work."

"Give it some time. Let her think about it. Remind

her you love her, and you can make things work," I suggested.

"I'm not so sure about that anymore. I'm going to let you go. Thanks for listening and sorry I woke you. I'll see you sometime tomorrow."

"I have to try and go into the office, but we'll get together after okay. We can talk it over then. You guys will be okay; you'll see. How did you leave things?"

"I told her there would be no funeral for now and to stay in the city."

"What did she say to that?"

He let out a long sigh. "Nothing really. She didn't seem to care about coming back here. Certainly, there were no tears, she sounded like she couldn't wait to get off the phone. I bet if I checked, her friends would tell me she's broken off our engagement."

"I'm so sorry," I said.

"Don't be, it's been tense for months. Like I said, I feel like she's using current circumstances to get out of something she hasn't been sure about for a long time. I'm going to let you go back to sleep," he said again.

"I'm here for you."

"Goodnight. I…" He stopped what he was about to say.

"Jake? You okay? Want me to come over?"

"No, that would be a bad idea. I'll see you tomorrow," he said.

As I tapped off the call, I questioned what he hadn't been sure about, whether he still loved her or whether he could make it work out. And then I wondered why going over there would be a bad idea. I was pretty sure I understood why.

Chapter 13

The banging on my door at eight a.m. had me dreading someone with more bad news. I was still jumpy about media and I sure wasn't in the mood for Agnes.

"I got it!" I yelled to Annie.

I took the time to check the side window, and then yanked the door open. "Jake, what brings you back so early? Is everything okay?" I asked, feeling uneasy.

"Sun's up, so are we, let's go to the beach for the day." He clapped his hands and stepped inside.

The Mr. Happy Guy had to be an act after essentially breaking off his engagement the night before.

I shook my head. "Really, I can't. I get it, you need to talk things through and there's nothing I would rather do than reciprocate the loving support you have shown me, but it's going to have to wait until after work. I promised Karen I would be into the office today."

"You owe nothing to them the way they've treated you. It's like summer out. You don't get days like this in October. I won't take no for an answer," he said.

Sunny had come to run circles around us, excited at the sound of Jake's voice. He crouched down to pat her, and I tried again. "There's still the odd reporter around. If you and Courtney are ever going to fix things, you don't need any more pictures of us out together, and I really have to get to the courthouse and do some work. Even if they don't want me there, I have so many cases still outstanding that need to be dealt with, either there or from here. I was just getting ready to leave. Really, I can't do a beach day today. Can we get together later?"

Jake interpreted my no way firm lawyer voice as invitation to walk right past me and argue. "Come on. The media has died off over the weekend. You said so yourself, that's why they said you can come back to work. If they're anywhere, they'll be down at the courthouse, not where I'm taking you. You could have a murderer on your tail, you shouldn't be out alone."

"I know, but—"

"No buts. You said they didn't want you there and now they need something, so suddenly you drop everything and go in? You haven't taken a day off that place since forever and you've been working to some extent every day since the fire. Under the circumstances, you should have weeks off. Cut yourself a break, Fenwick can handle it."

"Arnold Fenwick is an assistant crown attorney and there's a reason we call him Junior," I argued.

Jake's frustration showed as his initial enthusiasm dissipated. I felt badly saying no, but I'd psyched myself up to get into the office.

"He'll be fine, they're remands and a couple of easy plea bargains, let him practice, nothing big ever happens around here," he insisted.

"Seriously?"

He had the decency to wince. "Sorry, let that comment go. The kid can practice, and the rest of your work will wait, it's one day. I need you to come with me. We both need a day away from everything. Please, say yes, it's easy, one little word." He put his hands together and made a begging pout face, that made me laugh.

"I appreciate what you're trying to do, you're a true friend, and I know you're upset and want to get out of the house too, but I can't this morning. You're right I haven't called in sick in years, but things are shaky there. They don't know how to deal with something like this. And Karen said that Alexander said they needed me, and they expect—"

He silenced me with a touch of his finger to my lips gazing directly into my eyes and leaning inches from my face. "Karen said, Alexander said, blah, blah, blah. Today you should listen to Jake said. Let me be in charge for one day you stubborn woman."

He came even closer and his lips softly kissed where his finger had been. "Please call them now and tell them you'll try to send the files or list or whatever the hell to them later, or I'll call for you."

My face grew hot. "You kissed me?"

"Yes, ma'am, I did and if I'd known it would bring such a charming blush, I might have done it sooner. Now, I'm asking nicely one more time, may I please be in charge for one day?"

My hands went instinctively to my cheeks. The investigation and lack of sleep must be getting to me. *Blushing at a kiss from Jake Anderson, what had come over me?*

"Madam Crown Attorney, have I rendered you speechless?" he teased.

"Don't be smug, I'm going to change, unless your idea of a day away from it all requires a navy-blue suit."

I conceded as I climbed the stairs, he might be right. I shouldn't be jumping to their every whim. Maybe a day away is what we both needed and maybe I should rethink how high I jump for that office.

"Yes," he cried. "Make it jeans and a T-shirt and bring a sweater and don't make me wait," he yelled up the stairs behind me.

I leaned over the upstairs railing and called back. "Don't make you wait? I'll make you wait. You could be costing me my job for a day of goofing off with you."

"Get going, times a wasting!"

Holding my cheeks, I stared at myself in the mirror. "Did I really blush at Jake Anderson? Get a grip on yourself, girl, you've kissed him a million times, you're acting like a schoolgirl. And now I'm talking to myself in a mirror."

Lamenting got interrupted by Jake calling up to me again. "You about ready?"

"Keep your shirt on Mr. Troublemaker, I'll be right down." I hung up my suit with all the other matching suits, reminding myself to shop for more casual wear. I selected dark blue jeans and my favorite light blue sweater, that Dad said matched my eyes. "Why do I care what enhances my eyes? It's only Jake. Why are you talking to yourself again?" Tossing my hair clip on the bed and giving my waves a shake, I had to admit, I was a little excited for a day away from all the drama.

"Okay, maybe playing hooky isn't such a bad idea." I smiled at Jake who now leaned against the front door.

"There's, my girl, see you're more relaxed already. Let's go," he said.

"I'm not your girl, Jake, no more funny business. We talked about this. Can I at least have a hint where we're going?" I asked.

Jake beamed one of those smiles I had seen a million times since we were kids. Today, it looked different, too inviting, too sexy. Had he really changed or was my confused mind seeing things that weren't there.

"Nope, trust me," he said.

"I hate it when you say that." Putting full trust in someone else with no control of a situation was one of my toughest challenges, and he knew it.

He winked and grinned again before grabbing my hand. "Come on."

Annie came in from the backyard just as we were ready to leave. She dropped her gardening gloves on the kitchen counter and came through to the front hall with her dirt covered shoes, giving us a piercing stare, and starting again with a string of questions. "Where are you two going? You were dressed for work before I went out back. Does your father know what you're up to?" She glanced at our linked hands, frowned, and squinted her eyes.

"We've called a truce, remember? Don't start this again. Jake is right, I'm not ready for the office and he has stuff going on that you don't need to know, so we're taking off for a few hours." She accepted the explanation without further questions, but I expected to hear about it later.

I stopped Jake who had pulled on my hand and I ran back to hug Annie. "We're taking a drive away from all the drama for a couple of hours. I called work already and told them I'd get their stuff over to them later and be there in person before the end of the week. They're okay with it, really. I'll text Dad on our way. If anyone calls for me, tell them I can't be reached. Please, Annie, try to relax, everything is going to be okay." I tried to sound reassuring, despite my own uncertainly.

I also knew Annie would never be convinced where Jake was concerned, but she hugged me back which surprised me. "Be careful, I'll keep dinner warm for you."

"Please stop fussing. I don't need dinner. We may eat, I may be late. Do your own thing and put your feet up for today. I'm in good hands with Jake."

"I doubt that," she muttered, returning to the kitchen.

****

I hesitated when Jake held the truck door for me. "What are you up to?" I asked, with a side glance. He closed me in without reply and scooted to the driver's side.

"Why doesn't she like me? I can't understand it. Like, really, what have I ever done to her?" Jake asked.

"Well, if you remember the time when I was twelve and you were fourteen and you dared me to eat a whole Gino's pizza followed by a whole carton of ice cream and she was up with me half the night when I was sick. Then in tenth grade, you were a senior and I accepted an invitation to go to my first spring formal with Cody Tanner and he conveniently got covered in poison ivy after your hike up the falls, so you conveniently became available to step in as my date. Then, the time we went walking at the golf course and we brought back that little mouse—"

"Okay, okay, I get it; I was the typical boy next door. But lately, it's like an obsession, like I've done something to offend her. You should have seen the death stare she gave me over your shoulder when you hugged her, like she might throw something at me, and by something, I mean a dagger or a poison dart. What is it lately? And why do you keep defending her?" Jake sounded genuinely hurt.

I chuckled at the dagger comment. "Sorry, that's not funny. I don't know the answer. David's death must have her shaken too. We've talked and I'm trying to be patient and understanding. I'll talk to her again, I promise. She's been with us so long, she's like family to me and it's hard to dismiss her anger without trying to figure out where it's coming from. Give it some time. She'll come to like you." For the second time in a few minutes, I found myself saying words I wasn't sure I believed.

****

I watched out the window while Jake wove through the streets away from home. He headed west, but he wouldn't say where. Traveling in silence was never awkward with him but I wished my thoughts would silence. Although we had a murderer figured out, no one seemed to have any answer to the big question 'why'. *What had David been into? Who knew enough to want him dead? What happened to our marriage? I had the answer to that one. We were always too busy, too busy for the cottage, too busy for kids, too busy for each other. There never seemed to be any time. Now time seemed to stand still. When would they have answers? When would it all be over? What was I doing spending every day with Jake? Dinner had been one thing but going out for the day. What was I thinking?*

"Stop thinking about it," Jake said.

"It's like you read my mind sometimes. Will it ever go away? Every one of these homes with a carriage house like mine, every time I watch the news…" I trailed off to my thoughts again reaching to hold Jake's offered hand. We sat silent again for several minutes.

"Thank you for today. In case I forget to tell you, I had a really nice time. Thank you for knowing what I need better than I know myself," I said, smiling when he looked at me.

He smiled back and squeezed my hand. It was easy to be with someone so undemanding, and I kept holding his hand because it felt good. A lot of things felt good about Jake lately, and I questioned again if something had always been there or if the circumstances were toying with my emotions. I should be encouraging him back to Courtney not acting like a couple.

Again, he interrupted my thoughts. "Yes? See something you like?"

I hadn't realized I stared at him while I questioned my own motives. His question certainly brought me back to the moment. "What? Nothing, just looking at the scenery." Damn if my cheeks didn't heat up again.

"I bet and that's why you're blushing again. I know you want me."

"Funny guy. And wishful thinking. Okay, enough about me. When are you going to talk to me about Courtney? Where's your head at today, other than trying to pretend everything is perfectly fine in your life and be your old funny guy self who I know and love?"

He snatched his hand away and focused straight ahead. "I'm not pretending. This is me. This is who I have always been and who I want to be, my friendly, ridiculous, loving, idiot self. The pretending has been with Courtney. I've tried to be what she wants and it's not me. I'm not the suit wearing, expensive dinner party, champagne and a carrot, schmoozing type. At first, she seemed to like my wild side, hanging out the back, having a barbecue and a brew, taking off for a cruise in my truck, going to the lake to see my parents."

"I like that version of you, and you should be true to yourself, but marriage is about compromise, meeting halfway. Maybe you have to do the odd dinner party to help with her career goals in order to have her by your side when we're all hanging at the beach or doing the pool party thing."

"I get that, but I'm not feeling halfway anymore. I haven't for a long time. When we spoke last night, there was no halfway coming from Courtney. It's one hundred percent her way, as in move to the city, be a hot dog Toronto firefighter who never gets in any trouble, stay jacked to look good beside her at her fancy functions, support her career and give up all of myself, including my house and my dog. How could she not love Finnegan?"

"Or?" I prompted.

"Or, what? She didn't offer an option number two, just here's what I want and if you want me, this is how it will be. I can't lose my whole self for a life I've never wanted. I'm not sure she ever loved the real me or if it was just the bragging rights of a firefighter husband who compliments her in pictures and who put a ring on her finger." His voice grew louder as he explained.

"That's harsh." I winced.

"Yes, it is and unfortunately, I've known it for a

long time, but have been stupid enough to think I had the ability to change things. The last few days has nailed it for me. When things really matter, I mean really, life threatening, matter, you learn that surrounding yourself with what means the most to you, is what makes life worth living every day."

His hand held tightly, white knuckled on the wheel, his jaw twitched, and he focused on the road ahead.

"I'm sorry. I hate seeing you struggle like this. I don't know what to say to make it better," I said.

"You don't need to be sorry for me. You're the one consistent thing in my life that always makes things feel right. And that is why we need this day together and why we are not going to ask any more doom and gloom questions of each other for the rest of the day," he insisted.

He slapped his hand down on the console, palm side up, still avoiding eye contact. I slid my hand down onto his, entwining our fingers once again, warmed that the gesture made him smile. *Sometimes the simplest things show more support than a thousand words.*

****

"Fine, no more doom and gloom. But what I do need to know is where we're going and when I'm going to get another coffee," I said.

"I'll warm you up," he teased.

I chuckled. "And he's back. Caffeine, I need caffeine, funny guy."

I knew this Jake, and we had always been best friends, but I had to admit his hand did seem to warm me all the way through and that kiss in the hallway and the almost kiss in the den on Saturday were playing on my mind. Damn, I needed to stop thinking about him kissing me. *It was the stress, surviving a tragedy together. I had read articles about that kind of thing, complete strangers, unlikely couples connecting over a shared tragic event.*

Don't go wrecking the best thing you've had by getting all goofy on him. He's a friend. I left my hand in his just the same and enjoyed the ease of it.

After almost an hour of driving, we pulled into one of three parking spots in front of what looked like a large old silver Airstream camper in the middle of several blocks of small cottages. Directly next door was an old-style general store. A young boy ran out the front door with an ice cream cone in his hand, letting the wooden screen door slam behind him. A ponytailed girl ran out seconds later with a double scoop cone. "Hey, wait up, you almost hit me with the door."

I laughed. "That was us not so long ago."

"I was about to say the same thing. But we're grown up now and George here makes a caramel macchiato better than anything you'll find in the city." Jake released my hand and slapped my knee. "Let's go caffeine queen."

"How did you ever find this little hole in the wall?" I asked.

Jake smiled but didn't answer. When I didn't move, he waited with eyebrows raised and a tilt of his head.

"I'm afraid to get out of the truck. What if people know who I am? They'll whisper when I pass or call the cops or take our picture together to send it to the local rag. I'm getting paranoid to go outside anymore other than an immediate beeline from a parking space to the comfort of a bullet proof police station. Even when I'm there, people talk about me."

"No one will know you're here. These aren't cottages like you're imagining. People live here year-round and they choose to stay off the grid so that citiots as they call the big city folk, don't get in their way. You can't find rentals here and there are no park trails or reporters or gossipy bars. It's called a hamlet, not even half the population of our wee town of Arva, and you won't find it on a map. The hamlet of Lakeshore; there's a shore on the lake, original, right? Well, and a general store where we saw mini us who are probably on a recess break from homeschool. And of course, George here who takes care of everything from fancy coffee to the local beer drinkers. You coming in or staying here to sulk?"

"Guess I can't keep a good macchiato waiting. And again, I ask, how did you find this place?" My answer didn't match my apprehension, but I opened the door and jumped down with my best effort.

"You don't know everything about me. George is an old friend."

He once again reached for my hand. I was getting used to this comforting support from Jake. At least, it helped me through for now, no matter where things were going.

We climbed three wooden steps and opened the RV-type screen door, walking into what looked like a small-scale sixty's diner. It had five stools at a counter bar, little booths with red vinyl seats, one in front of each tiny side window and a larger one across the full-length back window, neon lights behind the small bar-top advertising various beer types, and one big red neon circle that went all around the ceiling of the unit. He even had a juke box at the other end and little metal napkin holders casually placed.

"Jakie, my man, how the hell are you?" asked a large man who headed straight for us. He wore a red and white checkered apron that had seen more than a few washings. His head was as bald as a bowling ball and his big grin lit up his face and told me that he made time for his people. He had no "too busy" in his life. It was impossible not to smile at his expression when he greeted Jake.

"Georgie, my man, I'm great. How's flashback sixty's life treating you?"

"Living the dream, just living the dream. And who's this, your little lady you've told me about? You must be Courtney." George smiled warmly, and extended his beefy, soft hand to shake mine.

It was Jake's turn to blush. "No, George, this is my friend Christine, who really needs one of your delicious caramel coffee city drinks."

I punched Jake's arm, then smiled back at George. "Plain coffee is fine. Really, don't go to any trouble."

"No trouble this time of the day, sweet thing. Plop yourself down on a stool and wait for a treat for your taste buds. And grab a slice of pie out of the server. I baked it fresh this morning with blueberries I picked myself."

"You're so full of it. Cathy did your baking and your berry picking, you old fart. But I will take a slice with two forks," Jake said.

"You know where they are, help yourself," he called over his shoulder and over the whir of the surprisingly modern milk steamer.

Jake and George chatted the usual guy small talk

about sports and work. George seemed particularly interested in the fire department gossip. At first, I worried he wanted details about my fire until I found out, George used to be a deputy chief in Jake's fire house and had since retired to this adorable little village, well hamlet.

I savored the flavor of one of the most delicious drinks I had ever had while contemplating how much Jake talked about Courtney to his friends and why he hadn't told me about George and why I was experiencing what I recognized as a tinge of jealousy at not being his girl.

"How's your drink, pretty lady?" George interrupted my thoughts.

"Truly the sweet vanilla and caramel, mmm mmm mmm, and the espresso is exactly what I needed. Better than any city drink I've ever tasted, I swear."

"Well, she has good taste at least, even if she is hanging out with a slug like you. Where are you two headed off to today? Not so many people land in Lakeshore by accident." George smiled.

Jake winked and smiled back at him, then threw down a twenty. "Thanks for the treats, say hi to Cathy for me." George smiled again with a nod that made me think they had some kind of unspoken language between them.

We drove a few more minutes before Jake pulled off the road again, this time alongside some trees and rocks. "Come on," he said, jumping out of the truck before I could argue. I climbed out my side as he opened the truck bed cover to retrieve a blanket and a basket.

"You packed a picnic? Pretty sure I would say yes,

weren't you?" I scoffed.

"Maybe it's fishing gear and I planned a day to myself." He grinned.

"Uh huh, since when do you fish?" I didn't believe him for a minute but was glad that I let him drag me away.

"So, are we picnicking at the side of the road?" I asked.

"Certainly not, follow me," Jake said, taking the lead down a barely visible path through a thick patch of trees. "And we're not picnicking for a while after all that sugar."

"Agreed, I'm not too hungry yet." In less than a minute, we came to an opening. Ahead of us spanned a long stretch of soft, light sand, with large areas of flat rock piles and a few driftwood logs, no people anywhere in sight.

"Here, is a private oasis on the shoreline of beautiful Lake Huron, where we can relax and forget the world for a little while." He swept his arm in a grand gesture.

"Wow, it's perfect. I'm going to stop asking how you know about this little hamlet of heaven and just enjoy. Let's go for a walk along the water," I suggested.

We left our basket in the shade and walked the shoreline. It seemed like we went for miles, but I'm sure it wasn't far at our slow pace. Talking and laughing about nothing had always been easy with Jake, equally as comfortable as our silence from time to time. He didn't hold my hand, but he never stepped more than a few inches from my side. On our way back, he seemed to be scouting the tree line for something specific. I got nervous there might be someone lurking.

"What are you looking for?"

"There," Jake said. He pointed to two large trees with a hammock swinging between. "That's George's property. He's had a rough go with PTSD, came out here a few years ago, and learned how to unwind and take one day at a time. Come on."

Jake climbed into the hammock and lay back like he meant to sleep the rest of the day away. I wasn't quite sure what to do next.

Opening one eye, he smiled. "Room for two," he said, extending his hand toward me.

Climbing into an occupied hammock proved to be an amusing task. I barely missed tumbling to the sand more than once. "Maybe this isn't such a good idea," I said.

He sat up and drew me to him, lowering us both down with ease. "Well, clearly you and George have done this before."

He chuckled. "Ah, no," he said and pushed my head down, letting me know it was time to rest. My face fit perfectly in the center of his chest. I lay comfortably enfolded in his embrace. With my eyes closed, I sensed every movement, sound, and smell around me. The lake was as smooth as glass, sending a tiny lip rippling quietly at its edge. The clear air had barely a whisper of breeze and slivers of sun sliced through the trees generating warmth like a blanket. The beach had a distinct fresh air smell with none of the polluting city smells. I was consumed by the perfection of our surroundings. I couldn't see his face, but knew Jake smiled too. He kissed me tenderly on the top of my head, his arms held securely around my back. He had one foot on the ground to keep us rocking gently.

Laying on my side, my leg curled naturally over his other leg. The moment felt like paradise. His steady heartbeat lulled me to sleep as we swayed slowly side to side, in the hammock meant for one, but heavenly with two.

I jolted from a sound sleep, unaware at first where we were, then embarrassed at the drool on Jake's shirt. He too, opened his eyes and stretched as best he could with me laying on him. I tried to ignore the feelings that stirred waking up with him. "I can't believe I fell asleep. So sorry about the, ah, drool on your shirt. It's been a while since I've slept well."

"You snore," he accused.

"You lie, I do not."

"Okay, it's not a snore, more like a moan. Were you dreaming about anything in particular?" He flicked his eyebrows up and down.

Knowing this conversation could be heading in the wrong direction, I tried to get myself awake and out of the hammock. This proved even more difficult than getting in. I dragged myself up on elbows, only to have him bolt away so I fell back down flat on top of him. "Stop! I'm trying to get up," I scolded.

"I didn't do anything; your elbow stabbed me in the chest." He laughed, but then his expression became more serious. He took hold of my face with two hands and pulled me to him for another kiss, soft at first like this morning, then stronger luring me under. His tongue touched mine, and I parted my lips for a deeper kiss. I reached one arm up around his neck, winding my fingers through his hair. A soft moan startled me when it escaped my throat. Jake's arm came down to position my body over him at the same time I stretched my other arm up. The dual movement caused us to flip and topple out of the hammock onto the sand with a thud.

We lay facing each other, sand in hair, arms and legs tangled, and burst out laughing. "Well, that sure put a damper on things," Jake said.

"Maybe that's for the best. We should get back to our picnic. Ants have probably carried off the basket by now," I said.

He smiled, but he lay still, staring into my eyes.

"What are we doing? I can't be responsible for breaking up you and Courtney. You have loved her for a long time, and I'm emotional and maybe you're only feeling sorry for me."

Jake's smile disappeared. "Don't ever say that. Pity is a horrible emotion, and you should know by now I care more about you than anyone else."

"Anyone? You know that's not true. You're engaged. We're only friends. We've been through a lot in the last week, month, okay, year, and our feelings are getting carried away. We can't let this get out of hand."

Jake stood and shook off sand extending his hand to help me up. "I don't know anything anymore. Let's go eat."

We walked back to the blanket in silence. The picnic was delicious. Salads and cheese and cold chicken all expertly wrapped with ice packs. He even brought wine, my favorite Merlot, and glass stems. "Because I know you're too fussy to drink wine from a plastic cup," he said. It was lovely, but the light mood of earlier had faded. Jake kept the conversation going but he seemed more withdrawn, almost sad.

I stared off over the water. "I wish I could give you the comfort that you have shown me. You have no idea how much today has helped," I said.

"Look at me," he said quietly.

"I can't." Tears were building and I knew if I glimpsed those beautiful blue eyes, I would be lost to him again. "We should get going. Annie will be having fits and maybe Dad has something new to tell us."

"I already sent him a text and told him you were safe with me. Annie can, well, she can mind her own business for a change. We don't need to think about any of that right now. I'm sorry if I overstepped, made things more complicated for you. I'm so sorry. The thing is, when I'm not with you and I think of you, I smile. When we're together and I look at you, I'm bursting with a feeling I can't explain, an excitement that I don't feel when I see anyone else, certainly not with Courtney, not lately or frankly, not ever. I don't know, I—"

I faced him and put a finger to his lips, like he had done this morning. Our eyes locked. Replacing my finger with my lips, I leaned into him once again. There would be no going back this time. We lay back together on the blanket, kissing like teenagers, tugging bodies closer when they couldn't get any closer. I tilted my head back, breath quickening, as Jake trailed kisses down my neck. This time the moan was clearly mine. He stirred passion in me I hadn't felt in years. He unbuttoned my sweater with trembling fingers, placing light sucking kissing all the way down my neck, my chest, my belly as each button came free.

"Jake no." I hesitated, balled my hands into fists, wanting so badly to reach out and draw him closer, angry at myself for not knowing my own mind. He stopped instantly when I pulled away and reached to put my sweater back together. “Oh God, I can’t, we can’t. What are we doing? You’re engaged, and I’m in so much trouble. This isn’t going to help.”

He leaned down to kiss me gently, then drew back hanging his head in confusion. I looked away, embarrassed at what I had started. He sat back on his knees saying nothing. My eyes couldn’t help wandering to the bulge in his pants. If only he knew I felt equally uncomfortable by stopping. “Please say something,” I urged.

“You’re right, absolutely, you’re right. I got carried away and I’m sorry,” he said.

“No this was all me. I crossed the line, I started it. I’m the one who got carried away. I’m the one who’s sorry.” I scooted out from under him and stood. “We should really get back.”

As he opened the door for me back at the truck, he brought me to him. I held him tight because it felt so good. He kissed the top of my head. “What am I going to do with you?” he asked.

I didn’t have an answer to that, nor did he expect one. We drove home mostly in silence. He didn’t hold my hand and I didn’t reach for his. Unsure what this day had meant, and less sure where to go from here, the only thing I knew for certain was if I lost my best friend, my life would change forever. I had so much to deal with and couldn’t imagine getting through it without him.

Chapter 14

I tried to sleep after my beautiful day with Jake, but my mind had been racing for hours. I had managed to avoid Annie after he dropped me off. The picnic had been a ton of food, so I grabbed some fruit and a box of crackers and went to my room.

I didn't hear Dad come in at night, but his car pulled away early in the morning, as I lay awake again or still, I wasn't sure. Attempts to go back to sleep after he left, failed and I finally gave up around six-thirty and went to put on a pot of coffee. Almost two hours later, I reached for my cup, with a shaky hand, a sure sign of stress, too little sleep, and too many coffees. Dad had come back and asked Jake to join us and Annie milled about too. I should have been at ease in my own kitchen with these three people. How could life change so much in such a short period of time?

The morning reminded me of my bad dream when we sat at the same kitchen table with Mom. Dad wore the same tense expression, like he had called us together for more bad news. And turmoil, was the best way to describe my feelings for Jake. Like a teenager the morning after a first date, I felt awkward making eye contact. It was only a kiss. We were both caught up in the moment on such a perfect day. I panicked that he wanted to ignore the desire between us and reconcile with Courtney as much as I was convinced that would be best for all of us.

I didn't like guessing how Jake felt. He seemed sincere but so had David and our whole life together had been a lie. Yesterday's passion left me wanting more, but distrust and self-doubt had become my biggest enemies. Up until this morning, David's murder had taken over every thought, but now I had a hard time focusing on what Dad came to say.

When Dad turned to pour coffee, Jake covered my hand with his. Our eyes locked. He looked tired and tortured too. Somehow it helped me to believe we were equally unsettled. I had to concentrate. There was so much more going on than the fact Jake and I had kissed.

I pulled my hands into my lap and took a deep breath, trying to calm myself. Dad came to sit beside me at the table. "I can handle whatever you've got to say. If you called Jake over too and made me stay home, it's got to be big. Let's hear it."

"Detective Scott said she was coming over to report but she has a lot on her plate so I assured her I could be trusted to pass on the latest. The girl is risking reprimand by telling me anything, but she knows you'll tell me anyway and what do you mean, made you stay home? You're barely out of bed and you look like hell by the way."

"Dad, please. Can we move on? Where are things at?" I snapped at him.

"Okay, okay. We already know the evidence they have against Wayne for a murder charge, but they're not close enough on who instigated him. And it gets worse."

"The worst is that they can't catch up to him. Why is he still out there? I can't even go for a morning jog.

He's a local guy who's been brought in for a steady run of petty shit over the years. He's not resourceful enough to outsmart the cops. Someone has to be hiding him," I said.

"I'm well aware. That's why I've insisted on staying with you. And that's their main goal, to find out who that someone is. They need to find Wayne, obviously, but when they do, they want to try to follow him for a day or two to see who his contacts are. Leaving him out there is a danger to you, I agree, and I don't like it, but they think maybe he'll slip up," Dad explained.

"Slip up, of course he'll slip up? This guy is a nut case. He could be laughing his way to another murder victim, me specifically. He killed my husband for Christ's sake, on our own property. I know David wasn't what we all thought, and we were splitting up, but he didn't deserve to die, especially at the hands of a loser like Wayne. What he does deserve is a proper funeral, and I can't even muster the energy for that or go out in public to deal with it because everyone thinks I killed him. There's got to be more going on and she's not telling us. They must have some evidence from that old shack that says where he lives or who he lived with." My voice grew louder, but I couldn't stop the tirade. Exhaustion and racing emotions overwhelmed me and made me want to run out on both of them.

Jake stretched from his chair, grabbing my wrist when I stood to walk away from the table. "Please, calm down and listen to your dad."

Dad motioned for us to sit back down. "Jake's right, you need to find a way to calm yourself and be patient. Why are you so miserable? What's gotten into you today?"

Glancing at Jake, I appreciated his sympathetic smile and slight shake of his head. I sat and tried again to focus on what was priority. "Sorry, Dad. I feel like I haven't slept for a week, and I'm having trouble concentrating. So, what you're saying is all they've come up with is Wayne Duncan strangled my husband, then torched my garage because he thought it might be a fun thing to do on a Friday night? And he and whoever he lived with coincidentally disappeared right when the cops figured out he did it?"

"The detectives haven't been ready to tell us much before this morning, you're right. So, yes, it sounds like that's all they have, but I'm certain there's more. You know what Wayne's like. Whoever hired him, if that's the case, likely had a good reason and is inevitably a whole lot smarter. I'm sure Wayne got a payoff to rough up Dave or maybe even to kill him. He's probably been told or paid or even threatened to stay out of sight. I don't think he's giving Jenny's team much to go on, and he sure didn't leave much behind in the carriage house or in the shack where he was last seen. But that doesn't mean they don't have leads," he explained.

Dad reached for my hand. I let him hold it. "I've had it, I'm so tired. I can't deal with this anymore. Wait, what did you say before? What did you mean when you said it gets worse?"

He stroked my hand like he used to when I was little. "Two things really. They decided not to go ahead with the press release about Wayne being a potential threat. Like I said, the advantage of that is they can try to tail him and see who he meets up with. The disadvantage is of course, he's still out there and like you said, he's been a little too close for comfort. I'm not sure pinning him with the murder really gets you off the hook anyway as far as the media is concerned. So maybe it's better this way, except for the danger factor.

"Frankly, if I hadn't assured them that I would keep you protected, they would have been out with a statement for the news this morning. But under the circumstances, it may help to keep Wayne in the dark that they're on to him so when he does surface, they can be all over him."

I started to protest when Dad held up a finger. "There's more. What I've been trying to say, that is, what I wanted to say to both of you is they may be looking a little harder at Jake."

"Are you freakin' kidding me? Jake? If that bitch Sharlene started this, she's going to have to answer to me. She told them he'd been angry at David and threatened them, didn't she?" I demanded.

"Honey, please, I don't know where it's coming from. Apparently, they had a tip, but Detective Scott wouldn't say from who or why. It could have been anonymous for all I know. They can't tell me anything more than what I've told you. She did us a favor giving me the heads up to pass this on to you." Dad's voice was much calmer than mine.

"Relax, both of you, please. This is ridiculous. I was on nights at the fire hall with a crew of seven other firefighters. I responded on the truck to put out the fire, remember?" Jake said.

Dad stated the obvious. "Doesn't mean you didn't pay Wayne to rough David up on Christie's behalf. Then Wayne took it upon himself to set a fire to cover up when he got carried away. Your alibi is a bit convenient and the media is clearly trying to make you two a couple. Maybe you wanted him out of the way. I know how things work; they're required to cover all the angles. I also know you like you are my own son, and this is as farfetched as it gets. You may have to answer some more questions for them. Like I said, I can't get any more details being on the outside, so I don't know what they're after. I wanted you both to know so you weren't blindsided if they came to your work."

"Bring it on. I'm happy to go talk to Jen or Detective Juzo or whoever else has questions. We need to know what's going on and to me the main goal is keeping Christie safe until Wayne and whoever paid him or contributed in any way to Dave's death are off the streets." Jake looked a bit thrown off, but he sounded confident.

"They're close and, trust me, Wayne will never come near you again. I promise you," Dad assured me.

"How can you say that? The weasel got right in my face two days after killing David. He has no boundaries. And now they can't find him."

"Trust me, love, you will never see him again," he promised.

I pursed my lips and gave Dad what I hoped was a stern glare. "Don't do anything stupid."

He flipped his hand at me, dismissing the warning. "In the meantime, you're right, if you want to have a funeral, make up your mind and get it done. You should decide now, and we can help you through it. You could try for visitation Friday to keep it brief and funeral Saturday. There's no way to fool the press. The police can try to hold them off for a day or two while they weed out Wayne, but after that, they're going to have to make a statement and the annoying reporters will likely be around all over again."

"The funeral can wait. I told you, I already made that decision. The coverage is finally dying down with nothing new and gory to report. I don't want to do anything to stir it up again. The headlines already pop up in my dreams. "Local Crown Attorney's Husband Dies in Fire, Is Cop Dad Covering?" - "Intimate Business Partners Seen Together, Did Angry Wife Want to Torch Them Both?" - "Firefighter on Scene Seems a Little Fired Up."

"Okay, honey, we get it," Dad said quietly.

"No, Dad. You don't get it. This is my career on the line, my life for that matter. Fired up? Really? I'll tell you what I'm fired up about. I spend all my energy putting away bad guys to keep people safe. You two spend every working day on the front line, risking your own lives to keep people safe. Then the minute the media puts one bullshit headline out there, everyone believes we've all conspired to murder to make our future more convenient. The world would be a lot better place if people had their facts straight before jumping to judge a stranger, based on speculation. People don't care when you do good things for others. But they sure pay attention when they think you did something bad. That's what I'm all fired up about, damn it!"

Dad nodded and patted my hand again. "You're not wrong. But, please, try to calm down, honey. It doesn't seem like it, but this will pass, and our lives get to go forward. The same isn't true for David or for whoever this deranged person is out there who wanted him dead."

"I appreciate that but going forward with a "maybe she killed her husband and got away with it" reputation doesn't work for me. Once the papers find out he was murdered, like you said, it won't matter if they pin it on Wayne. Until whoever hired Wayne is in jail, my life at the courthouse will be a sham. People believe what they want to believe. They judge and become hateful without knowing anything about a person. I see it every day in court. People are driven by misinformation and gossip to do bad things to good people. If this doesn't get solved, I'm going to be one of those people. Before I know it Junior will be sitting at my desk and I'll be moving to Lakeshore."

"Huh? What Lakeshore?" Dad asked.

Jake chuckled but stood and paced. "I don't think it will go that far. They can't drive us all out of town. I'm getting some of the same judgment from the guys at the station. Seems like city people who have nothing better to do, like to call in to ask why hard-working people like us still have paying jobs when there's a murder investigation going on around us. The fire marshal's office called and asked me a lot of questions. I thought I was helping with the arson investigation, doing something constructive. Now, I'm wondering if they've been giving the homicide unit the impression that I know too much," Jake said.

Dad's voice stayed calm. "We know Christie didn't kill him and neither did you Jake and neither did I. When the truth comes out, the media will be onto another story within a week, probably within a day and our colleagues will be gushing all over, assuring us they never had any doubt. We'll figure it out and it will blow over, I promise."

"This is ridiculous. I need to go to the fire hall and steer these people in the right direction. Enough already, I'll see you both later." Jake leaned to kiss my cheek, nodded to Dad, and headed to the door without another word.

Chapter 15

Annie had finally agreed to go home for a night, although she assured me, she was only getting more clothes and would be back in the morning. I didn't want her to be a permanent roommate, but for now, we were at least getting along, and I sure didn't mind having her around to help with the housework. She'd been surprisingly pleasant when she left, hugging me and leaving a litany of instructions about warming food.

I was attempting to remember those dinner directions when Jake called. I had scarcely thought of anything but him all day. My hand trembled when I answered. "How did it go?"

He sounded defeated. "Horrible. I met Jenny and Nick at the fire hall. They spoke to the chief behind closed doors, treated me like a damn criminal. The chief and the guys backed me of course, confirmed my upstanding reputation, but they sure didn't seem happy about the invasion or the annoying guy who hung outside the fire hall all day with his camera."

"Welcome to my world. I'm so sorry. Like everyone keeps telling me, this will pass, we need to let the whole thing run its course. Neither of us has anything to hide. The hard part is waiting around until they find the guy who does know what went down." I tried to sound reassuring.

"They asked me to take some time off, personal

leave, can you believe it? Like they didn't say come back when you're ready this time. More like, don't come back until we say. Now I can truly appreciate how you feel. You think you're part of a big family at work, until, well, until you're not."

His frustration was clear when he didn't pause for my reply. "That's not even the worst. Then they came to question me in a private office. I tried to be cool and answer their questions but when Nick started pushing my buttons about our relationship, I wanted to punch him. I had a hard time convincing him you and I are only friends. I can't stop thinking about you. I want to keep my distance and let everything sort itself out, but I'm a wreck. I need to see you."

"Want me to come over? Annie went out for the night, finally."

"No, I'll come to you. Finnegan and I will. Give me a few minutes to wash up and we'll be there," he said.

"Annie left me enough food for six people. I was just figuring out what to do with it. We can sit for a bit, have a drink, try to make normal," I suggested.

"Normal would be amazing. I'll be right there," he said.

Jake was at the door twenty minutes later. He handed me a bottle of wine then stooped to untie his shoes. He hung up his coat then reached for me. Hands on either side of my face, he gazed into my eyes without saying anything. He looked nervous and sad at the same time. He didn't kiss me, didn't seem sure as he pulled me into a hug. We held on like our lives depended on it.

He set me back and walked over to open the wine,

finally speaking for the first time. "If you hadn't asked me over here tonight, I'm not sure what I would have done. You're my life rope right now. And listen to me, I haven't even asked about your day. What happened at work? Did you show Junior the door?"

I shook my head. "I sent what they needed for today from my home computer and told them I'd try to be in early tomorrow before there's too much of a crowd. I'm getting paranoid to go out the door. Now that you know how it feels to have people invade your privacy, you can understand how quickly a person can change from kick-ass confidence to second guessing every move. I'll get back to working that pace again someday, it's what I do. But, like you said yesterday, having meaningful people and important things nearby really makes everything right. There's nothing meaningful enough at my office to draw me there right now."

We lit a fire in the den, had our wine and started eating. "And how did you manage to be alone tonight? I'm glad you are, but I don't think it's such a great idea," Jake said.

"Dad stayed here for most of the day, but he had plans tonight, and Annie told me she was going home for some clothes but would be back in the morning."

"Really? Does she need to hover?" he asked.

"No, actually it's okay. Well, it's better at least."

"I feel guilty enjoying this great meal. I'm sure she didn't make it with me in mind," he said.

"She'll come around. We've had a few talks. Maybe David's death brought back bad memories of living through Mom's death, and she's reverted to her protective nature from my younger days. There's something there and I'm determined to figure it out, but I need my own head on straight before I can consider her issues. For now, don't worry, I still love you, and I'll share my food with you any day." I grinned at him when I got up to put another log on the fire. The sparks crackled and jumped, and tiny flames immediately enveloped the new fuel.

Jake put his plate on the side table and held his hand out to me, drawing me onto his lap. His hand behind my back, I expected him to pull me in for a kiss. Instead, he held my gaze. "Christie, I have always loved you. It's taken me this absurd situation to admit to myself and to you that I have always loved you."

"Oh no, I meant, I love you enough to share my food, like we always say I love you to each other. Maybe this isn't the time—"

"No hear me out and then if you want me to go, I'll go."

I didn't make any move to get off his lap or dismiss his confession, so he continued. "Maybe it's just that it's never been good timing. High school we were too young, and we were too, I don't know, expected to be together. It felt forced and we always seemed to be in the friend zone. We both had goals to achieve and I suppose I always thought you would be here ready to jump into my life when I had grown up and made something of myself. I never told you how much I missed you when we were away at university, or how much I anticipated hometown holidays to see you again. When David came along, I'll admit, it threw me. I was the idiot for taking you for granted, for not making a move sooner. That's when I realized how much I really cared.

"When you finished law school, you were so beautiful and fun and accomplished, and you seemed so content. I presumed the glow came from his attention, from your life together. I loved you enough to want you to have everything you dreamed of. It seemed like David would provide that, so I stepped away, forced myself back to friend zone to keep you in my life. Things never would have worked with Courtney or with anyone else. I will never know someone like I know you. No one will ever know me the way you do. I will never love someone the way I have loved you all along."

"Why didn't you say sooner? I had no idea. If I had—"

Again, he put his finger on my lips to stop me. I was melting inside. "I'm almost done, I promise. I should have given you more credit. I should have recognized David couldn't be responsible for that happy, beautiful confidence. That was all you, that is all you. You're amazing and beautiful inside and out, and I love you, Christine Montgomery. I always have."

I had tears in my eyes that threatened to spill over.

"My fear now is the happiness and the confidence have disappeared. I realize David didn't put those qualities there in the first place, you did all that yourself. But I can say, with certainty David is responsible for taking them away. My beautiful love, will you let me help you get back that happy glow you once had when you loved life and all it had to offer?"

I was speechless. I stared at Jake, and the tears let loose, running down my cheeks. No one had spoken to me like that before, no one had seen me for me, loved me for all that I was, all that I had become, certainly not

David, certainly none of my friends.

"You don't have to answer me. You sure don't have to cry." Jake wiped tears off my cheeks with the back of his hand and brought me to him for a slow, tender kiss. When I slid off his lap, he frowned, and his shoulders slumped until I reached for his hand and pulled him along with me to the soft rug in front of the fire. The gesture brought a warm smile back to his face. My pulse quickened as he positioned himself between my legs, his full weight on me. We kissed, deep passionate kisses that seemed to go on forever. The fire crackled beside us. Our heavy breathing was loud in the silence of the room. I was frantic, feeling his desire pressing against me, wanting to feel skin on skin more desperately than anything I had felt in years.

He raised himself up on his elbows, gazing at me with the same desperation I was feeling. "Are you sure? I'll have a rough time walking away if we go much further."

I answered by arching against him and pulling his face back down to mine. He began where we left off yesterday, lifting my sweater over my head and leaning down to trail kisses on every inch of exposed flesh. I leaned my head back and couldn't help a pleasured moan while he sucked and nibbled his way from my neck to my belly button. He made what sounded like a growl as his arm came around my back drawing me closer.

"You are so beautiful and so soft. I want to kiss every inch of you." Finally, he reached to undo my bra, freeing my aching breasts, fondling one side while his soft kisses found the other.

"More, oh God, Jake more," I demanded. His

sucking deepened, he moaned, and I felt him rigid against my thigh. “Please don’t stop.”

Our breathing was heavy and loud drowning my thoughts. I fumbled to undo his pants with trembling hands. He pushed himself up on outstretched arms, hands either side of my head, staring intensely. “Are you sure? God, please say yes. You feel so good. I’ve wanted you for so long.”

I didn’t answer, couldn’t digest what he had told me tonight. I needed him on me as much as I needed air to breathe. I reached down to unzip my jeans. He pushed my hands away and shimmied my jeans down over my ankles. “Jake, I need you naked.”

Out of his own jeans, he knelt back down between my legs. I stared. His body was amazing and strong. I knew he kept in good shape, but what sat before me blew me away. His muscles were chiseled perfection making me ache with anticipation to feel skin on skin. The soft dark hair covering his chest drew a gentle line downward over perfect abs, inviting me to follow it with a trembling hand, to the rock-hard length of him.

“You’re so beautiful. I need you, please don’t make me wait,” I begged.

He leaned down to kiss me again. I felt him trembling too and knew he struggled not to go too fast. “Christie, I—”

“Please don’t say anymore, I need you, please, I want you in me.” I reached between us and guided him.

“You are so ready for me; I can’t stand it,” he said.

The frenzy we had denied all day, maybe all week, or all our lives, took over. He felt so good inside me, filled me, made me ache. I arched against him providing all the invitation he needed to pick up the rhythm. He kissed me urgently and moaned against my lips when he drove in me, slowly at first. It was torture, beautiful torture, and again I begged for more.

"Oh, I can't, I'm going to…" I yelled out, biting my lip to calm my wild reaction. When I thought I could take no more, he stopped and pulled out of me. I whimpered at the sudden pause, alarmed until he flipped me over in one swift move, and drove in deeper and harder from behind me, hitting a sweet spot that sent me over the edge. "Mmmmm, I can't stop it, oh, God you feel so good," I cried out.

He answered my pulsing shudders with one last thrust before he collapsed on my back. "Oh God, I'm so sorry," he said between breaths.

We rolled on our sides, him behind me, still in me. I was afraid to face him, afraid what expression I would see. "Why do you keep saying you're sorry? I'm the one who needs to apologize, it's not like you took advantage of me; more the other way around," I said.

He pulled me around and on top of him and held my face, so I stared into his beautiful eyes when he spoke. "You never need to apologize to me. Oh no." He suddenly glanced away like he searched for something. "We didn't ah, think about, you know…"

I chuckled and finished for him. "Safe sex? Really, it's pretty much a household phrase. Since I'm lying naked on top of you, I can confess I had tests last year after I became suspicious about David. Everything was fine. The truth is we haven't been together since the first time I accused him of having an affair last summer. And I have been on the pill for years. I can only assume since you're not married yet, you must still be a virgin, so no worries there, right?"

"Ha, good one. Well, no, I can't say that, but we do go through a thorough physical each year, and I had mine recently, so it's safe to say we're both okay from that angle."

I smiled and brushed his bangs off his damp brow. Leaving my fingers in his hair, I kissed him gently. "Well, that was awkward. And there seems to be a few more pressing issues we should really discuss, but if it's okay with you, can I enjoy laying naked on top of you for a few more minutes before I have to think about tough stuff?"

Jake rolled me onto my back causing a jolt of disappointment. I gasped, and he looked at me brows knit. "What is it?"

"Nothing, it's okay, I thought you were getting up to leave," I said.

He retrieved both our wine glasses and the bottle from the table, setting them on the floor behind us. Stretching to the back of the chair, he grabbed the blanket, which he now wrapped around us, laying behind me, so we both faced the fire.

"You need to trust me. I'm not leaving until you throw me out, or I suppose until Annie shows up and points a gun at me," he said.

"Jake!"

"Okay, that wasn't funny, but not entirely impossible in my mind."

"She won't be home tonight I'm certain. She made a big deal about leaving everything for me for the night and for breakfast, like I was eight years old. Apparently, she had some things to take care of. She was acting strange, flitting around like a bird. I would have asked her about it, but I didn't want to keep her here. I feel guilty saying that, but I really wanted her out of my hair."

"No guilt in that. She's been in your space every day since the fire. I'm glad she finally left you alone."

Jake pulled me tightly against him, so I felt every inch of him along my back. I hadn't felt so comfortable and safe ever in my life. "Mmmm, this is amazing, almost as nice as the hammock. You feel so good against me; let's stay here all night," I said.

We lay silent for a while. Jake's breathing got louder. He pulled my hair aside and kissed my neck. "I thought you had dozed off back there," I said.

"That would seem somewhat impossible with your beautiful naked backside teasing an unruly part of my anatomy." His kisses trailed across my shoulder.

I turned to face him with a smile, entwining our legs and reaching my hands into his hair loving the feel of my breasts rubbing on his chest. "And what unruly part might I be able to assist in taming?"

"You little…mmm, let's go." Jake stood and pulled me up from my cozy spot. I shrieked when he bent down and picked me up under my knees.

"Put me down, we can't walk through the house naked. The curtains are open and, someone—"

"Shit, your Dad." Jake stumbled and dropped me back on my feet.

I chuckled at his panic.

"Is your dad coming back? You said he would be out for the evening."

"You can relax. He's out for the night. I called him after I talked to you, told him you were coming over. I promised him no funny business, although he said he wouldn't mind if there was some funny business. But no, I assured him, you would either stay here or I would be at your house. I wanted him to have a night with Luisa. He doesn't need to babysit me every damn day."

"Well, hooray for Luisa." Jake smiled.

"Ah, this is a little odd. Standing here naked carrying on a conversation. It's freaking me out a bit." I grabbed the blanket, which had fallen to the floor and wrapped it around me to maintain some decency, while he stood appearing quite comfortable with his nudity.

"You get the wine. I'll grab the clothes." He walked back to the den.

I followed behind him. "Someone has to let the dogs out. And the fire, I don't usually leave the fire burning unattended. A fire fighter friend told me that's a bad idea."

"Damn it, you're taking all the romance out of my moves, with your logical thinking," he said.

I laughed. "Okay, I'll close the fireplace doors on these embers, it's almost out anyway. I'll grab the wine and if you promise to kiss my neck again, I may even stop for some chocolate."

Jake groaned, jumped into his jeans without doing them up, picked up the rest of our clothes and headed to the kitchen to let the dogs out the back door.

I followed a few moments later, shuffling with the blanket wrapped around me and dropped our dishes in the sink. I took a bag of dark chocolate covered almonds, the full wine bottle, and our wine glasses up to my room. When the back door closed, I called over my shoulder. "Don't keep me waiting."

It was hard to believe it was only yesterday morning he had called the same thing up to me before our beautiful blue-sky day. Prior to all the shit hitting the fan I reminded myself. "Don't go there, Christine. At least enjoy one night before everything blows up in your face again."

"Who are you talking to?" Jake asked, walking into my room, and dumping our clothes on the chair in the corner.

"I tend to give myself heck from time to time so I don't get out of line," I said.

"That makes no sense. Can I help get you back in line instead?"

"You can do anything you want when you walk around shirtless with your jeans undone. You're straight out of the calendar."

"Stop it; I'm a regular guy, the boy next door. It's more important to love a guy for who he is," he scolded.

"Don't give me that line. I've always loved who you are, but right now, I'm also loving what I see, and I'm going to assume you're okay with that." I chuckled.

He grabbed my face, drawing me toward him. My blanket dropped and we fell on to the bed, never letting go of our kiss.

We made love again at a slower pace, both exploring each other with hands and lips until the pleasurable torture reached its peak. It was me again who begged to have him in me. We were both in such a frenzy of heavy breathing, I didn't know how he could hold back. I pushed him onto his back holding his arms above his head as I rose up on my knees straddling him. He groaned deeply when I lowered onto the length of him.

"Sweet Jesus, what you do to me," he said.

Pleasuring him added to my own passionate

urgency. I sped up the pace, riding him faster, feeling my release. Almost reaching my peak, he stopped me again, grabbed my arms, and flipped me onto my back, completely halting our rhythm by laying his full weight flat on me. "Stop," he panted through clenched teeth.

"I can't. What? Why? Don't stop, please." I was frantic.

He pulled up on elbows, inches from my face. "Savor the pleasure, my love."

"I can't take it. Let me up. Let me have you," I demanded.

His hips moved back slowly pulling out of me and driving in again with slow tortured progression. I was pinned under him. He held my arms above my head with one hand, exploring my body with his other hand, heightening my pleasure, tormenting my need.

"Please, Jake," I begged.

He groaned; his head tilted back. "I'm trying to make this last but you're not making it easy."

He pulled my legs around his waist and drove deeper and faster until I could take no more.

"If you stop right now, I swear to God, this will be the last time you ever touch me." I crossed my ankles behind his back ensuring he had no escape.

He almost choked on a laugh deep in his throat, but he didn't stop this time.

I called out his name, not able to hold back, never having felt such extreme release. Jake followed as I pulsed around the length of him, his moan of pleasure coming out more like he was in pain.

His full weight fell on me still connected, legs entwined, gasping for normal breathing.

He lifted his head, gazing into my eyes with a

tenderness I hadn't seen before.

"You laughed at me," I said, trying to sound in charge, but my smile giving me away. "I'm about to orgasm and you laugh at me."

He smiled that beautiful smile not taking his eyes off mine. "Yup."

"Although, I appreciate that you weren't willing to risk my threat."

He laughed out loud, bringing me with him when he rolled onto his back, releasing our intimate hold. "Can I sleep over in your bed tonight?" he asked.

I leaned down to kiss him. "I was hoping you would but tell Dad you slept in the guest room. And whatever you do, get the hell out before Annie gets back."

"Now that is one threat I will gladly adhere. Come up here with me," he said.

"Wait, I need to plug in my phone, and I have to pee." I squirmed away from him.

"Logical thinking, ruining my romance again, but would you grab my phone out of my pocket while you're at it, please."

"Sure, now who's taking care of business?" I asked.

"I really just want to see you bending over in front of me so I can have sweet dreams tonight," he said with a flick of his eyebrows.

I threw his phone on the bed in front of him, shaking my head. "You're too much. There's a charger in the drawer, plug is on the nightstand."

We leaned against the head of the bed drinking our wine and talking non-stop for another hour, my head resting on his chest, his arm holding me there comfortably.

We were silent for a few minutes when his wine glass started to tip. I gently lifted it from his hand and set both glasses on the bedside table, pushing the button for the lights. I curled on my side under the sheets. Jake said a groggy "thank you" and pulled me to spoon against him.

Chapter 16

I slept more soundly than I had in months, certainly more than any night since the fire. The alarm went off at five a.m. I had every intention of getting to the office before anyone else arrived, doing what I absolutely needed to and getting back out before any media or even staff knew I had been there. Jake woke up with a gasp. “What’s going on?” he asked.

“It’s okay. It’s early, sorry I woke you. I want to get in to work before too much crap is in my way, then get back home and out of sight again. You can go back to sleep for a while,” I suggested.

“Well, good morning, beautiful,” he said with a mischievous smile.

I smiled too and let him pull me into his arms for a welcoming good morning kiss. He was hard against me and my pulse quickened when he dove further under the covers trailing kisses lower and lower.

“I’m not sure this was part of my early morning plan,” I said.

“Revise it,” he said, as he climbed on top of me circling an aching nipple with his tongue.

His cell phone rang startling us to an immediate stop.

He reached for it and I rolled away from him.

“Damn it, who calls at this hour? Someone with rotten timing that’s who,” he grumbled.

"Hello!" he said, abruptly. "Henry, are you okay? Take a deep breath; settle down, I can't understand what you're saying."

I heard only Jake's side of the conversation but knew from his tone that something crazy was going on, again. I jumped up and scrambled into leggings and a sweatshirt from my closet.

"Okay, okay, sit tight, I'm on my way. I'll be there in a few minutes. Sit down somewhere and take some deep breaths and don't touch anything," he instructed.

Jake tossed his phone on the bed, tripping as he tried to get into his jeans while searching for his shirt.

"What is it? What's happened now?" I asked.

"It's Henry Dirksen, the butcher, through the trees back of my place," he explained.

"I know who Henry is. What happened?"

"He said there's a dead body in his shop."

"His place is full of dead stuff. Why did he call you? He should call the cops."

"He thinks he's having a heart attack. He's probably in shock. I'll see what's startled him first before we bring too much attention on all of us again. Call your Dad though in case something's up and I'll message you soon to fill you in," Jake said.

"Oh no, you're not running into another incident without me. I'm coming with you."

"Christie, whatever forget it. I don't have time to argue. Shit the dogs, I don't have time to let them out either."

"Let's run with them on the path to your house, they'll pee on the way and I'll dump some food, so they'll stay and eat. We can run through the path behind your house to his property. Do you still have that emergency bag in your truck?"

"Yes, I do. I'll grab it while you feed the dogs. Logical thinking again, sometimes it comes in handy. Let's go," he said.

I called Dad while we ran across to Jake's, encouraging the dogs to do their business in a hurry. They didn't seem to mind an early morning run.

"Dad, we need you at Dirksen's farm, like now," I said.

"What the hell's going on? Where are you? Why are you running? And who's we?" His demanding string of questions didn't help to calm me.

I took a deep breath and blew it out before I answered. "Henry called and said there's someone dead in his barn. He also thinks he's having a heart attack, which is why he called Jake, but hopefully Jake read it right that he's in shock. I'm hanging up because I'm running in Jake's back door and we need to go. Can you get here?"

"I don't want you involved in that. And why are you running with Jake at this time of the day? What the hell was that noise, it sounded like shots fired?"

"Jeez, Dad, stop with the questions, it's not helping! I'm feeding the dogs; it's the food in the metal bowl. I wouldn't be on the phone with you if someone was shooting at us. I don't have time for any more questions. I'm not letting Jake go alone. Just get here as fast as you can."

"I'm fifteen minutes out, please be careful. I don't like this. I'll have a cruiser there in less than five," Dad said.

"Can you hold off on that? We don't know what's what. If it's an animal or something that's scared him in the dark, then we'll deal with it. We don't need cops and reporters all over the place again if it's nothing. Please," I begged.

"I'm already in my car. Don't do anything crazy. I'll be right there."

I punched off and ran to follow Jake through the trees. Nerves making me clumsy, there were a few spots I had a hard time keeping up to him. I thought back to our childhood adventures when we dared each other to peek through the windows at Henry's farm. I visualized the inside of the barn, the rooms where he did the butchering. They had always made me feel like part of a horror movie. There were long plastic tables, stained brown with old animal blood. Rows of large knives and cleavers stuck to a magnetic board between the two tables so he and his helper could do the butchering on either side. The floor was littered in sawdust to help sweep away the blood and unused animal bits.

Of course, we had returned many times since those adventures to buy his excellent meat. He took care of the butchering for all the hunters in the area and a lot of farmers too, and he packaged and sold everything from pigs to moose. He was a kind man, always polite and obviously proud of his business. I shook away the gory images from childhood when we got to the clearing and saw Henry looking distressed. He sat on the ground, leaning against the side of his biggest barn, the one closest to Jake's property. He was an average-height man, appearing his age of about fifty, with slightly graying hair, and a bit of a belly no doubt from good home cooking and daily trips to the pub with the local farmers and businessmen. Today he seemed paler than I had seen him before and had a wide-eyed terrified expression.

"Oh, thank God. Jake help me. Christine don't go in there." He pointed at the barn door, shaking his head quickly.

We both crouched down. Jake spoke calmly having years of practice in emergency situations. I opened his emergency bag but didn't know what else to do, so I sat beside Henry and stroked his hand like Dad always did to soothe me.

Jake checked Henry's pulse, then pulled the blood pressure cuff out of his bag and attached it to Henry's arm, all the time reassuring him in that composed voice he was so good at. "We're not going anywhere Henry. Tell me where it hurts. Do you have chest pain? Are you having trouble breathing?"

Henry shook his head in answer.

Jake smiled when he spoke to him. "Henry, my man, your pulse is bounding, and your breathing seems pretty even. I don't think you're having a heart attack literally, although you are kind of pale, so I'm guessing what you saw has given you a real shock."

"I don't want you kids to go in there. It's a nasty sight, something you don't need to see. You've had enough going on from the sound of things. I really appreciate you coming. I expected to die out here all alone. Thank God I had your number in my cell phone." Mr. Dirksen started to cry. Clearly, he was in shock and bordering on hysteria.

"I'm glad we were close by. You're okay now. We can help, but, where's your family? Who can we call for you?" Jake asked.

"That's the thing, my Emily is off at college, gone

last month to live on campus and young Thomas took his mother and her friend off to some quilting bee for the week. It's in Florida, so they get their crafting friends or whatever the women do and Thomas and his buddy who went along, get the beach and the bars for the week. They were so excited last weekend to get away from here for a whole week, missed the fire at your place and everything. They're not going to believe the week we've had. Nothing like this ever happens, let alone two deaths."

"Okay, try to relax. Your heart sounds as healthy as a horse. We can call the police if we need to and an ambulance for you and they can be here in a few minutes. Can you try and take some big breaths for me? That's it. Now, tell me what's got you so scared. What do you mean when you said two deaths?" Jake prompted him.

Jake held Henry's arm at the wrist, keeping gauge of his pulse. I jumped up when Dad arrived, his dash light still flashing. Bright red light reflected off the barn and the trees making things seem more urgent than necessary. He had arrived in record time; no doubt the light had cleared any traffic, and he had obviously driven at an outrageous speed.

He jumped from the car and ran to me. Holding my shoulders, he checked me up and down taking inventory of injuries.

"I'm fine, we're all fine, I think. Turn off your dash light. It's going to freak Henry out even more. How the hell did you get here so fast?" I asked.

He hit the switch, turning quickly to Henry and Jake ignoring my question. "Mr. Dirksen, what's going on?"

"We were just getting to that. We'd like to keep Henry calm if possible. Maybe, you could come down here with us and we can figure out what's really happening." Jake motioned downward inviting Rick to crouch to Henry's level.

"Oh, thank goodness it's you, Rick. I opened the door of my big cooler at five this morning, like I always do, flicked the light switch ready to get at some work and there he was, dead I'm sure of it. I stumbled back and tripped over the door ledge, thought for sure I would have a heart attack; I could hardly get my breath. I called Jake here with my cell phone, figured he'd be the closest to come help me," Henry explained.

"Okay, you did great. You didn't step near the body, near the dead thing? Are you sure it's a person, not an animal got in the barn in the night?" Dad questioned.

"No, God no. I stumbled out of there like I said. Dear God, I'm glad my Joyce and the kids weren't here to see this."

"Okay, you catch your breath for a minute, Jake and I will go see what we're dealing with. I can get the police here real soon. If it's a person like you say, they're going to have lots of questions, so I want to make sure you're okay. Do you want us to call an ambulance for you?" Dad asked.

"I think I'm okay. I trust Jake that I'm not having a heart attack. And my breathing is coming okay now. I just needed someone here to help me settle down is all."

"You said you touched only the barn and cooler doors and the light switch. Did you touch anything else, the dead thing?" Dad asked.

"No, I mean yes." He took a deep breath and

huffed before he started again. “No, I didn’t touch the body. Yes, I touched the doors, and flicked the light in the cooler, but it didn’t come on. You’ll see from the main light in the barn, though, there’s nothing to step on. Trust me, you’ll see what I mean when you go in there, and I’m absolutely certain it’s no animal. It’s a human, although I sure didn’t stay in there long enough to tell you who. You better see for yourselves. Christine, dear, maybe you ought to stay out here with me,” Henry suggested.

“If you’re okay for a minute, I’d like to accompany them. Unfortunately, we’re all involved up to our ears after last week and dead bodies are nothing new in my line of work.” I left Henry and followed Dad and Jake to the barn where they were already investigating.

Death and destruction were nothing new to these two. Seasoned police officers and fire fighters like them had seen it all. Despite experience, the sight before them when they opened the meat locker clearly shocked them like it had Henry. I was a few steps behind as they pointed the flashlight Jake had taken from his bag. Fully opening the door, Dad looked away almost immediately. It was too dark to read his expression, but his jaw tensed, and his head shook slowly. Jake covered his nose and mouth and staggered back. The smell of raw meat was overpowering, but I guessed his reaction came more from what they saw.

I stepped between them expecting a body on the floor or perhaps tied to a chair, curious how Henry could be so sure the person was dead. Dad tried to hold me back, but I pushed past his arm, gasping when I saw what had them staggering back. I too had seen a lot of murder photos and horrible footage of criminal incidents, but this scene made bile rise in my throat. I bit into my fist through my sweatshirt, preventing my scream. My knees buckled so that I slumped against Jake.

"Hang in there." Jake put his arm around me, holding me steady.

Safe against him, past my initial shock, I ventured a second glance. He had a blue tinge to his face and hair caked in ice as thick as a January windshield. His head stuck out of a black body bag which was zipped up to his chin like a winter parka that was one size too small. He had been wrapped in chains which led up his back to a large hook allowing him to revolve slowly like a curing hunk of beef.

Wayne Duncan, the only lead to David's murder, the only proof to set me free, hung in front of us as dead as the rest of the butchered meat in the cooler.

"Shit," Dad said. His eyes closed and his chin fell to his chest.

"This frozen hunk of murderer was all we had. Who the hell was supposed to be tracking him?" Jake asked.

Rick ignored the question, clearly lost in his thoughts.

Jake kept talking like his own mind raced, but his theories came out loud. "Obviously, whoever hired him to torch Dave, decided we were getting too close. Why did Wayne disappear exactly when Jenny told us they were onto him? Wayne couldn't have known. Whoever hired him couldn't have known. Only we knew. Nothing has been in the media to say they were on to him. This doesn't make sense. He couldn't have been hanging here long. Henry is in here every day, sunup to sundown. I'd put money on it, Wayne was alive up until last night. One thing for sure, whoever did this had to be pretty strong to string him up."

Rick reached for his cell phone. "Let me get the team in here. Now the fun begins. We'll have to defrost him before we find out what really hung him up. For his sake, let's hope, he died first. And let's hope forensic can find something on him to point us to whoever is on this killing spree."

Jake gripped Dad's arm stopping him from calling. "Maybe we need to think this through. Let's go back to yesterday's conversation about following Wayne. No one in town's going to miss him, except for whoever freeze-dried him in the first place. If we keep this out of the news another day or two, we might be able to ferret out something that can help us. Now that he's gone, what else do we have? Can you walk away quietly like we were never here, you know, call Jen directly instead of dispatching police and ambulance and the coroner over every reporters' scanner in the area? I can convince Henry to keep things to himself if he thinks it would help Christine. He doesn't seem like a social media kind of guy. He can even stay with me where I can keep an eye on him."

"Damn it, Jake. I'm sure neighbors are already running to see what the commotion is about. People see flashing lights a mile away. Come on, let's get out of here before our marks are the only ones they can find. It's impossible to keep things away from media. People want to know every damn detail of everyone else's life.

"Think of what you're saying. I'm a cop and this is a murder investigation, I can't leave a dead guy hanging in a meat locker and not say anything. There's a killer out there somewhere, probably watching each move we make. It's damn obvious whoever did this knew we were on to Wayne. Someone close to us, the fire guys or the cops had to have tipped off whoever did this. That's too close for me to leave this alone, even for a day. And in case you forgot, I'm not lead on this case. Scott and Juzo need to know about this and I can't convince them or anyone else how to run the investigation. And since they're already sniffing around your door, you'd be wise to keep your suggestions to yourself," Dad said.

"We're talking about clearing Christie. I'm not saying ignore it or leave him hanging. Just keep all the speculation and bullshit and the fact we were here, out of the papers and social media. Tell them to come in quiet instead of lights and sirens. If no one knows he's here, but the homicide unit, as in Jen and Nick and the coroner and of course us and his killer for maybe one more day, someone is bound to come back to the scene. I see it at fires all the time. Arsonists come back to admire their masterpiece. Wayne murdered David and he was right there on scene to watch. If we can't clear Christie, they're going to be all over every inch of her life again for a really long time."

"Hello, I'm here people, right in front of you. Stop talking about me like I don't exist. No damn it, we're not ferreting out anything. You sound like you have an agenda, Jake. You're a fire fighter, not a cop. Murderers don't act like arsonists and murder scenes need immediate attention before crucial evidence gets destroyed by time passing. I know you're trying to help, but I've seen enough, heard enough. We're going to do this the only way we can and right now. Dad get your team in here and do this by the books, damn it."

"I don't have an agenda; I'm only trying to think things through. They can take the damn body away for forensic to do their thing. It doesn't need to be a shit show back in our faces again is all I'm saying," Jake said.

"This isn't about you two. It's about solving a murder. We can't leave a dead guy hanging and we can't walk away. We're in this and we have to deal with the backlash whether we like it or not!" Dad's voice was loud now confirming his frustration, but I knew it was aimed at the situation not Jake or me.

Jake's irritation clearly equaled Dad's and he had no trouble yelling back. "I didn't say leave him hanging. I said keep it quiet so maybe the murderer would show up again, and maybe Christie could have five minutes peace, damn it. There's a difference."

"Both of you stop it." I stepped between them. "This is a complex investigation, with two murders now. I don't want you covering for me. I don't need covering. I didn't do anything. Yes, the media will have a heyday with two dead guys in less than a week but think about what you're saying Jake. It will come out even worse in the news when the death is reported, and someone finds out we were hiding that we were here. And it will come out, everything always comes out. Trust me, a perfect crime doesn't exist, there's no hiding anything in this world anymore. I know your team will figure out the fire and, Dad's team will find out who's on a murdering rampage around here. There is no backdoor way around this. Call your dispatch and get everybody the hell over here, now."

My tears fell unchecked. I swiped my face with the

back of my hand, feeling overwhelmed by too much emotion in such a short period of time. Unfortunately, the swept-up sawdust pile with the animal bits was right under my feet and the stench made me gag. I ran from the barn and puked in the bushes while Dad called Jenny relaying the details of another nightmare.

Chapter 17

Less than an hour later, I had once again landed in an interview room with Jenny and Nick. They read my rights; I again refused a lawyer.

"Can we do this later? I'm worried about Jake. I know the law so I can refuse representation, but he should have somebody. Can I make some calls for him? Your team is treating him like a criminal frankly and I don't want him taking any of this hassle because he's my friend."

Jenny wasn't as friendly this time around. "Sit down, Christine. He's in holding and we'll be doing the questioning. You don't get to come in here and start telling me what to do with my team."

"Jen, I'm sorry, really I am. I'm at the end of my rope. This can't be happening. You have no idea," I pleaded.

"Give us the answers we need, and we'll sort it all out," she said firmly.

"Can we start with you and Jake? You were adamant last time you were here that you two were only friends. Can you tell me how you came to be present when Jake took the distress call from Mr. Dirksen at five this morning?" Jenny asked.

"Fine, he stayed at my house. You're the one who said I needed to be with Dad or Jake every minute of the day. It's not what you think."

"Tell me what I'm thinking," Jenny said.

"The truth is, well, the thing is—"

"Yes, the truth would be refreshing." Nick piped up.

"Nick, come on. I have told you both the truth all along and so has Jake. How about someone finds the truth for us? What am I here for because I slept with Jake? Both of us have been through hell and back in the last week and okay, we've become close, closer, than we were, well, we've always been close, damn it. Last I checked my Criminal Code there's nothing illegal about that. We were together last night; we can vouch for each other. Henry can likely vouch that I was there when Jake answered the phone, so what's the big deal?" I threw up my hands and shook my head, glaring at them.

They didn't reply and I resumed. "You questioned him at the fire hall yesterday. He came to my house right after he got home. I had been at home all day and Annie too. When forensics finds out Wayne was hung up last night while we were in the middle of a lover's tryst, then we'll all be back at square one, won't we? We have nothing. No one knows why David scammed investors' money or who it went to. No one knows who hired Wayne and now we may never know. It's not Jake. Dad knows it's not Jake. You need to look somewhere else. Can I go now?"

"It's not that simple and you know it. We're getting nowhere here. Go find Jake a lawyer, but don't talk to him and don't leave yet, damn it." Jenny scoffed.

"Thank you," I said.

I stormed from the interview room straight into Dad's office. "What the hell has gotten into these—"

A detective sat across from Dad's desk writing notes. Dad glanced up and shook his head. "Not now. Go sit in the hall." He pointed me out the door.

Like a misbehaving student sitting outside the principal's office, I plopped myself on the closest bench. I was shocked they were interviewing Dad again. I needed to see Jake. I waited not sure what to do next, imagining the reporters who had already shown up at the Dirksen farm. Like Jake had warned, those paparazzi types had a channel on their scanners for every police, fire, and ambulance dispatch so they could run off to each gruesome scene capturing pictures of families in every desperate state of death and destruction, to entertain the morbidly curious over their morning coffee. *"Oh no, that poor family has been through so much."* I pictured the wife saying. *"Deserved it, if you ask me,"* the husband would argue. *"All that money those types have, they can cover up anything they feel like doing."*

I was losing my mind sitting and waiting, creating absurd scenarios in my mind. What took Dad so long? I picked up my phone to call my friend Lynn Spencer. We had been to law school together, and she had a great reputation for criminal defense. She had been my toughest competition when it came to winning the big cases, but we always came out shaking hands.

"Lynn, hi it's Christine. Can you call me back as soon as you get a chance? It's urgent, as in this is the only phone call I'm allowed to make. Only kidding, but not really. Call me please soon if you can."

It was only a few minutes before she rang back, an agonizing long few minutes to me but an amazingly quick reply for someone with her work schedule.

"Christine, what it is? What's wrong?"

"Thanks for the quick call back. It's my friend, Jake Anderson." I summarized the whole ordeal quickly, trying to stick to the important bits without sounding desperate. "Please, Lynn, I need your help."

"I don't know. My expertise is fraud, you know that; corporate, the big money guys."

"Please, I'm begging you. You're the best I know. I'll pay you up front. I'm asking as a friend, a personal favor, one I will be thrilled to reciprocate any time you name it," I pleaded.

"The thing is, to be perfectly blunt, they're not painting you with a pretty picture. The word is the Crown's office, and the homicide family are covering for you, and you're coming off like the spoiled little rich girl."

"I've read the paper. What are you getting at? Is that really what you think?" I spat the questions, angry at her accusations.

"Of course not, I respect your work. You are an amazing Crown Attorney, and we've been friends for a long time, but I have a family and my career is solid. I don't want to get tangled up with the media and get labeled the lawyer who got paid to help cover—"

"That's crap and you know it. I didn't do anything and neither did Jake. You have a job to do. You should be happy to land in the paper as the competent lawyer who helped free an innocent man."

"I'm sorry, Christine, I can't," she said quietly.

"Thanks for nothing." I regretted saying that as soon as I hung up.

Next, I called Karen. She answered on the first ring. "Great, I've been waiting to hear from you. Are you coming in today? I need a name. Remember that case, the one with the guy in the shower and the roommate got in and started coming on to him, and then they got in a fight and the roommate ended up—"

"Not now, Karen, stop talking and listen to me," I demanded.

"What the hell is wrong with you?"

"Wrong with me? I'm not the one who answered the phone with a rambling question. Can you check your index and find me that lawyer who took on the Buckley case, the one with the drunk guy who stole the truck, then hit that farmer? Remember?"

"Oh, so it's okay for me to have to remember names, but not to ask you to remember?" she asked sarcastically.

I had lost my patience by this point. I answered her through clenched teeth. "Karen, I don't have time for this right now. I'm at the police station. There's a second murder victim and I'm in interview with Jake Anderson. Get the guy from the Buckley case on the phone and if he can't get his perfect pin stripe suited ass down here in the next half hour, then find me someone who can, damn it!"

I punched the off button and threw my phone down on the bench. Jenny and Nick came through the door holding Jake's arm like he was a wanted man. I stood. "Seriously guys, is that necessary? Jake, I have a lawyer on the way for you, and I told Scott and Juzo that we slept together so don't try to be a hero and cover anything for my sake, okay?"

Jenny squinted, clearly unimpressed with my outburst. "Unfortunately, yes, it is necessary and Christine, you need to keep your mouth shut or you're going into holding yourself. You know the rules with questioning."

"Jen, those rules apply to suspects. We are witnesses. There's a big difference. We were in bed together about to have sex when a neighbor called saying he thought he might be having a heart attack because he saw something scary in his barn. We ran to help him and arrived on scene faster than an ambulance could have, I should add. Explain to me where we became murder suspects in all that."

Jenny glared at me, along with most of the people in the office.

Jake spoke in his soothing firefighter voice, maintaining eye contact with only me. "Take a deep breath. I'm going to answer a few questions. I have nothing to hide. I'll be home in time to barbecue for you and your dad. Please stop talking."

"But—"

He held up his hand warning me to stop. "Look at me. Everything is fine. We're all going to get through this."

"Let's go," Nick said to Jake walking him away to the interview room.

Dad stood in the doorway of his office shaking his head. "Get in here," he demanded.

I sat down where the detective had been as Dad closed the door. "Honestly, what the hell is going on?" I asked.

He sat behind his desk. "Does the whole precinct need to know that my daughter is sleeping with the fire fighter from next door five days after her husband was killed? Murdered, in a fire no less. Can you add anything else to make it look like a cover up, do you think?" He glared at me.

"Oh, that sounds bad when you say it like that. But it's not like that. Really, Jake has been there for me for like a year through all this crap with David, through all the murder investigation, through everything, really forever."

My anger had been replaced by exhaustion and nerves. I cried, more like sobbed on my arms on Dad's desk. He didn't speak or make a move to comfort me. I lifted my head. "He told me he's always loved me; can you believe it? All this time, I didn't think, and he didn't say."

"Yes, I can believe it. I've known all along and so have his parents," he said, more calmly now.

"What? Why didn't you tell me?"

"Well, I think I did, many times, but you needed to figure it out yourselves. That's not the biggest issue right now. You need to focus, listen to me," he insisted.

"What do you mean? So, your staff thinks I'm a cheap date, whatever, it will pass like all this media bullshit." I flicked my hand to the side.

"You are not helping." His jaw clenched.

"Stop it; what is it now? What are you angry about?"

"The detective in my office wasn't interviewing me. He was one of the sweepers at the Dirksen's. They found something and they have questions."

"Dad?" I felt uneasy.

"Something of Jake's, a fire department toque."

"That's ridiculous. I'm sure he gave it to Henry or Thomas to wear. He has a million of them. I wear one of his fire department hats every day I go out jogging," I said.

"They tested already; it has his hair. Recent, healthy hair. And none of Henry's or anyone else's. Your little outburst would back up the accusation that you've been intimate a little longer than one night. You may have a wonderful, loving history, that you're finally figuring out, but no one else knows that. It sounds a whole lot like you've been, well, doing that, for a lot longer. Also, it lends to the media stories that Jake or maybe even both of you wanted David out of the way and with Jake being a firefighter, he knew how to set the carriage house going. Then, when the police started nosing around Jake, Wayne shows up hanging the next day, in a body bag that Jake has access to and then he's conveniently alibied over at your house with no one else around, having sex with you for the first time."

"Do you think I would have blurted out that Jake and I were in the sack if all that was really going on? We really were, ah, just waking up when Henry called. Why would he run over to help if he had hung Wayne up there or taken me along with him for that matter? He would have called nine-one-one, would have dispatched whoever was working instead of going himself. And you saw his reaction when he saw Wayne. He almost threw up. And who wears a toque this time of year? It was sunny and hot yesterday. This is ridiculous." My anger was taking over my misery once again.

"I'm not accusing him, and you don't need to be defensive with me. I'm only telling you. It didn't help that his personal belonging showed up, of course our prints are all over, probably covering whoever's did this, and now his only alibi is the person they say he's trying to protect."

"This can't be happening. We were together last night, I swear. I can prove it," I insisted.

"I'm sure you can vouch for last night, but he had a lot of time between when Scott and Juzo were at the fire hall questioning him and when he came over to see you. Enough time to strangle or drug or hit someone who has given you a whole lot of grief and hang him up in a barn that Jake would know would be empty."

"That's ludicrous and you know it. How would he know if Henry would be working in the barn or had gone out?"

"The property is almost in eyesight of Jake's back door, and he would know when Henry knocks off work and goes to the local pub. He said it himself, you heard him; Henry is in the barn sunup to sundown. They've been neighbors his whole life. It's also a bit convenient that Henry's wife and son were away this week. The way the detectives see it, he had knowledge, the strength to do it, easy access to the barn, and motive."

"He was upset when he called me. He had just come from work. The media had been there, and the cops questioned the Chief and him directly. This is impossible. He only wanted to come and see me because he couldn't stop thinking about me, not because he needed an alibi. Why would he want to kill the one person who can get us both off the hook? It can't be him. He couldn't strangle a guy, hang him up in a meat locker, wash off, and come and have a romantic evening with wine and dinner and, well…it doesn't fit Dad. I would know. Dear God, I would have known. Annie can't be right. Jake doesn't have a malicious bone in his body. It's impossible."

"I'm doing everything I can, and they really don't

have much, but he got pretty defensive at the fire hall when they questioned him, especially when they brought up your relationship. You and I trust him with our lives, but in their minds, two murders have taken place essentially in Jake's backyard; and both dead men have been a threat to the woman he loves. I'm telling you; they think they have enough to at least keep him overnight and search his place," Dad explained.

"He got defensive because he values his integrity and they called that into question. You know how you would feel if it were you. And then Nick pushed his buttons specifically about me, goaded Jake on purpose. I know it's upsetting because he did the same thing to me," I said.

"That's his job honey, to get suspects defensive enough to figure out what or who they might be passionate about; enough to kill for."

"Jake loves me, damn it. I didn't even get to enjoy that for a whole day and now it's going to be his ruin. Are they really keeping him overnight? What the hell? This is horrible."

"They're getting a warrant, they'll search his place, make sure there's no washing up evidence, which of course I know there isn't. But even the hat and the proximity to the property and your relationship is enough to get them a warrant."

"I need to talk to him. I need to get Finnegan and Sunny. I need to do something."

"You know you two can't talk." Dad shook his head.

"Can you Dad? Can you at least tell him we'll get the dogs, and a lawyer is on the way and tell him to call me the minute he's home? And tell him I, no, never mind. Tell him, things have a strange way of working out. Tell him that please. And they will, right?"

"What's that?" he asked.

"They will work out, right?" I asked.

"Sit tight. I'll go talk to them and to him. I'll let him know you'll take care of things and you'll see him tomorrow. Then I'll take you home."

"I have to go to work. This is going to make things even worse. I'm going to lose my job."

"Breathe. Work can wait one more day. Go tomorrow, early and sort what you have to. It will take that long to process Jake and his house search. You can't be there either. I will accompany you to get the dogs but then you have to stay away from his house. And I'm coming to stay with you. We both know it's not Jake, so that means there's still a murderer out there and you're not going to be alone. And no more nonsense trying to save the day or figure things out yourselves. Understand?"

"Yes, I get it. We're not criminals, and we weren't doing anything wrong. We were helping Henry. This has to stop." I lost it to tears again as Dad closed his door and left me.

****

Dad took me to Jake's, and accompanied by another officer, we retrieved the dogs and took them home. I was angry and upset, nowhere near a mood to focus on work. I took the dogs outside and let them run around the yard while I sat on the back step staring at the burned remains of the carriage house. On the verge of tears once again, I didn't know what to do next. My whole life had revolved around too many hours of work and way too few hours of marriage and happy times with friends. David had not only died but had been violently taken away from us. *Who hated him that much? Who hated Jake and me that much to make it seem like either of us would do such a thing?*

Before the fire, I cared about nothing but work. I dedicated most of my energy and time to seeing my cases through to a successful finish. I had complete control over every aspect of my day. Now, I realized I had avoided coming home because work appreciated me more than David. It's like I had an affair with work while he was having an affair with Sharlene. It made sense, but it still made me sad.

Now my situation had been reversed. I had a hard time leaving home. Work seemed irrelevant, impossible to focus on. Their simple requests drained every ounce of my energy. My life revolved around figuring out details of David's life instead of ignoring it. I had become more aware of people instead of cases, myself included, my future, my life, and Jake's life too. I had lost sight of all that in the shadow of marriage to David. I worked double time because the caring part of my life had been missing. Jake was right, surrounding yourself with what's meaningful, is what makes life worth living. Jake, my steady, through thick and thin, we grew up together. He had always been there for me. I had always been there for him. How had we not appreciated the depth of our relationship before now? Who knew? And now, what now?

I held my head. It throbbed from crying and lack of food and too much trauma for one day and it was only early afternoon. I whistled the dogs back inside and put an extra water bowl down beside Sunny's. Dad and Annie were both staring at me from the family room.

Annie spoke first. "I'm here for you, I told you—"

I squinted my eyes and held up my hand for her to stop. "If you say one, I told you so, it will be the last time you ever step foot in this house."

"I'm trying to help," she defended.

She stood ready to come to me. I watched Dad put a hand on her arm and shake his head slightly to stop her. I appreciated his gesture so I wouldn't say something I might regret. Excusing myself, I patted my leg so both dogs would follow. I needed comfort even if it came in animal form. The last thing I wanted was a lecture from Annie.

By the time I reached the top of the stairs, I felt beaten. I opened the door and glanced around my bedroom as Jake and I had left it, mid lovemaking, turned panic when we ran off to help Henry. The sheets were crumpled in the middle of the bed. My clothes from last night were still piled on the chair. Jake's T-shirt lay on top, left behind when he jumped into his jeans and hoodie in his rush this morning. I picked it up and inhaled his familiar scent. It was enough to put my emotions over the edge. I sat on the side of the bed holding his shirt to my face and broke down sobbing. Sunny licked my hand, then put her head down on my lap, while Finnegan seemed less sure, and came to lay across my feet.

I chuckled despite my grief. "You two are all a girl needs."

I patted both their heads in thanks and lay back on the bed hugging Jake's shirt, trying to calm my emotions. Loud voices rose from the kitchen below. I could only guess what insulting words Annie spewed about Jake.

It surprised me when I woke up and it was only early afternoon. I felt like I had been asleep for hours. The minute I opened my eyes and lifted my head, both dogs jumped up, panting, and wagging their tails like they hadn't seen me in days. "Hey, guys, guess I better get up and see what disaster faces me now. I won't solve anything crying in bed all day."

The dogs followed me downstairs and took off past me at the sight of Dad sitting at the kitchen counter, working on his laptop.

"I'm really glad you're here," I admitted.

He stood and came to hug me. "You okay?" he asked, stepping back.

"Not really. Is she still here?" I peered around the corner, into the family room, then back toward the basement stairs.

"I think I scared her away." He shrugged.

"I'm not sorry to hear that, thank you. I heard you guys yelling, but then I kind of passed out for a while. What was she on about? Never mind, I can answer that myself. I'm glad she's not here, at least for now. Have you heard anything from Jen or Nick?"

"Nothing yet, love. Make a coffee or get us a beer or some chocolate whatever will make you feel better. It's going to be a long wait to hear from them or Jake. Like I told you, they'll be checking his place and keeping him overnight, so you can bet it's going to be an even longer night for him."

Chapter 18

There were no reporters confronting me this time when I pulled into the parking lot across from the courthouse. They had moved on or they weren't expecting me back having been away all week. Of course, I didn't miss them and was relieved that I had a reprieve for the time being.

As I approached the front door, a uniformed security guard reached to open the door. "Good morning, Ms. Montgomery," he said, bowing slightly to me as I entered the building. That was a refreshing change from last week's arrival.

June from the lunch counter called over. "Hey, Chris, finally made it back, did you have a nice week off?"

I gave her a half wave and a puzzled look. Rose stepped up and elbowed her in the back. "Idiot, she hasn't been on holidays."

"What?" June asked.

Rose ignored her and smiled warmly. "Welcome back, Bella."

"Thank you," I said, and headed straight to my office.

I had been at my computer almost an hour trying to sort out my cases and review what Fenwick had entered, when Karen came to stand in my doorway.

"Did Fletcher show up?" she asked.

"Good morning Karen. Who?"

"Mr. Perfect Ass. Did he show up to get your boyfriend out of jail?" she asked with a smirk.

"I said perfect pin striped suit, not perfect ass and Jake's not my boyfriend, and he's not in jail and I'm not in a position to talk about anything. Did you see Mr. Walker on your way in?"

She tipped her head to the right. "He just walked in, but he has an 8:30 meeting, so go now if you want to plead your case."

"Jesus, Karen, I think you have Jake and I both serving life sentences already. Do you remember the phrase, innocent until, you know? We use it a lot around here."

She didn't answer, only rolled her eyes upward, and went back to her desk. I wasn't sure I wanted to talk to Alexander, but if I expected to keep my position, which I also wasn't sure about, I needed to make him understand that the investigation was coming along, and I still had nothing to hide.

He was on the phone when I inched his door open after knocking quietly. I took a step back, relieved to postpone the inevitable, but he waved me in and pointed to the chair. I closed the door quietly behind me and sat.

He finished his call then walked around from behind his desk, perching on the corner in front of me, hands folded, resting on his leg. "So?" he asked.

"Good morning, sir. I'm not sure what you want to hear. I came in to sort, well, I've been trying to come in all week, but it's been a nightmare. I needed to get in here and get at some of these files, before, well, what can I say? Fenwick, you know, has it been horrible?"

"Your cases are fine and what you've been sending from home has been enough to keep things going. He's working with it and we're managing. Why are you really here?"

At first, I was relieved at his show of support and appreciative they were handling my absence. But then I suspected he may be doubting my motive. "Wait, what are you asking me? Why do you think I'm here? I've been through hell and back, and so has my Dad and my friend Jake Anderson. The police department is getting a bad rap like they're covering something as is the fire department and now you're implying that I'm trying to use my position here to work some angle to get all of us off? Am I correct in this assumption, sir? Because I really hope I'm wrong." My apprehension had quickly been replaced by irritation.

"You are wrong. I don't suspect you of any wrongdoing in the murder or that you're here to use your connections to cover anything. You, better than anyone should know not to make assumptions. I'm asking why you feel the need to be here when there's so much else going on and frankly, when I told you to stay home until this was all over."

"You still don't believe me a hundred percent do you, Alexander?"

He looked away and then got up to sit behind his desk. "It's not up to me to be your Judge, and I don't expect I ever literally will be either. I have complete faith that you had nothing to do with your husband's murder, or the more recent murder of the suspected killer."

"How did you know about that?" I asked.

"I'm privy to things. That's not relevant. I'm not

talking about these investigations, and you're not supposed to be either. I'm concerned about you. I'm talking about what you have become and what has become of your life. You have worked these kinds of cases for the last several years. I see what you have sacrificed, your marriage, your youth. You are what I was many years ago. I didn't like what I became back then, and I don't like what I see in you today. You look like hell and you shouldn't be here.

"I'm sure I seemed abrupt last time you came in, but I did that for your own good so that you would stay home and face the situation you're in instead of hiding behind your work. I know you. You're in here to make sure Fenwick isn't destroying your cases, and he's not. I won't let that happen. But I also know you're hoping to find answers in past cases, similar M.O.s. It's not here, the answers are not here. Take care of yourself for a while and let the police do their job. Then and only then, when you're ready, when your confidence is back, when you believe in yourself, that's when I want you to come back and be the best you can be for our victims who need you."

I hung my head and made an effort not to cry. I'd done too much of that in the last week. "That means the world to me. I was starting to doubt my career, my everything. I honestly don't know what to do at home. The police won't let me investigate anything. Jake and I, well, it's complicated, but he's been great. Dad too, he's my rock. But I had to come in. It's what I do; I need to know everything is on track. And, okay, maybe I wanted to check for a few similarities. You're right, though, I have realized this week that I need to step back and approach my life from a different angle.

Thank you for reinforcing what I'm already figuring out. You're an incredible mentor and I hope you know how much I value what you say. I promise, promise, promise, I won't work all weekend. But for today, I need to write a few points for Fenwick about next week's cases and then I'll go."

"Make it point form and get the hell out of here." Alexander stood and again came from behind his desk, motioning me to stand, signaling our meeting was over. In a rare show of affection, he put an arm around my shoulder as he walked me to the door. "I mean it, Christine. I need you back, not like before in overkill mode, but calm, with your confident expertise, your thinking mind, and your efficient jury addresses. No one can win a jury like you do. Finish what you must and leave. I don't want to see you when I come back from court at the end of the day. Get out, get healthy, and don't come back until you know it's absolutely what you want to keep doing."

I shook his hand with both my hands and answered with heartfelt appreciation. "Thank you, words to live by."

"Out." He pointed me down the hall.

Walking back to my office, I smiled, feeling valued for the first time in a long time. I worked through the day with little interruption, writing notes for Fenwick of details I had planned to use when prosecuting, but had never written down.

Even with Alexander's encouraging words and my focus on the cases, I was on edge waiting to hear from Jake or Dad. Finally, at four, Jake called.

"Hey," I answered at a loss what to ask.

"Hey, yourself. Where are you?"

"At work. It's tough, but Alexander made me feel appreciated so that was good. How are you? Where are you?"

"They let me go, no charges of course because, duh, what the fuck were they thinking? And I'm home now that they rifled through my stuff and didn't find anything."

"I'm so sorry. I can't believe they're doing this to you."

"We'll get through it, but I can't talk now. I'm too angry and I feel disgusting. I've been up for more than thirty hours and that place smells and God knows what vermin are running around on me."

"Vermin?" I chuckled.

"Seriously, it's nasty in the holding area. Cops and drunks and druggies are coming and going all night. These sketchy guys getting arrested for God knows what, were all yelling and punching walls and spitting and trying to out tough each other when they're probably so scared, they're actually shitting themselves. It was ridiculous and talk about smell. Not exactly a five-star accommodation if you know what I mean."

"I'm so sorry," I whispered.

He was silent for a minute and I didn't know what else to say.

"I need to see you, both you and your Dad. I don't want to talk on the phone. I really need a shower. And then we need to talk about some theories I came up with."

"I'm almost done here. Maybe another half hour," I said.

"When you're done, when all this is done, I'm going to hold you and I'm never going to let go. Do you hear me?"

"I hear you. I think you might need some sleep but I'm happy to let you hold me while you're doing that." I smiled at the thought.

"I got Finnegan back from your house. No one was around so I took the key from under the fake poop, but I locked up again. I'll see you soon, okay."

"I promise." I ended the call smiling. I could get used to someone wanting me close. It was something I hadn't felt with David. He acted happy to see me most of the time, but Jake didn't act. I truly felt in my heart that he was genuinely happy to see me, and I ached to see him and talk through all the latest with him and Dad.

Chapter 19

When I finally left work, a different security guard opened the door. I smiled and thanked him, then scowled when I walked directly into a flashing camera on a reporter's phone. "Ms. Montgomery, why are you back at work so soon? Have you been cleared of murder? Why haven't you buried your husband? Has Jake Anderson been arrested?"

The guard followed me out the door and forced the reporter away, waiting outside until I had crossed the street toward the parking lot. I punched Dad's number on my cell.

He answered on the first ring. "I can't believe I'm still newsworthy. Why are people so mean? No one knows me and they're still bashing me on social media, calling the Crown's office, saying I'm not fit to fight for justice. Why can't I be old news? Like, enough already. I'm tired and I just want to be home and see Jake."

"I didn't expect you to stay at the office so late. Get home, sweetheart. I think they have some leads."

"Nothing to do with Jake, I hope. You believe him, don't you, Dad?"

"Of course, I do and I'm pretty sure they feel the same. They have—"

"I can't believe it! I try to come to the office for one lousy day and they trashed my car. Holy shit! My tires are slashed, and someone keyed it and there are eggs all over, fucking eggs. My nice car is wrecked. I can't take this anymore."

"Get out of there now." Dad's voice sounded calm, but I caught the nerves. "Back out of the parking lot, now. Get in a cab and I'll meet you at home. Go now," he demanded.

He told me enough times that I realized my emotions were taking over my common sense. "People are ridiculous out here. I'm used to dealing with irrational, but this makes no sense."

"The people you deal with are cuffed and escorted by security into the courtroom. Whoever did that to your car clearly knows you and has it out for you."

"David was the one screwing people over for money. Why is anyone after me?" I asked.

"I don't know but keep talking to me. Keep walking and talking and hold your keys like I showed you, firm hand, and strong key down in your fist. You've got lots of power in your elbow if you need it. Key down, remember?"

"I know, I'm good, I see the cabs out front of the building. I'm almost there. Hey, it's Bruce, your buddy. Hang on one second, Dad."

I waved to Bruce and held my phone down to speak through his open window. "Hey, Bruce, am I glad to see you. I seem to have some car trouble. Can I get a lift home?"

I put the phone back to my ear. "I'm good, it's Bruce. I'll call you when I get home."

"Call me yes, but Jake's home. I talked to him this afternoon before he left, told him we would both go over when you were done with work," Dad said.

"He called me when he got home too. He said he got the dog, and he needed a shower and we all needed to talk."

"Listen to me. Get Sunny the minute you get home and go over to Jake's house. I'm sending an officer and I'll be there myself within half an hour. And I'm not taking no from you. That crap nails it, you both have twenty-four, seven watch until this is all wrapped up."

"I'll see you soon," I said before hopping in the cab.

****

"Hey, Bruce, nice to see a friendly face."

"Heading home, are ya?" he asked.

"Yes, please, my house is down—"

"I know where you're at. Prit near know every house in twenty miles of my own."

"How are your kids doing? I haven't seen them since high school."

"Awe, you're sweet to ask. Well, they got jobs, not the like of you, mind, or your wee friend Jenny, but all three are doing okay. Got themselves married and we have a total of four weeuns between them so far. My Stella loves to fuss over her grandbabies."

He leaned over like he would tell me a secret. "To be honest, there's nothing like a baby falling asleep on ya for a wee nap. I ain't got no trouble being a grandpapa either. Sweet wee things."

I was glad he hadn't brought up the murder or asked anything hard like why I hadn't had kids yet. I tried to pay him, along with a hefty tip for calming me down.

Initially he took the money, but then stuffed it back in my purse. "You put that money right back. I'll be happy to take full fare someday when things are goin' more your way."

I walked to the door smiling at his kindness, wishing there were more in the world like him. I looked up from retrieving my keys, to see my house in darkness. The days were shorter now we had reached late fall, and it was getting dark earlier. I appreciated that Bruce waited in the driveway with the car lights on the front of the house, providing light while I unlocked the door. I considered asking him to come to the door with me but reminded myself I shouldn't be paranoid. I clearly hadn't thought to put the outside light on when I left this morning not having planned to stay at the office so late.

I removed the keys from the lock, holding them up ready for attack, feeling somewhat foolish. I flicked on the outside light and the front hall light before fully opening the door. Sighing in relief when nothing jumped at me, I waved to Bruce who was slowly backing down the driveway.

Ahead, to the right of the front entrance was Annie's room. She hadn't been around since she and Dad had argued about Jake. I jumped with a gasp when a light came on from under her bedroom door piercing the darkness. Any other time I got home after dark, and certainly lately with all her nurturing, if Annie had been there, I always entered a hallway of welcoming lights. I reminded her often that she didn't need every light on in the house. I also generally walked into the smell of food cooking and occasionally the smell of a fire started in the den. Tonight, there were no familiar lights, smells, or sound, not even the TV in her room, like she had fallen asleep watching something and forgotten to turn lights on. Tonight, something was definitely off. *Why wasn't Annie up? Why had she even come back for that matter? Please God, don't let me find another dead body.*

Even though Wayne was out of the picture, I still felt jumpy. They seemed a long way off solving the case and now there were two murders to figure out. Obviously, that meant Wayne wasn't the only one capable of killing. My heart pounded as I looked and listened.

The slam of a door sounded like a gun shot in my frazzled state. I screamed and clutched my chest. "Annie, is that you?"

"I didn't expect you home so soon, dear. I'll be right out," she called.

"Oh, thank God," I whispered.

"Are you okay? Why are all the lights out and where's Sunny?" I called louder so she could hear through the door. I hit every switch on my way to the kitchen, arms laden with my purse, my briefcase, and my keys still clutched and ready for attack. "Sunny, here girl. Sunny?"

"Annie, where the hell is the dog?" I yelled back over my shoulder.

"I'm coming dear," she called back.

Something felt dreadfully wrong. Despite Annie's presence, the house felt eerily unwelcoming, and my apprehension mounted.

Temporary relief washed over me when I heard a familiar, distant bark. I dropped my bags on the counter, ran to the back door, and called again, worried Sunny had been accidentally locked outside. It wouldn't be the first time Annie had let her out and forgotten about her.

"What the hell?" Realizing the barking came from the closed shed, I cursed the darkness and the state of things.

I flicked another switch to the outside light, kicked off my pumps and ran in bare feet over the damp grass to the shed. I tried, unsuccessfully to open the jammed door, while Sunny barked furiously. Behind me, the house lights went out, and the sliding door slammed shut, leaving me in the darkness of dusk. Searching for an intruder, I saw nothing but black.

Chapter 20

"Sunny, shush, it's okay, girl. It's me. Settle down." I struggled with the wedged door, cursing when I sliced my hand on the latch.

Once released, Sunny bolted out of the shed and circled me, jumping up almost knocking me over. With trembling hands, and blood dripping from my cut finger, I grabbed her collar, pulling her behind the shed. My mind raced with questions. *Who could be in the house? Did someone have Annie hostage?* My cell phone rang from my suit pocket, startling me, and causing Sunny to bark again. I yanked her collar quieting her, saying a small prayer of thanks that I still had my phone with me. I pushed ignore to lose the caller and dial for help.

It rang again by the time I steadied my hands enough to make a call. "Hello," I said, as forcefully as I could in a hushed tone. It was Bruce Elroy, the taxi driver. "Bruce I can't talk right now. I have to hang up and make an important call."

"No, Miss Christine, wait, this is important. You have to wait one minute; this may be important to the investigation. 'Member you gave me your card, said to call iffen I had somethin' else to add."

"Another time, Bruce, I can't talk right now. Someone is here in my house; he may have Annie. We may be in danger; I need to call my dad. I'll call you back I promise."

"Please, Miss Christine, that's the thing, there is someone there, that crazy lady, the one from the porch, that I was tellin' you and Ricky about with the pink bumpy robe and the hair thing, and the long gun, the skinny guy's Ma, that's who was in your winda just now."

The hair on my neck stood on end. My palms were sweating, and my hands trembled. Sunny started to whimper sensing my terror. I wanted to answer Bruce, but my voice wouldn't come. He kept talking while I put two and two together.

"I swear when I parked in your drive just now with the lights on the house so's you could see to get unlocked and then a light came on in the front winda right after you went in and there was that lady peeping out. At first it didn't register, but now I'm sure, I'm positive it's her. My car lights shone right on her face, then she spun away real quick. She's the lady what was with them two drunk dudes the other night. The skinny one, her boy Wayne, what she told not ta come near ya, the one who we did the sketch about and then that Frank with the hundred dollars. 'Member, Christine? She's the one I'm sure of it. Christine, are ya there?"

I sat stunned, unable to speak, so terrified, I felt sick. *Annie? Could it have been Annie all along? Annie killed David. Why? She loves us, this doesn't make sense. Could there be another old lady holding Annie hostage?* Surely, I was in another nightmare.

"Miss Christine, are ya there, do you need me to come back to help ya?"

Bruce got louder now, his voice piercing my dark, quiet hiding spot. "Yes, Bruce, I'm here, but no, I don't need you to come back. I'm going to hang up now and call my Dad for help. He's already on his way, so don't do anything heroic. I'll be in touch I promise." I kept my voice much calmer than I felt.

I hung up and dialed direct to my Dad. He picked up on the first ring once again. "Sweetie, you okay?"

"No, I'm not. It's Annie."

"What's wrong with Annie? Is she hurt? Where are you? What's wrong?"

"Please, Dad, stop and listen to me. It's Annie, she's the wild lady who had the gun pointed at Wayne when Bruce dropped him off at the shack on Townline. Bruce saw her just now in the window when he dropped me off. He called me, said he's certain she's the one with the gun who asked Wayne why he came near me, told him that he'd get caught. She knew he murdered David."

"What the hell?"

"Dad, she heard me talking to Jake after I got back from jogging that morning. I admitted to her that Wayne came at me. She knew the police were on to him from the first day he was watching the fire because she's been listening every time we were talking about it. And she heard me talking to Jake and to you about Bruce dropping Wayne off on Townline Road. At least she heard enough to guess when and where they were looking for Wayne and that's when he disappeared. It's her Dad, this is all her. That's probably why she's been hanging around so much since the fire. She wanted to be close to hear about the investigation." I was spewing words so quickly I wasn't sure Dad would even understand.

"Take a breath and calm down. What did she say

when you came in? Did she come at you?"

"She was shuffling and banging around in her room, and all the lights were out in the house. She flicked a light on and said she'd be right out. I kept calling for Sunny and yelling to Annie. Then the dog barked out back. I went to find Sunny and she had been locked in the shed. Jesus, Dad, why would Annie lock the dog in the shed? Then the patio door slammed, and the back light went out when I was trying to get the dog out. I don't know if she's still in there or if she's out here." I whispered now. "Dad, my heart is beating so loudly, if she's outside, she's going to hear it."

"Listen to me carefully. Jake texted me before you called and told me to come urgently. I've been trying him back to get him over there until I get to you, but he won't answer. Damn it, I don't know what the hell is going on out there, but I'm already on my way. I'm only a few minutes out. And backup is behind me. Go to Jake's. Can you get there without being seen?"

"I think so. It's already pitch dark around here with no streetlights. I'll go through the trees instead of the path. I haven't seen her since she shut the back door, but I'm behind the shed. I can't see the house. I had to fight the door to get Sunny out and then I talked to Bruce after that, so it's been several minutes. Maybe she ran, maybe she's still inside. God, I don't know. My heart is beating so hard, it's making me nauseous. I have to put the phone down or the light will give me away when I start walking. I don't know if she's out here, but I know my way in the dark, and I can hide at Jake's. We've been sneaking around this property since we were kids."

"Good girl. Hang up now but keep your phone in

your hand. Wait. If you see her, act like everything is normal between you two, like you're worried for her. Ask her if she's okay and who else was in the house. She won't know that Bruce called you and outed her. I'm calling backup to let them know where you are and who to look for. I'll meet you at Jake's. I'm less than five minutes now. Get there and both of you hide and be safe. I'll be there soon, I promise. We'll find her and we'll figure this out."

I thanked God for the darkness. Sunny knew the way and pulled me through the trees. I tried to hold her collar so she wouldn't bolt ahead and start barking. The lights at Jake's were on, the most inviting thing I had ever seen. Loud voices pierced the quiet when I got closer the house. *Great time to run into Jake and Courtney arguing. No, she wouldn't have come back.* I recognized Annie's angry voice before I was close enough to see her face. *No, please don't let her hurt Jake.*

I couldn't risk Sunny barking and giving me away. Staying lower than the window ledges, I crept around back to Jake's garage. It was big and had windows that would let in the outside deck lights. Sunny would stay calmer in there, and more importantly it sat far enough back from the house so Annie might not sense where the barking came from if Sunny got excited. I opened the door just enough for Sunny to squeeze in then gasped when I saw Finnegan lying in the middle of the garage. Sunny pulled from my grasp and bolted to Finnegan, whimpering, and licking his face. I snuck in behind her and crouched to check him, my tears flowing, afraid what I would find. He appeared to be breathing, and I didn't see any obvious injuries. It seemed like he had been drugged.

"Sit, stay here and protect Finnegan, I'll be right back with help, good girl." She seemed to understand the importance of my terrified commands. She whimpered once then lay down beside Finnegan, her head resting on his middle. There was nothing else to do until help arrived. I closed the door behind me and crept back to the house.

I snuck up to the only vantage point beside the kitchen window. Jake's head slumped looking like he might fall forward had his arms not been tied behind him. I gasped when Annie came into view, standing beside him, long gun in hand. She glanced briefly at the window but returned her focus to Jake. She smacked him across the face, causing him to jolt upward. Jake's jawbone twitched.

Annie laughed, inches from his face. "Who's the big hero now, Mr. Fireman? You'll be next, just what you deserve for trying to take my place in her life like the rest of them."

Had she drugged him, hit him on the head? She couldn't have tied him up without drugs; he would have overpowered her in a minute. The pieces were starting to come together. She had to be the one with the drugs that overtook David, possibly Wayne too, even Finnegan. The big question was, why? Jake kept clearing his throat, like he fought to stay awake or tried to find his voice.

He lifted his head and glanced at his cell phone on the table. I shared his frustration knowing he had no way to reach for it. Annie's stance shifted wider and her vacant stare changed to an angry, deranged squint. I trembled, terrified she would pull the trigger.

Her voice sounded higher pitched than normally when she spoke. "Damn it, why did she have to come home. If she'd stayed at the office a few minutes longer, I'd be done with you and away from here. No one would have seen me since that idiot Rick threw me out."

At this Jake's head lolled back; keeping it straight, appeared to be a struggle. "What have you done? Where's Christie?" His voice was slurred but loud. "Damn it, you crazy fuck, where is Christie?" he yelled again.

"What do you think you can do about it? You have enough Thiopental to keep you senseless for a long while yet. Don't get all excited, she's locked out with that stupid dog. I'm sure she thinks someone is in the house trying to kill me. She's either circling around trying to find a way to sneak in and save the day or she's hiding until the cops show up. By the time that happens, and they find a way into the house, you'll be looking like a suicide case, obviously distraught because Christie knows you're a murderer, not to mention that wench from Toronto dumping your sorry ass."

"Enough. Let's call Rick, we'll call him together. Rick can help you. He always makes you feel better. Rick and Christine are your life." The soft tone of his voice told me he was attempting to calm her.

"I don't need him. I'm fine. A slight headache, that's all. Nothing that won't go away once you're out of my life. You want to call Rick? You can't. He's dead," she snapped.

"Dead? How? I don't believe you."

Annie laughed. I shook watching them. I knew she

lied, but Jake didn't. I was terrified he would try something, and Annie would shoot him. I wanted to rush in, tackle her but knew that would likely end with both of us dead. *Please Dad hurry and bring the whole damn cavalry.*

"He talked too much, just like you," she said.

"I had it right all along. You are nuts. Christine's going to put you away for the rest of your life. She'll be here any minute, with the cops. You won't get away."

Jake's comment about putting Annie away brought me back to reality. I needed evidence in case she got out of this and disappeared like Wayne had. I pulled my phone from my pocket and started the video button, holding it slightly below the window ledge so the light wouldn't give me away, but high enough to record what she said.

Annie sneered at Jake. "She's not here now, I am, and I'm feeling really bad about old Rick. He said you and Christine are lovers. That's when I killed him. The thought of your slimy hands on my precious girl makes me sick. You make me sick. You two were so quick to jump to the rescue, Mr. Fireman and Mr. Big Cop.

"I had enough of Rick's hard-to-get attitude. He was making friendly with that Luisa witch, says she's *adorable*, wanted to have her over for dinner with Christine. Did he think I'd do the cooking, clean up after the two of them and their make out session? And who does she think she is working him, after I cleared the way?"

"Cleared the way? What are you talking about? I don't understand," Jake questioned.

"Ha, that got your attention Mr. Tough Guy. Of course, you don't understand. I helped Julie along to get to my rightful place, but I don't want to talk about her. I was talking about my Rick. He wanted Christine all to himself too. He talked to that new bitch girlfriend about kicking me out of Christine's house altogether. You all wanted me out. Who the hell does he think he is?"

Annie walked toward the window. I pinned myself against the wall and clutched my phone to my chest. She stayed quiet a moment before her voice distanced again. "Big cop and fireman now, aren't you?"

Returning to record, I saw Jake staring at her, looking more angry than shocked or nervous.

"I want to see you squirm your way out of this one. My plan to rope you both in at once is working out fine, he's out of the way and in a few more minutes you can say nighty-night too. Too bad my boy's not here to do the dirty work for me. I trained him so well. He wanted to use something fun to torch David. He wanted to make a big bang with gas or gunpowder. Useless boy, he was almost as stupid as you, Jacob Anderson."

Jake's eyes were wide. "Your boy?"

"Yes, Wayne's my boy. He lived with my brother Raymond Duncan and his idiot son Frank out in the woods. Can't you figure out anything? He started high school with Christine, right when I came to take over her mother's place. Wayne and Christine were both juniors. You were a big-shot senior jock. Am I the only one who remembers anything important? Rick didn't even recall our high school days. Oh, the love I gave him. That Julie came along and ruined everything, brainwashed him, took him away from me. I vowed revenge from that day on.

"I followed those two and watched the fake lovey-dovey show they put on. I even followed them here to this hick little spot in the country. Rick never wanted that. He could have lived with me in the city. But noo, she wanted trees and fresh air. She wasn't right for him. She didn't know him like I did. I was meant to raise his children, love him, be by his side. I read their plea for someone to nursemaid that sick, helpless bitch and knew it was my calling to jump into my rightful place by his side. It was easy enough to hurry her little cancer along, miss a few meds, double up a few, mix up a few special remedies of my own. Blood count got way off and bam, it was Rick and Christine and me, like it should have been all along."

"Oh—my—God." Jake's reply seemed to startle Annie from her rambling.

Shaking my head in disbelief, tears running down my cheeks, I wanted to jump in screaming and ripping at Annie. Dad came up behind me and clamped a hand over my mouth. I flinched but knew it was him. He let go and put a finger to his lips. He pointed to indicate he would go to the back door when I grabbed his arm and pulled him down. "Wait, listen. She said she killed Mom! And she admitted she's Wayne Duncan's mother. She was in love with you in high school. And she has a gun on Jake," I whispered.

His jaw clenched, his eyes closed briefly, and he took a deep breath letting it out slowly.

"Wait, listen with me for a minute, she's confessing and I'm recording. You have to wait for back up; she wants to kill you both."

Dad didn't answer my whispered plea. He seemed torn, hesitating before he stood to the side of the window so he could listen too, pulling his handgun aimed to fire.

Annie kept her confessional rant going. “Listen to me go on. I do tell a good story, don’t I? Yes, Wayne was my boy. I tried to get him and Christine to be friends. In my heart they were both my children. Silly boy wouldn’t even talk to girls, took his father’s death real hard, sobbed like a baby for months. At fourteen years old, he should have been able to deal with it. I explained it had been an accident. Then, he’d get all in a fuss when I stayed overnight to nursemaid that Julie. Wayne used to tell me his uncle took comfort with him when I wasn’t there. Stupid little liar. He would have been a real man and fought back if he’d had Rick’s blood like I intended all those years ago. I called Rick after high school, you know, told him I needed his help, confessed my love, tried to convince him to raise my baby as our own, together like a family. He said he didn’t even know me. Can you imagine? After all I did for him, he denied my love. What could I do but marry Wayne’s useless idiot father? No loss getting rid of him, such a terrible accident out hunting one day.”

Dad was shaking his head.

“Unbelievable,” I whispered.

"Once I realized Christine would be the ideal child for Rick and me to raise in proper style, I left Wayne with Raymond. They did okay together but don’t worry, I went back. When Wayne got old enough, I put him to work for me, and what a special relationship we had then. He got to be useful after all. Did you like the tortilla chip fire starter idea? It should have been obvious to you. You’re a stupid fireman. I came up with that little trick, of course a cook would supply food to start a fire. Why use something difficult when there are so many nice flammable things right in your own kitchen?"

Dad mirrored Jake's frown and puzzled expression telling me they shared my shock and confusion. "You killed all of them, didn't you? You killed your own husband and you forced Wayne to kill David, then you killed Wayne, your own son?"

"Oh, don't get all dramatic. I did it for love, my boy. Yes, I did it for love. And look at the years I've had with Rick and Christine. I've loved them, nurtured them like my own family, made them what they are, as it was meant to be, like fate; do you belief in fate, Jake?"

She didn't wait for his answer. "Now, they'll think you killed David and Wayne to protect Christie but couldn't bear it when she sent you packing, so you shot yourself. Then I'll have Christine all to myself. Perfect cover for me, again. I'll tell them I heard the shots, then I found you and you confessed right before you died. Easy sell to the cops and the papers. They believe anything that makes their job simple, like when I planted that fire department hat at the Dirksen's butcher barn and gave them a tip to investigate you. Stupid cops, one suggestion and they're right off your trail sniffing at someone else."

She started to wander away. "If you love Christie so much, why would you let her be blamed for killing her husband? Why make her go through all this adversity?" Jake asked.

"Brainless police, they would never pin it on her. I got away with murder for years, of course she would too. If Wayne hadn't got so mouthy in front of that damn cab driver, we could all have let him take the fall. Now it will have to be you. I always said you were sloppy seconds."

There was silence again and I panicked. Then Jake spoke. "Do you honestly think you'll get away with this? You are one sick lady."

"You insubordinate little moron. I have no intention of spending time behind bars. Precisely why I get rid of people who get in my way, people who know too much, people who don't see the love Christine and I share. That wily little Wayne got too smart for his own good, tried to turn the table on me, just like his old man. I taught them, didn't I? Where the hell is Rick? I'm tired of talking to you."

"Rick? You said you killed Rick." Jake's brow knit again. He tried tilting his head, but it lolled to his shoulder instead.

Sirens wailed far in the distance. "Damn it, no lights, no sirens," Dad cursed into his radio.

A gunshot and Jake's cry brought his attention back to the window.

Sunny barked from the garage. I jumped and ran to the door, losing Dad's grasp when he tried to pull me back. "Jake," I screamed, as I ran0 through the back door, Dad right behind me.

Annie bolted for the front door, Dad just seconds behind her. "Call nine-one-one," he yelled, over his shoulder.

Blood oozed down the front of Jake and pooled by his feet. His head sagged to his chest without any sign of life.

"Oh, please Lord no. Jake talk to me, where are you hurt? Please, talk to me."

I made a terrified nine-one-one call, for the second time in one short week, interrupting the operator once again. “Ambulance, please dear God, ambulance and fire rescue whoever can get here the fastest. My friend’s been shot, I’m not sure if he’s still alive, there’s blood everywhere.”

I untied Jake as I gave instructions to the operator. He grunted when I lowered him from the chair.

“Okay, Jake,” I pleaded. “Please come back to me, I love you, please don’t die on me.” I found the wound below his ribs on the right side. “That’s good, she missed your heart. You’re good, stay with me.” I grabbed a towel and pressed hard to stop the bleeding. Sirens grew closer. I expected a stretcher and paramedics when the back door opened.

In walked Annie, gun in hand.

Chapter 21

I gasped, then screamed at her. "Annie, where's Dad? What have you done with Dad? Why did you shoot Jake? What the fuck is wrong with you? Answer me, you lunatic!"

She had a dazed expression I had never seen before. I was petrified but I had never been so angry. She slowly moved her gun, taking aim at me. Jake started to moan and move around, bringing her focus back to him. I tried to keep pressure on his wound while I moved between Annie and Jake. I was scared for Jake and for Dad, but some strange adrenaline kept me from being afraid for myself.

She tilted her head and lowered the gun. "You don't understand. I did it for you, my dear daughter. I raised you, I love you!"

"I'm not your daughter. My mother is Julie, and she loved me and my dad very much. Where is Dad? Tell me, damn it. Where is Rick?"

She stared at me with that trance-like face but didn't speak.

"Damn you. Snap out of it. Where's Dad?" I screamed.

It felt like an eternity before Dad came to the door behind Annie. He raised his finger to his lips once again. The next few moments seemed to occur in slow motion. Annie raised her gun, taking aim at Jake. Dad flung open the door entering with his hands up drawing Annie's attention toward him. Her back turned, I jumped up, yanking her arm behind her so she dropped the gun. I stretched my free arm to the wooden block on the counter, grabbing a knife and pulling it around her neck, pinning her in place.

"Christine, my love, please. How can you put a knife to my throat, after all I've done for us? You're my daughter, I love you."

"There is no us, Annie," I said through clenched teeth. "You have hurt people who mean the most to me in the whole world. You know nothing about love. You are a housekeeper and a murderer. You are nothing like a mother to anyone. And now you're going to jail."

The deranged Annie responded to that, starting to squirm and fight me. Dad had taught me well how to keep a choke hold. He drew his handgun out of the waistband of his pants and pointed it at her.

"You can't pull a gun on me, you stupid cop, you've got nothing on me." She spat at him.

I yanked tighter on my hold. "Shut up, Annie, no one is planning to shoot you. You were the only one killing people. Why go out with a big bang when there are so many nice things for arresting someone right in your own kitchen?" Dad actually chuckled when I quoted Annie's earlier comment.

Jenny's eyes widened when she came in the back-door seconds later, gun raised, followed by several other officers. "What the hell?"

"I've never been so happy to see someone in my life." I sighed.

"Drop the knife," she demanded.

I happily surrendered my hold and let the knife

drop to the floor, shoving Annie toward the officers. Dad and I returned to Jake's side. His eyes were open now, and he smiled at me. He slowly lifted his hand, which appeared to take effort. I was on my knees in a second. "The paramedics are right here. You're going to be okay." I brushed the hair off his face and leaned down to kiss the tears off his cheek.

He whispered so I had to lean closer. Gazing into his beautiful eyes, I teared up, so happy to see him conscious. "What did you say?"

He cleared his throat and spoke slightly louder. "I said, I always knew teaching you to hide in the dark would come in handy someday."

"Mmm hmm," Rick said.

Jake surprisingly chuckled, which changed to a cough as the paramedics and firefighters came in, bags in hand. "He's full of Theopent something or other, as well as the gunshot wound," I reported, stepping out of their way.

"Thiopental? How is he still breathing?" the paramedic asked, eyes wide as he reached for a stethoscope.

"Yes, that's it. I was listening." I pointed to the open window. "And I'm guessing she gave some to the dog too, if you have a spare guy who can go check poor Finnegan, he's out back in the garage with Sunny standing guard," I said.

Dad kept his arm around me while they did their assessment. Adrenaline crashing, my legs felt like they would give out if he hadn't been holding me.

Since they all knew Jake from work, the paramedics tried to lighten the situation by calling him a weenie and letting him know this would cost him a case of beer for the hall. Despite the teasing, their concerned expressions and quiet exchanges told me they were worried too and taking extra special care of one of their own. They gently loaded Jake onto the stretcher.

"His chest wound doesn't seem to have gone deep and Thiopental will wear off in a few hours," the closest EMT assured us.

Jake reached his hand out. I walked over to hold it. Once again, I leaned close to hear him. "I love you too, Christie."

I kissed him gently, then let go so they could get him out the door. Dad smiled down at me. "Haven't I been telling you all along that he's the one."

"Don't you remember what Mom used to say? Sometimes it better to be quiet than to be right."

We walked out arm in arm and were greeted by a wagging, whimpering Sunny. One of Jake's colleagues carried Finnegan toward us. I ran to them, Sunny at my heels. "Is Finnegan okay?"

"He will be. He has a strong pulse. We gave him some oxygen, and he's starting to come around now. Guessing the shooter gave him a hit of whatever she gave Jake. The dog may have a bit of a hangover for a day or two, but he'll be chasing squirrels with this one in no time. Do you want me to take him back to the station?"

"Oh, I don't think Sunny would like that," I said.

Dad took Finnegan out of the firefighter's arms. "I think we can we settle these two brave pups back home safely, and then we'll head to the hospital and see how our human is making out."

Chapter 22

I sat at Jake's bedside the next day trying to convince him of the healing effects of hospital food when Dad stuck his head around the door. "Up to visitors?"

"Of course, come on in," Jake said.

"I brought a friend who's heard a lot about you two," Dad said.

I jumped up without waiting for an introduction and reached with a welcoming hug. "Luisa, I'm so glad to finally meet you."

She stood almost as tall as my five feet, ten and appeared several years younger than Dad. She had clear, soft olive colored skin and shoulder-length straight, black hair. Her smile reached her beautiful brown eyes when she replied. "I was beginning to wonder if you two really existed. The stories Rick has told me sounded kind of farfetched."

Luisa and I both looked to Dad for explanation. He rolled his eyes. "What? You're both here now." He waved a hand at Jake in introduction. "Jake, this is Luisa."

She came closer, and they both extended hands. "Is it Louisa?"

"No, Luisa. Mom and Dad expected me to be a boy. I was supposed to be Luigi, so when they had a girl instead, they traded the gi for a sa and left it at that.

I've spent my whole life explaining that one. Silly Italian Ma, she still doesn't know how to spell," she said with a smile.

"That's funny, well Luisa it is. Nice to meet you." Jake smiled back.

Rick perched on the edge of the bed. "So, how're you doing? You look a whole lot better than you did last night."

"I'm okay. Good thing Annie's a lousy shot. She missed anything crucial. The bullet went in one side under my ribs and out the other. Everything will heal in time, and I'll have a sexy scar to show when I tell the story."

I rolled my eyes when he flicked his eyebrows to me before continuing. "Mostly, I'm thrilled to have all that behind us and have Christie safe again. Who would have thought the trouble would be right in her own house all along. What I don't get is why kill David when they were already splitting up? He would have been out of Christie's life and that's what she said she wanted."

"Once Annie got into interview, she became a singing canary. They wouldn't let me in the room, but I stood on the other side of the glass. It took hours. Scott and Juzo did a relentless job provoking her to get her talking. Initially, she tried to pin it all on David, said it was his con from the start and she only tried to protect Christie. She got herself so mixed up in her lies, but they finally got it out of her how far back all this went.

"Like she told you, she had a crush on me back in high school that she obsessed over for years. When Julie got sick and we looked to hire a helper, Annie saw the ad because she essentially followed our every move from high school on. I should have checked her credentials, but she hit it off so well with Julie from the first day, I didn't think we needed to dig further. Who gets a criminal record check for someone to do the dishes and help a kid with homework? She was always so friendly to all of us, I never picked up."

I glanced at Dad when he paused. He had tears in his eyes. Luisa put a hand on his shoulder, and he covered it with his own.

"None of this was your fault. She had us all fooled. She played a convincing role, one she had us all believing," I assured him.

He swallowed down his emotion and cleared his throat before he continued. "Yes, well, anyway, she didn't have anything to do with Mom passing. I called Dr. Levine last night after listening to your phone video. He assured me the cancer had spread through her and there's no way Annie could have made that any better or worse no matter what Julie had taken in the end.

"That aside, Annie had it in her head that she got Mom out of the way and we were all one big happy family until you started dating. She needed some control over how that would go too. So, when you were in university, she picked David specifically to pull the whole con starting several years ago when you were in your final year. She paid him quite a lot of money to charm you and wine and dine you and eventually, he was supposed to leave and then you would be desolate and run back home to her. She didn't count on him marrying you and sticking around, but he must have liked the idea of how much money you had from Mom's trust fund and how much a prosecuting attorney would earn. He obviously cared for you, even if he didn't completely fall in love, so he went through with it. Annie got pretty riled up when they talked about that part.

"Then a couple of years back, she started blackmailing him, not much at first, but the last several months she really pressed him. It seems, she had him convinced that she would tell you and the press that he had set it all up and he would lose you and his business he had built with Sharlene and it would be a big scandal and he would have nothing and so on and so on."

"So that's what the fake mortgages were for, to pay Annie to keep quiet? I presumed he wanted it all for him and his lover," I said.

"Probably a bit of both, but mostly to pay Annie. And that worked for a while, but he was running out of properties to mortgage, and he knew you wanted a divorce. The night of the fire, apparently David called Annie and said you had found the mortgages and the gig was up. He told her he wouldn't pay her anymore, and he had nothing to lose since you were leaving him anyway, and he was likely going to jail on the fraud charges. When she knew she would get caught in the scheme and might get in even more trouble than David, she sent her dear son to do some dirty work.

"Annie said Wayne wasn't meant to kill him. She sent him to drug David enough to rough him up, tell him to leave town. But Wayne got carried away. He had been abused and was a loose cannon, must have taken his anger out on David and strangled him when he fought back. When Wayne told Annie he'd killed David, she actually went out to the carriage house and they started the fire together with his damn nacho chips."

"My God, that's right, she was already outside when I went out after calling nine-one-one. How did I forget that?" I shook my head.

"Well, things were a little hectic that night. It's not surprising. Anyway, then when Wayne was placed at the scene, Annie had to kill him too so he wouldn't blow her cover. Imagine killing your own child?" Dad asked.

"I don't think she ever thought of Wayne as hers, because he wasn't yours, Rick. That's one sick obsession. She said she dumped him with the uncle so she could raise Christie with you. She even changed Wayne's name last name to Duncan so no one would associate the two of them. Did they finish the forensics on Wayne's death? How did she ever string him up there by herself?" Jake asked.

"It sounds like she coerced him to the barn, easy enough; then she drugged him with this Thiopental. The same drug was in his system and yours and David's. It's a barbiturate that slows the activity of your brain and your nervous system and kicks in quickly, like in seconds, so none of you would have much time to react.

"It wouldn't be enough to kill Wayne, but enough so she could get him to move where she wanted him without him really knowing what she planned to do, or at least enough to fight back. There was a chair that got kicked out of the way, so Jenny figures she must have got Wayne to stand on it, after giving him the shot, then stood on a chair herself to get the body bag and the chains around him and then kicked the chair out from under Wayne. The sick part is he would still have been alive, although I'm sure barely, since he hung there full of drugs. But she left him to freeze to death whatever life he still had in him. That's some serious punishment when he probably never would have squealed on her.

"There's no doubt she meant to kill you, Jake, and me too. They believe her plan was to make it appear like you killed me when I confronted you about the murders and then you killed yourself. If I hadn't been stuck at the office, she likely would have tried to kill both of us before Christie got home."

I shuddered. "Jeez, Dad."

He nodded slowly; eyebrows raised. "Yeah, it was that close. I got a text from your phone, Jake, asking me to come urgently. She must have sent it right when she drugged you. You're also lucky she's sick enough that she wanted to see you squirm or maybe watch me die before she killed you. She only gave you enough drugs to have the opportunity to tie you to the chair so she could get in your face. A bit bigger dose and the drugs alone could have killed you. Wayne must have given David the same, just enough to make him weak in their fight, so he could overpower him," Dad explained.

"I didn't even hear her coming. I was standing at the kitchen sink, right at the window where you guys were listening. Thank God I didn't close the window. I turned around right when she jabbed me. I got tied to a chair before I was with it enough to know what happened. She must have got the dog before she got me, or he would have been barking his head off. Wayne probably snuck up on Dave the same way. Good thing he didn't give enough for him to pass right out or we never would have had Wayne's DNA evidence under Dave's nails from the struggle."

"Very true. And also, good thing Christie got home

before I finished work; and even better that Bruce happened to drive her home and see Annie in the window. He saved the day," Dad said.

"Where would she get drugs like that?" I asked.

"She was happy to take her brother Raymond down with her, pay back she said for abusing her boy, because that makes sense. What a screwed-up bunch. Anyway, Raymond works at Grantmark Pharmaceuticals in their shipping department. He somehow managed, with the help of some of Annie's extra funds to get his hands on a few rounds of drugs she needed over the years. So, he's also in the slammer now awaiting a bail hearing on drug and theft charges as well as accessory to murder.

"Raymond also paid a pretty penny to one of the drug salesmen to steal a black body bag from the hospital. She really had thought it through how she could try to frame you with the body bag and the hat and her tips to the cops. I know they questioned you a lot and I'm sorry for that, but trust me, they never suspected you and they made your fire chief completely aware of that. They did all that to ferret out who might be trying to frame you, to see if the killer followed you.

"The anonymous tip that started the questioning at the fire hall and then the FD hat at the crime scene of Wayne's death were a bit too obvious. They knew you were smarter than to leave something like that behind if you were involved. It also got left in a spot too far from the body to have fallen off in that kind of incident. Also, like Christie mentioned, it's way too warm this week for you to wear a winter toque. I hope you know the homicide team is a lot smarter than Annie suggested."

"Well, I…of course I do. At least, I should have known. But jeez, did they have to be so convincing. They put me through hell. Hanging out in holding overnight was not a pleasant experience."

"Well, your idea to keep Wayne's death quiet made them think using you for bait might have the same affect. If they appeared to suspect you murdered Wayne, at least until they got some forensics on him, then the real killer might relax a bit and surface. So really, you brought your overnight stay on yourself with your smart idea. And as luck would have it, that's exactly what happened. Annie figured they were suspicious of you, so she could make her move and get away clean," Dad said.

"It's unbelievable that Annie plotted against Jake while she played nice at home giving me dinner instructions. And frankly I can't believe Jenny and Nick would set Jake up so convincingly. Waiting for Annie to surface that way took it a little too close to the line, don't you think? I expected to be the one in danger, not you two."

Dad nodded. "I agree that got a little too close for comfort. I'm also mortified we thought you were protected when you were home alone with the killer; the irony of that. But they have most of the answers now and with your video, Annie's direct confession and Raymond happily filling in any details of the past, well, she'll be away for a long, long time, my guess is the rest of her life."

"What about Sharlene?" I asked. "If David called Annie to tell her I figured out his con, why wouldn't he tell Sharlene their business scam was up? She must have known."

Dad shook his head. "I'm not sure he ever brought her in on the mortgage thing. They can't find anything that ties her in with it. The photo of the two of them must have been in the pile with the mortgages because he obviously couldn't leave their picture on his desk. When your pretend marriage faded, he really did fall for Sharlene. She's devastated, like legitimately, she can't believe he lied to her, which is kind of strange really, knowing he lied to his wife every day of the week. But I believe her.

"She said they had a long talk after you called him about what you found. He told her about the mortgages, that he had even mortgaged her house, but that he did it for them so they could run away together and put the rest back into the business so they could make more to pay it all back. She believed he planned to leave you and they could start over together somewhere else and live happily ever after. He never said anything about the blackmail or Annie or the initial con. She really trusted him, and frankly, he may have convinced himself he could work it out. Maybe he thought once he got far enough away, Annie would let it go and they would all be content. Dave and Sharlene really did seem to have a thing, sorry."

"It's okay, Dad, no need to feel sorry. Our marriage was long over. Apparently, it never really started. I should have known better too. That's likely why he kept putting off having kids. He never intended to stay." I waved it all away with a flip of my hand. "On to better days, shall we?"

"Tell Christie about her car," Luisa said.

"Right, I almost forgot. Jenny called me, said she tried to call you, but your phone didn't pick up."

"I've been here all night. I turned it off. What did she say?"

"She wanted to tell you about your buddy, Mr. Jordan. He got released on bail yesterday, must have remembered your car from the cemetery and apparently didn't like the idea that you were back at work while he had been charged with assault and forcible confinement. He thinks you should have been charged for assaulting him. The guy is thick as a brick, slashed your tires, keyed your door, and threw a bunch of eggs right in front of the courthouse camera and right after being released on bail with the first condition that he stay away from you and your property. Doesn't get any more dimwitted than that. Needless to say, he's back in the can with additional charges of breach of recognizance and mischief over five thousand, on top of the charges from last week. He won't be getting out on any promises this time. Oh, and they towed your car over to Clausen's so call him today and let him know what kind of new tires you want. And you're going to want your insurance involved since he keyed the whole side of your car."

"Wow; sounds like I'll be on the other side of the bench for a few upcoming trials down the line. That should be interesting. But in this Jordan guy's case, I'll say it's a good thing once again. If he hadn't taken his anger out on my car, I wouldn't have taken the cab ride home with Bruce. Things could have ended a lot differently." I shook my head trying to grasp the reality of the last week of my life.

"Yes, you're absolutely right; and speaking of you appearing in court, call Detective Scott when you're up to it. She needs statements from both of you the sooner the better, and she said that she owes you both a dinner."

"She doesn't owe us anything, but I'll look forward to the night out. Can you ask her if we can wait until tomorrow for any more police business?" I asked, reaching for Jake's hand.

"I'm sure that will be fine. Annie's not going anywhere," Dad said.

I smiled at Jake. "I don't want to think about that right now. The doc says I can spring you in a couple of days, and I'm going to take you home and make you eat my cooking and watch romantic comedies until you beg for mercy."

"I'll be begging all right, but mercy isn't what comes to my mind." He grinned at me.

Dad cleared his throat and got up to leave. "We'll leave you two alone to ah, mend."

"Um, Dad, speaking of leaving you two alone, why did delusional Annie know more about you and Luisa than I did when you said you just started seeing each other?"

Luisa laughed and looked to Dad too. "I'm guessing Annie did a lot of eavesdropping and formulating stories in her mind that she wanted to believe herself. I don't remember telling her anything about Luisa."

Dad winked and reached for Luisa's hand. She smiled tenderly in return. "My lovely Luisa is, however, coming over for dinner tonight, and your old dad is cooking. So, on that note, we're heading for a hike and then to the market for some fresh steaks and veggies."

He pointed at Jake. "Get better."

Luisa hugged me again. “So nice to meet you both. Jake I’ll hug you next time we meet, when you’re standing, and I won’t hurt anything. I hope you’re feeling better soon. Let us know if there’s anything we can do to help.”

“I appreciate that, great to meet you. Have fun you two, you deserve a day off,” Jake said.

Dad appeared more relaxed and happier than I had seen him in months, maybe years. He kissed my cheek. “Love you.”

I kissed him back. “Love you too, have fun, Dad.”

“Yeah, have fun, Dad,” Jake said.

Dad walked out the door shaking his head.

“Jake?”

“Get used to it. I’ll be calling him that sooner than you think.”

I stared, eyes wide.

He grabbed my arm and pulled me to him for a long, slow, healing kiss.

A word about the author…

My career has spanned many years in a mix of criminal and civil law and hospital surgical administrative work. Along with my work and life experience, I hold a Bachelor of Arts Degree in English and a Creative Writing Certificate, both from McMaster University, Hamilton, Ontario.

I am thrilled to have had the opportunity to take early retirement and pursue a career in writing, a pursuit I have entered with energy and enthusiasm.

My husband and I share our home in Grimsby, Ontario, with our youngest daughter, her boyfriend, our dog and two cats. I also spend a great deal of time at our cottage in Kincardine, Ontario near our daughter, son-in-law and first grandson. On these shores of Lake Huron, with some of the best walking trails in the country, my imagination soars and my best stories come to life.

Find me at:

www.suejaskula.com
www.facebook.com/sue.jaskula
www.instagram.com/suejaskulaauthor
twitter.com/JaskulaSue

Thank you for purchasing
this publication of The Wild Rose Press, Inc.

For questions or more information
contact us at
info@thewildrosepress.com.

The Wild Rose Press, Inc.
www.thewildrosepress.com

CPSIA information can be obtained
at www.ICGtesting.com
Printed in the USA
LVHW022326020521
686271LV00016B/785